A Note on the Author

Allan Gaw studied medicine at Glasgow and trained as a pathologist. Having worked in the NHS and universities in the UK and the US, he took early retirement and now devotes his time to writing.

His non-fiction publications include textbooks and articles on topics as diverse as the thalidomide story, the medical challenges of space travel and the medico-legal consequences of the Hillsborough disaster. His poetry collections, *Love & Other Diseases* and *The Sounds Men Make*, are published by Seahorse Publications.

To the Shades Descend is the third novel in the Dr Jack Cuthbert series. You can read more about Allan and his work at his website: researchet.wordpress.com.

Also by Allan Gaw

FICTION
The Silent House of Sleep
The Moon's More Feeble Fire

NON-FICTION
Born in Scandal
Trial By Fire
On Moral Grounds (with M. H. Burns)
Testing the Waters
Tales From an Oxford Bench
The Business of Discovery
Our Speaker Today
Abstract Expressions

POETRY
Love & Other Diseases
The Sounds Men Make

Praise for the Dr Jack Cuthbert mystery series

The Silent House of Sleep

**WINNER OF THE BLOODY SCOTLAND
CRIME DEBUT PRIZE (2024)**

'This murder mystery makes for compelling reading . . . Cuthbert himself is a finely conceived and drawn character'
Allan Massie, *The Scotsman*

'The first in Allan Gaw's Dr Jack Cuthbert mysteries . . . has a gritty historical edge'
Rosemary Goring, *The Herald*

'Heartbreaking and harrowing in equal measure. Dr Jack Cuthbert is a brilliant, damaged genius you'll want to follow to hell and back'
Pauline McLean, BBC Arts Correspondent

'The central character perfectly expresses the damage of both the period and his environment, and the author's pathology background was skilfully deployed'
Tariq Ashkanani

'Deliciously dark, vividly visceral, heartbreakingly harrowing'
Sharon Bairden

ONLINE REVIEWS

'Dr Jack Cuthbert is a compelling and comprehensive character in a beautifully crafted world'
CrimeBookGirl.com

'There's a sense of doom, there's a complex and damaged main character . . . vivid and well researched life of LGBT people and the medical procedures'
Scrapping & Playing

'I couldn't put it down . . . Jack is a wonderful character'
Lyndas_bookreviews

'Excellently paced and full of tension'
BooksbyBindu.com

TO THE SHADES DESCEND

A DR JACK CUTHBERT MYSTERY

ALLAN GAW

This revised paperback edition first published in Great Britain in 2025 by Polygon, an imprint of Birlinn Ltd. Previously published
by SA Press in 2024.

Birlinn Ltd
West Newington House
10 Newington Road
Edinburgh
EH9 1QS

www.polygonbooks.co.uk

1

Copyright © Allan Gaw, 2025

The right of Allan Gaw to be identified as the author of this
work has been asserted by him in accordance with the
Copyright, Designs and Patents Act 1988.

All rights reserved.

This is a work of fiction. Names, characters, businesses, places,
events and incidents are either the products of the author's
imagination or used in a fictitious manner. Any resemblance to
actual persons, living or dead, or actual events is purely coincidental.

The narrative takes place in the 1920s and 1930s and contains language
and prevailing attitudes of the time which some readers may find offensive.
The publishers wish to reassure that such instances are there for reasons
of historical social context.

ISBN 978 1 84697 725 1
eBook ISBN 978 1 78885 804 5

British Library Cataloguing-in-Publication Data
A catalogue record for this book is available on request
from the British Library.

Typeset by Initial Typesetting Services, Edinburgh

Printed and bound by Clays Ltd, Elcograf S.p.A

For Margaret

summus nempe locus nulla non arte petitus
magnaque numinibus uota exaudita malignis.
ad generum Cereris sine caede ac uulnere pauci
descendunt reges et sicca morte tyranni.

What else but his immoderate lust of power,
Prayers made and granted in a luckless hour?
For few usurpers to the shades descend
By a dry death, or with a quiet end.

Juvenal, Satire X.
Trans. John Dryden, 1693

Chapter 1

Glasgow: 9 February 1931

The small, brown leather suitcase had once been used to carry samples from door to door. Indeed, there was still some faded commercial lettering on the lid, but now scuffed and scratched, it was barely legible.

The man carrying it was short, and his clothes were as old and well-used as the case. He moved slowly and unnoticed through the thin crowd that was gathering for that night's event, speaking to no one as he went.

When he got to the front, he spent some time looking over the temporary wooden platform that had been erected earlier in the afternoon for the candidate. It had been built of rough pine, high enough that a man could stand beneath it, and the sides were draped with swathes of cheap cotton, dyed in the party colours of amber and black, to hide the poverty of the workmanship. A public address system had also been set up and already some popular music was being played on a gramophone and relayed through the loudspeaker to the right of the platform.

None of the dignitaries had yet arrived, but there were already some familiar faces in the crowd – some who had no intention of allowing the speaker to be heard and others who were recognisable from their grainy photographs on the crime pages in the evening papers.

The open space at the centre of Glasgow Green, not far from the river, had always been a popular spot for political gatherings. Just beyond the cast-iron railings and the line of large horse chestnut trees, and in the shadow of the huge stone obelisk that the Glaswegians had erected more than a century before to mark the passing of Lord Nelson, there was a clear space. It was readily accessible from both main roads, but sufficiently far away from the tramlines and the traffic to keep the police happy.

That evening, the gas lamps around the perimeter of the wide-open space were being lit as twilight fell, and there was a definite scent of carnival in the air. Anticipating the size of the crowd, food stalls were setting up and a fortune-teller had even pitched her tent hoping to earn a few much-needed coppers.

The evening rally had been timed to catch the hundreds of workers streaming out of the Templeton's Carpet Factory on the other side of the Green, as well as those travelling home from the shops and offices of the city centre to the tenements of the Calton and nearby Bridgeton.

A tall, anxious-looking young man caught sight of the case and the man carrying it in the distance. He called out to him, but his voice was lost in the music blaring from the loudspeaker. The young man pushed his way through, drawing dark looks from those he jostled, but he could no longer locate the man carrying the case.

He was tall enough to see over most of the people, but his search was in vain and he shook his head before moving off in the direction of the platform. In a moment, he too was lost in the throng.

On the other side of the growing crowd, banners were

being unfurled and flags hung from the branches of trees. A dark-haired man was shouting instructions. There was a flurry of activity as a breathless youth carrying a heavy duffel bag was immediately whisked out of view.

The dark-haired man appeared concerned, checked about him for any sign of a police uniform, and then started shouting orders even more loudly than before at those around him.

A firecracker went off near the platform, and heads turned to see a gleaming black car roll up to the park gates. Necks were strained, and cheers, muffled by heckles and catcalls, met the man with the large rosette on his lapel who got out. He exchanged some words with the woman who had accompanied him in the car. They laughed, then kissed, and he bounded over to the platform and up the short flight of wooden steps to take up his position at the microphone stand.

The people got their first good view of their candidate, and some, having seen him, decided that was enough for one evening and started to leave. Others, intrigued, surged forward to get even closer. The crowd was now large and dynamic, heaving this way and that — much like the flock of starlings overhead who were weaving and swirling their sky-dance before roosting for the night.

The candidate raised his arms, partly to welcome the crowd, partly to bring it to heel. He took a folded sheaf of handwritten papers from his inside jacket pocket, cleared his throat and opened his mouth to speak.

There was a sudden, deafening squeal of feedback, and he stepped back a little from the microphone to silence it and began again. Despite the loudspeaker, the crowd had difficulty hearing him because of the noise now coming from the trees. In the branches, waving flags and banners of different colours, young men and women were screaming at the top of their lungs while beating drums and clanging metal sheets with hammers.

The crowd were amused by this battle for their attention and enjoyed deciding which faction to support. When stones were thrown at those in the trees and a woman fell to the ground, bloodied and dazed, some of the onlookers cheered. Others booed and whistled loudly.

Around the edge of the gathering, the few uniformed policemen who were in attendance started to sense the kind of trouble they had hoped to avert. The rally could only take place on the Green at all because the City Corporation had granted it permission, and the officers present were beginning to wonder what palms had been greased to make that happen.

The bylaw forbidding gatherings like this in the park had been passed in the middle of the war. Although it was regularly flouted by individual evangelists and the odd crackpot anarchist on a soapbox, the officers could not remember anything on this scale being authorised.

Through the crowd, smartly dressed young men in suits and flat caps now pressed forward to form a circle around the platform, facing out towards the crowd. Those whom they pushed past to take up their positions could see they were armed. Pulling their jackets back as they passed, the men made no attempt to hide the folded cut-throat razors in their waistcoat pockets.

Some of the crowd moved away as they approached; others patted them warmly on their backs, offering words of encouragement. A few even began to sing. There was a whistle and a movement, but the police officers kept their distance, not wishing to ignite a situation in which they would be so outnumbered.

The candidate, having lost his train of thought in the commotion, shuffled his papers and made to start over again when he thought he might be heard. He tried to mask his irritation as he straightened the amber and black rosette on his lapel and adjusted the knot of his tie. He was clearly not at ease being this close to his electorate.

He had readied a speech full of the kind of populist venom that passed for political discourse, and he was determined to unleash it. At last, as those in the trees caught their breath, he found a brief moment of calm and opened his mouth to speak.

When it happened, the flash was silent and blinding. It was only in the split second that followed that the thunderous explosion burst eardrums, tore organs apart and ripped flesh from splintered bone.

Chapter 2

London: 23 January 1931

When his name was called, the next witness rose from his seat in the row behind Dr Jack Cuthbert, paused to adjust his cuffs and walked slowly across the well of the Central Criminal Court to mount the stand to the left of the bench. As he passed Cuthbert, he glanced down at the much younger man who had just completed his expert testimony and made the smallest of sounds.

Only Cuthbert could have heard what sounded like a disappointed sigh mixed with a faint groan of disdain. And it was only for Cuthbert's ears that the elderly pathologist had intended it. Cuthbert did not look up, nor did he acknowledge the man in any way for he was well aware of what was about to take place.

On the stand, the next expert witness stood erect and allowed the court to take in his demeanour. He turned to survey the barristers, the gallery, the press tables and even eventually the judge, but only so that they all might have a better view of him before he spoke. His oath was administered quickly, and the clerk of the court asked the witness to identify himself.

'For the records, please state your full name and occupation.'

'Auberon Reginald Flincher. Chief of pathology at St Mary's Hospital and senior Home Office pathologist.'

The judge, who was of the same vintage as Flincher, leaned forward and smiled as he caught his old school friend's eye.

'And a knight of the realm, if I am not mistaken.'

'Oh, your lordship, I'm sure such titles are neither here nor there in a court such as this, but you are really too kind to mention it.'

The counsel for the defence watched the jury as Flincher modestly acknowledged the compliment and was encouraged by their nods and smiles. With the wind now firmly in his sails, the barrister pushed on with his questions.

'Sir Auberon, the court has already heard a version of the findings from the first post mortem performed on the deceased from . . . let me see, now . . . ah, yes, from a Dr Cuthbertson. My apologies, that should of course be Cuthbert. Please would you now tell the court what you found during your meticulous re-examination of the body.'

Cuthbert was seated not more than a few yards from the barrister and the witness. He was watching the proceedings and listening with interest, but with no confidence that the court was about to hear anything other than a distorted and heavily biased account of the findings.

He had encountered Flincher on several occasions when, as today, they had been positioned on opposing sides of the argument. Only minutes before, Cuthbert had completed his testimony, having been called as an expert witness for the prosecution, while Flincher had now been called by the defence.

Whenever he attended this courtroom at the Old Bailey, Cuthbert always watched the games the barristers played with the jurors, using every trick at their disposal to sway and influence them. And he was always quietly appalled.

He, and by extension his testimony, was about to be diminished in the eyes of the jury in favour of the celebrity pathologist now on the stand. Flincher's name was familiar to anyone who could read a newspaper, and he had been associated with many of the most notorious cases in recent years.

Everyone recognised his thin face and closely clipped grey moustache from his photographs, but now he was here before them in the flesh. Cuthbert had watched the jurors' eyes widen as they first saw the famous figure take the stand, even though he had neither looked their way nor acknowledged their presence. Now, his entire gaze was directed to the judge with occasional knowing nods to the press seated at the back of the court.

Flincher described his findings without ever looking at the jury. His voice was loud and clear, and every syllable was uttered with authority. An authority that Cuthbert knew to be misplaced.

As expected, Flincher came to very different conclusions about the forensic details of the case, all of which, if believed, would exonerate the accused. While comparing and contrasting his findings with those of Cuthbert, he never referred to the younger pathologist by name, preferring that the jury should have only one expert witness to remember.

Flincher spoke to a silent court. Everyone listened when he was on the stand, such were the weight of his opinions and the almost hypnotic tone of his voice. Only when he had completed his testimony, did the barrister standing opposite him dare to speak.

'Are you saying, Sir Auberon, that in your professional opinion Dr Cuthbert is wrong?'

Flincher frowned and looked slightly pained by what he felt compelled to say. The jurors almost sympathised with him for the difficult professional position in which he found himself.

'What must be understood is that these are fiendishly complex matters, and it requires a great deal of experience to be able to interpret such post mortem findings accurately. I am not saying any deliberate misdirection was intended, but the expert witness for the prosecution is a young man, and all young men have much to learn. I myself have been a practising pathologist now for almost forty years. With those years comes a certain understanding that is quite impossible to obtain merely from reading textbooks.'

'Thank you, Sir Auberon. You have been most enlightening. No more questions, m'lud.'

'Mr Withers, do you wish to cross-examine?'

The counsel for the prosecution stood and collected his thoughts before speaking. He had faced down this particular pathologist before, and he knew that he had to start as he meant to go on.

'M'lud. Dr Flincher, old dogs do not necessarily find it easy to learn new tricks. Is it not the case that your methods are antiquated in comparison to the most up-to-date forensic methods employed by the eminent Dr Cuthbert of St Thomas's Hospital?'

Flincher smiled benignly and shook his head just enough to let the jury see that he was in a forgiving mood.

'New and, I might add, highly experimental methods must pass the test of utility before they can be considered superior to anything that has gone before. Just because something is new-fangled does not make it better, no matter how many people might tell us so. Every person in the jury is more than acquainted with that notion. How many new face creams are claimed to work wonders on the complexion? How many new diets are claimed to help shed the pounds? How many new ideas are claimed will change the world? And every one of them turns out to be no better than what we had before.

'My methods are tried and thoroughly tested. They have survived both the test of utility that I mentioned and the test of time. The question you should be asking me is how robust my methods are, not how new they are.'

Few witnesses who took the stand at the Old Bailey had the temerity to instruct the cross-examining counsel on how they should phrase their questions, but Sir Auberon Flincher was sure not only of himself but also of his position as the most eminent medico-legal expert in the country.

He would only see fit to answer the questions he thought sensible and shrugged off anything less as an annoyance. While this was surprising, what was even more remarkable was that the judges allowed him to do so despite the pleading of the barristers in question.

Cuthbert had seen and heard enough and had no intention of finding himself in the position of having to speak with his opposite number. As Flincher stepped down from the stand after being thanked by the judge and the next witness was called, Cuthbert took advantage of the short break in proceedings to make his exit.

He left the Old Bailey by a side door he often used to avoid any of the press who might be waiting at the main entrance, and made his way out onto Newgate Street. He chose to walk down to the Scotland Yard building on the embankment where he was due to meet with Detective Chief Inspector Mowbray.

The senior police officer had been in charge of the investigation, and although they had initially been at loggerheads over the guilt of the main suspect in this case, Cuthbert had managed to demonstrate through the forensic evidence, to the chief inspector's satisfaction, that once again he was right and the police were wrong.

Mowbray was a young high-flyer at the Met and one of the secrets of his success had been his ability to find and work with talented people. Cuthbert was one of them, and from their first meeting the chief inspector had realised this was someone special. Their personalities were, however, too alike for it all to be plain sailing and there had been many cross words along the way.

Cuthbert was going over Flincher's testimony in his head as he walked. He was now angrier about the court proceedings than he wanted to admit even to himself, and, in his irritation, failed to watch where he was putting his feet. Stepping off the pavement in the Strand, he plunged his right boot up to the laces in a gutter filled with muddy water from that morning's rain.

He immediately shook his foot to get the worst of it off and took out a handkerchief there and then to start wiping it dry. All he did was remove the shine from his boot and end up with a filthy, wet rag that he discarded in the first bin. If he was angry before, now he was furious, and he marched on at double the pace to reach Scotland Yard.

As he entered the building, he was still far from pleased with his boots. His grim expression was enough to make the constable on the reception desk sit up and quickly admit the visitor.

'You know your way, sir?'

'Well, laddie, I've only been coming here for the last two years, so I sincerely hope so.'

Cuthbert always mounted the stairs to the second floor two, sometimes three, at a time but never arrived at the duty room out of breath.

Mowbray, who was standing by one of his junior's desks, saw him arrive. 'Another one over?'

'Not quite, chief inspector, but I suspect it will be very soon. Although I doubt my testimony, or your hard work for that matter, will do much good.'

Cuthbert did not smile, and Mowbray could see he was distracted as he spoke.

'What's the matter with your boots? Somebody spit on them?'

'It's this damnable weather. Forgive me, chief inspector, I know you're busy. What was it you wanted to see me about?'

Mowbray invited Cuthbert to join him in his office, and then closed his door. He went to his cabinet and took out the bottle of single malt he kept for trial days. He poured himself and Cuthbert two generous measures and sat at his desk.

'To what do I owe the honour, chief inspector?'

'No honour, just a little ritual that needs to be observed. Do you remember the first time you were in this office? I'm not sure I was especially polite to you.'

'You were downright rude, but that's all in the past.'

'I'm glad to see you've put it behind you. I suppose I just wanted to acknowledge that I think we're a good team, Jack.'

'You've never called me that before.'

'Isn't it about time we were on first-name terms? After all we've been through?'

'Yes, you're right, chief inspector, it probably is. It's just that I'm old and stuck in my ways.'

'You're not old. You're only a couple of years older than me and I'll have you know I'm still the young gun around here.'

'I felt old today in that courtroom, I can tell you. We do have to deal with some very unpleasant aspects of humanity.'

'But you love it. Anyone with eyes can see that. You love the challenge of a puzzle. It's what gets you going.'

Cuthbert took a long, slow sip of the amber spirit, and smacked his lips as it hit the back of his throat. 'Puzzles, yes, but not sifting through the sins of those who live in the gutter.'

Mowbray had not seen Cuthbert like this before and wondered what had really prompted it. He knew the pathologist worked tirelessly both at his department at St Thomas's and at the university, when he wasn't assisting Scotland Yard, but he had always thought he thrived on the work. Today he looked wearied by it all. He sat with his head back on the chair and his eyes closed, and he drank down the whisky without needing the usual encouragement to finish his glass.

'Chief inspector . . .'

'Jim.'

'It will take me a while to get used to that but, yes, Jim. Does it get to you? Do you ever think about doing something else, just to get away from it all?'

'What exactly's brought this on? Here, let me top you up. I've never seen anyone in greater need of a second drink.'

'It's the whole rigmarole of the court. I mean the games that are played with people's lives. Today was just another example. Forensic science should be an objective search for the truth. And that truth should be presented to the court in a clear and comprehensible manner, not manipulated to skew justice.'

'You look like you need a break. When was the last time you took some time off?'

'I don't have time for holidays.'

'Oh, I'm sorry, I keep forgetting you're the only pathologist in London. Or is it that you think you're the only one who can do the job? Don't be seduced by that particular siren. Believe me, nobody is indispensable, Jack. And if you start to think you are, it won't be long before you end up on your own slab, and then not much longer before they forget you altogether.'

Cuthbert leaned forward, his broad shoulders hunched, and cradled the whisky glass in both hands. Mowbray was starting to think this was serious. He had met Jack Cuthbert for the first time in this office two years before, and that day the giant of a man who walked in uninvited and sat down unasked was a very different one to the sorry figure now sitting opposite him.

'What's this really about, Jack? The door's shut and you can talk in here. You know I'm not about to share anything with the minions out there so why not spit it out?'

Cuthbert remembered where he was and unwound slightly, but he was still embarrassed that he had put himself in this position. He was an intensely private man, protective of his real thoughts and feelings. In part it was the way he had been brought up; in part it was the consequence of many years of practised deception so necessary for a man like him.

Now, he was cornered. The fatigue and the whisky on an empty stomach had made him vulnerable and he needed to talk. Mowbray was hardly the sympathetic ear he would have chosen, but the hard-nosed East Ender was all he had.

'The truth of the matter is, I'm finding the job difficult. Damn it, I'm finding everything difficult. I don't seem to have the energy I had. Life doesn't excite me the way it did, and I feel lost in it all. And when I try to make sense of it, my head starts to spin and I end up in some even darker place.'

'For God's sake, man, you really do need a break. And just so you're clear, there's nothing wrong with you that getting your end away won't solve. Look, I don't know about your personal life, and I don't want to know because it's your business, but you need something more than the work to excite you. You're young, and look at you. Don't get me wrong, you're not my cup of tea, but there's plenty who wouldn't throw you out of bed.'

Cuthbert winced at the suggestion, but Mowbray knew better than Cuthbert about his personal life and cared less about the details than the wellbeing of the man whom he had come to regard as a friend. Cuthbert was the most intelligent and valued colleague he had met in his fourteen years on the force, and he wasn't about to watch him go under.

'I know you think me crude, but I'm a man and so are you. We're from different worlds, Jack, but we've both been through the mill, and I like to think we have a bit more in common than anybody else might realise. I look at you and I see a man who's burning out through overwork and lack of purpose. More work isn't going to give you that; you need to find it somewhere else, with someone else. Now, finish that drink, 'cause you're cluttering up my office and the lads will think I'm going soft. And you know I can't have that because I'm their worst fucking nightmare and that's the way it needs to stay if I'm to get any work out of them.'

Cuthbert half-smiled and handed Mowbray his glass. He stood and straightened to his full height, looked down at the chief inspector and took his hand to shake it.

'Thank you, Jim, for the whisky and for the talk. I'm just sorry you had to listen to all that.'

'Come on, what is it you Jocks are always saying? "Awa and bile yer heid."'

Cuthbert could not help grinning at Mowbray's woeful attempt at a Scottish accent. He collected his hat and coat, and as he was opening the office door, he looked back at the strong, stocky man who was perched on the edge of his desk.

'Yes, we do say exactly that, so I will awa and dae jist that. And thanks again, but just to avoid any misunderstanding, Jim, what with that broken nose of yours, you're not exactly my cup of tea either.'

*

At the breakfast table the following week, Madame Smith poured his coffee and brought him hot croissants in a basket wrapped in a white linen napkin to keep them warm. She was Belgian and would not countenance the thought of fried foods in the morning. Indeed, Cuthbert's early suggestion that she might serve porridge occasionally was met with the kind of sneer she normally reserved for the nightsoil in the gutter.

'Porridge is what we feed to the farm animals in Belgium.'

Cuthbert did not ask again and had learned to savour the lighter, sweeter breakfasts she provided.

She worked about the table in silence, allowing him to read the morning paper and deal with his post. She had already collected the letters from the mat in the hallway and placed them on a tray at his side. She always studied the stamps and postmarks before laying them out for him, so she was unsurprised when he called her over to listen to the contents of a typewritten letter.

'Well, this is a turn-up for the books, madame. It's from Glasgow – they want me to pay a visit to the university, "to discuss a possible appointment".'

Madame Smith could see his face light up; he was excited by the prospect. 'Are you being invited to interview for a new job, monsieur?'

'Not an interview exactly. That's not really how these things are done. But if I go, I will be under scrutiny, I have no doubt about that.'

'If you go?'

'Oh, I'm far too busy to go traipsing off to Scotland. Besides, it's not the right time to be thinking about a move like that. I'm perfectly happy here.'

Madame Smith, who had been Cuthbert's housekeeper for five years and who had never really conformed to anyone else's idea of a domestic servant, put down the tray she was carrying and drew up a chair to take a seat beside him at the breakfast table. Silently, she poured herself a cup of coffee from his pot, and he knew he was about to receive one of her regular lectures.

'With respect – and why do you always say that in this country as a prelude to something that isn't in the least respectful? – you are not perfectly happy, monsieur. These past weeks you have been tired, somewhat irritable and increasingly discontented with your work. I do not suggest that you leave us here to work in such a cold, wet country as Scotland, but would it not be a good idea to consider taking some days off, to take a trip and perhaps even relax a little in new surroundings? They are offering you an excuse to get away – take it, even if it is only to find some new energy.'

Cuthbert studied the young woman and could see that she was calculating the consequences of him leaving London. Theirs was an unconventional working relationship which suited them both perfectly, but she knew she would be unlikely to find another Dr Cuthbert if he left her to work in Glasgow.

At the same time, here she was encouraging him to go, if only for the change of scene, but surely in the knowledge that if he did, he might be offered the job and he might accept it. He knew she served his food and changed his sheets and cleaned his house, but he also knew that she was concerned with his wellbeing and his happiness. He knew because she had told him so on more than one occasion.

'It would be quite a disruption to the department if I were to go away for the week.'

'For whom? Dr Morgenthal has been more than an assistant to you for months now. You have trained him well, and he is as concerned as you about the quality of the work. He is certainly capable of coping on his own for a week, is he not? In fact, does it not occur to you that it would do him good if you were to show some sign of your confidence in his abilities?'

Cuthbert was forced to agree with everything she said and realised that he was not going to be able to use Simon Morgenthal as an excuse.

'Tell me more about this job, monsieur. When you read the letter, you looked excited by the prospect. I do not imagine it is just any position.'

'How observant of you, madame. No, this is Glaister's chair.'

With that, Cuthbert paused again to savour the moment. Professor Glaister was the doyen of medico-legal medicine. His textbook, now in its fourth edition, was on the shelf of every pathology department, not just in this country, but throughout the world.

Cuthbert had met the great man only twice, although he had heard him lecture on a number of other occasions. And now, the letter from the dean of the medical faculty at Glasgow University informed him that John Glaister, regius professor of forensic medicine, was about to retire.

There were bound to be a number of candidates to fill his position, but even to be considered in that field was, for Cuthbert, an honour. Lawrence Quinn, the dean, had written that he would very much like to meet him and personally show him around the university, if he was willing to consider the long journey from London. Cuthbert passed the letter to Madame Smith and urged her to read it.

'I see he would like you to come for the week beginning the ninth of February. That is only two weeks away. I can certainly have your clothes ready and your bags packed. All you need do is inform Dr Morgenthal that he will be in charge for a week.'

'I haven't said I'm going, madame, and as long as I'm at St Thomas's, Simon will not be in charge.'

'Nonsense, it is decided. Please make the arrangements.'

With that she began clearing the table and told him he would be late for the hospital if he did not leave soon. Cuthbert did not protest further for he knew he wanted to go to Glasgow, if only to satisfy his curiosity about the old man and his department.

When Madame Smith came back, she was perturbed to find him still at the table re-reading the letter. He looked up and somewhat dreamily asked her about her own aspirations.

'Aspirations? To live, monsieur, just to live – that is miracle enough for me.'

*

When he arrived at St Thomas's, he walked the long way around to the pathology department, through the hospital garden. It was bare and waterlogged, but there were already some signs of life.

The small green shoots of crocuses had broken the soil alongside the thicker blades of the daffodils to come, and in the corner sheltered by the stone walls of the hospital he saw the unmistakable white flowers of early snowdrops. His spirits were always lifted by the first sights of spring, and he entered the department with a smile on his face.

Dr Simon Morgenthal, his assistant and trainee, was already at his bench in the laboratory adjacent to the dissection room. He was setting up further tests to complete the lead absorption studies that had been prompted by a recent case. Although Cuthbert had already obtained the information necessary to support his testimony, he had encouraged Simon to perform additional studies under various conditions in order to make their planned research paper all the more robust.

The young doctor had realised almost as soon as he started working with Cuthbert that his mentor took nothing at face value and always insisted upon irrefutable scientific evidence. Morgenthal had also learned that acquiring such evidence was inevitably slow, difficult and painstaking work. However, he had already published two papers with his mentor and was being encouraged to work on a more substantial research project in order to submit his M.D. thesis.

When Morgenthal saw Cuthbert smiling, he was concerned. His mentor was not an unusually gloomy man – on the contrary, he was lively, quick-witted and always pleasant to be with. It was just that in the last few weeks, he had seemed tired and worn down by the caseload. This sudden change of mood needed an explanation, and Morgenthal did not have one.

'Good morning, Dr Cuthbert. What a beautiful spring day, sir.'

'Indeed, Dr Morgenthal. There are even snowdrops in the hospital grounds. What do you make of that?'

'Spring is just nosing her way around the corner, sir, and will be here before we know it. May I say, sir, how well you look. Has something happened?'

He asked as politely as he could, knowing full well that the determinants of Cuthbert's mood were really none of his business, but his curiosity was getting the better of him. And hadn't his mentor always encouraged curiosity?

'Actually, Simon, it has, and I need you to do something for me, when you've finished setting up those lead analyses, of course. Come into my office when you have a moment, will you?'

Now Morgenthal's concerns were redoubled. What had he done, failed to do or simply forgotten? Had he gone awry? His mind raced through everything he had worked on in the last week – the post mortem examinations, the studies of victims' clothing, the analyses of hair and soil samples.

He always worked hard and tried his very best to impress Cuthbert, but he also knew that he was far from being his equal either in intellect or experience. He turned his attentions back to setting up the apparatus for the lead analyses on the bench before him.

An hour later, Morgenthal knocked firmly on Cuthbert's office door and entered straight away as he had always been instructed to do.

'Ah, Simon, good. Now, I have to go away for a week in

February and I'm leaving you not quite in charge but certainly responsible for the day-to-day running of the department. Do you think you can manage that, young man?'

Morgenthal was caught off guard by the request. He had been expecting some well-deserved carpeting for missing a key point in his post mortem report or some lack of precision in his laboratory work. Instead, here was Dr Cuthbert handing him the reins, albeit for only a week. The young man beamed, and Cuthbert was warmed by his smile as he remembered Madame Smith's words.

'I won't let you down, sir.'

'I know you won't, Simon, because if you do, you'll be working somewhere else when I get back.'

It was only the glint in Cuthbert's eyes that made Morgenthal realise he was joking. First a morning smile and now a joke – Morgenthal had to know what had prompted all this, but he asked as subtly as he could. 'When you are away, sir, do you wish to be contacted about anything? If so, would you leave me the details on how I might get in touch?'

'Or, in other words, Simon, where am I going and why?'

'Not at all, sir. That's entirely your business.'

'Don't worry, Simon, I'm not angry. In fact, I'm feeling rather good today. I've been invited to visit the University of Glasgow, and I thought I would make a trip of it. I haven't been back in Scotland since Professor Littlejohn's funeral a few years ago. That was a bleak affair, and so I thought I might take a look at the city while I'm there. I really don't know Glasgow that well, and they tell me it's worth seeing.'

Morgenthal did not appreciate the significance of this trip to Glasgow and assumed it was simply one of the many requests that Cuthbert received to teach or examine his subject.

Most of his academic work was in and around the London hospitals and medical schools, but occasionally he was called further afield, so Morgenthal put his mentor's good cheer down to being able to visit his homeland. It did not even cross his mind that Cuthbert might be readying himself for a more permanent move.

Chapter 3

London: 8 February 1931

Even after fifteen years, Cuthbert still had trouble sleeping. There were times when he would try to evade sleep altogether, fearful of what it might make him remember.

He knew that he was far from alone in this, and the medical journals of his day were full of case reports of so-called shellshock, regimens of corrective therapy and even heated debate from some quarters about the authenticity of his suffering. Although he read the medical and scientific literature avidly to maintain his knowledge and understanding of medical practice, he avoided such papers, preferring not to give a name, a diagnosis, to what he was enduring. The nights had become easier with the years, but like so many others, he had not completely come home from the war.

*

The sleeping berth on the overnight train to Glasgow was comfortable but cramped, and as soon as the train pulled out of Euston Station, Cuthbert chose to sit in the lounge area reserved for first-class passengers. The steward offered him a drink after welcoming him, and Cuthbert took the whisky from the tray more out of politeness than need.

He walked carefully along the moving carriage, and it was only as he was about to sit down that he realised he was not the only one unable or unwilling to sleep on the train. There was a man, about Cuthbert's age, sitting alone staring out into the darkness as it rushed past.

His head was turned away, but Cuthbert could see his face reflected in the glass. The man wore no expression, but his features were strong and angular, and Cuthbert found himself looking for rather longer than was polite. The man, sensing his presence or perhaps catching sight of the tall Scotsman in the window, turned, smiled and immediately stood up. Cuthbert was met with warmth, and he took the proffered hand and enjoyed the heavy touch of his grip.

'My name's Jaeger, Erich Jaeger. How do you do? I thought I might be the only insomniac on the train tonight.'

'Jack Cuthbert. Very pleased to meet you. Indeed, I'm not sure why I take the sleeper at all. It seems curiously misnamed, at least for me.'

'Please, won't you join me? I use it a lot. My work, you know. Always up and down to our offices in Glasgow. But you're Scottish. Going home?'

'No, I live in London. I have some business at the university in Glasgow. Just a short trip.'

Cuthbert watched the man who was now sitting opposite and found himself appraising him. He was careful not to allow his attention to stray from the conversation or to reveal what he was thinking, but he was unable to stop himself thinking it.

He studied the man's large hands and watched how he used them to emphasise a point. He followed the line of the sharp crease in his trousers and assessed the shine on his shoes. He was impressed by the crispness of the knot in his silk tie and the tautness of his neck muscles. His fair hair was oiled and slicked back and his bright, interested eyes were green. But most of all it was his smile that drew Cuthbert in.

Jaeger had appeared distant and almost melancholy when lost in his thoughts. Now, his face was animated, and he appeared genuinely pleased to have found some company.

The fellow night owls chatted with good humour and the steward served them more whiskies. Cuthbert relaxed into the conversation and found that there was little for him to do because his companion was so convivial.

He was Austrian by birth but had spent much of his adult life in London. His English was perfect, with only the trace of an accent that did nothing other than complete the allure. Sipping his drink as the train thundered north, Cuthbert listened with interest but enjoyed looking at the man opposite even more, taking care to control his breathing.

On many such occasions before, he had found himself secretly savouring the masculinity of a stranger, all the time quite certain that his discretion would protect him from any charge of impropriety. Despite his worldliness, never once did Cuthbert consider that he might similarly be the object of desire.

However, this was exactly the situation he now unwittingly found himself in. Jaeger was studying the dark stranger with just as much interest as Cuthbert had invested in his gaze, but the difference was that he knew exactly what the tall Scotsman was thinking, perhaps even more than the man himself.

Jaeger had met men like Cuthbert before, and he knew that things had to proceed slowly, or all would be lost. The more he looked at Jack Cuthbert, the more he realised he wanted this powerful, charming but ultimately innocent man.

Words like seduction seem out of place when all that hangs in the air between two people are the merest murmurs of familiarity. There was no flirting, no suggestion, no invitation, but Cuthbert could feel himself being drawn into the space

Jaeger occupied. The very air about him started to catch in Cuthbert's throat as he tasted the scent of the man, and he swallowed hard.

His glass was empty, and noticing it, Jaeger immediately hailed the steward and ordered another for Cuthbert.

'I'm sure I've had my quota for the evening. Thank you all the same.'

'Nonsense, old chap. We've barely left the lights of London behind. There's plenty of time. Although I'm sure I must be boring you with all my gab. Listen, what do you say to a game of cards?'

Cuthbert was not a card player, but he wasn't at all sure he wanted the evening to end. In fact, he had no idea what he wanted, for his imagination was never better than vague when he tried to flesh out his fantasies.

'I have a pack in my berth, you know. Why don't we take our drinks there? Change of scene, and at least we can take our jackets off. Relax a little.'

Cuthbert quite suddenly realised what was happening, and his discomfort was acute. He always prided himself in his social grace because that was the way he had been brought up, and he would rather have hacked off his own thumbs than be thought of as rude. But he was unprepared for this. Despite the feelings which he had wrestled with his whole life, he found it impossible to submit to them.

Confused and barely coherent, he offered his apologies and made to leave. Jaeger caught Cuthbert's arm with a strong grasp and held it for more than a moment.

'I know – it's all so very difficult, but if you should change your mind . . .'

Jaeger almost whispered the words close to his ear and the tenderness of his breath made Cuthbert tense even more, but he managed to nod and smile awkwardly before turning to walk quickly back to his own berth where he closed and locked the compartment door.

He slumped on the floor with his forehead resting on his knees and his hands in his hair. He felt like a fool, not knowing if he was more disappointed in himself at not going to Jaeger's berth or for even considering it as a possibility. He was as confused in that moment as he had been all his life, and he knew he couldn't sleep.

After rummaging in his briefcase, he found his leather-bound copy of Catullus. It was an old friend, and the Latin verse had helped him navigate many such nights. Perhaps, he thought, it might help him through this one.

*

Not long before dawn, the train eased its way into Platform 1 of Glasgow Central Station. For convenience, Cuthbert had chosen to stay at the Central Station Hotel in Glasgow, and after dressing and breakfasting on the train, he found he could walk without getting his feet wet across the station esplanade to the glass entranceway.

The top-hatted commissionaire saluted and held the door open, and Cuthbert dealt with the formalities at the reception desk. His luggage was taken to his room while he decided to enjoy another coffee and the morning papers before heading to the university for his first appointment.

In the reading room that overlooked Hope Street, he watched the trams, liveried in orange-yellow and green, clatter and spark over the points. It was the beginning of the morning rush hour, and Glasgow was doing its best to live up to its reputation.

This was a warm, vibrant city densely populated and full of opportunity. Even the teeth of the Depression had not bitten too hard here yet, and the throngs of shop and office workers that were trooping from tram to pavement to building were testament, if any were needed, that Glasgow was certainly open for business.

But, as in any city, on the street corner opposite the station, there was a beggar. A thin, dark smudge of a man, bareheaded with his hat in his hand, on a makeshift crutch, was leaning heavily against the wall behind him. His left trouser leg was pinned up, unneeded. Cuthbert reflected that the war had certainly not ended for men like that, if indeed it had ended for any of them.

By his second cup of coffee, Cuthbert watched the bustle of the morning begin to slow, and after checking his waistcoat watch, he decided that, although still early, he could afford to set off. First, however, he summoned the bellboy and whispered his instructions before he pressed the ten-shilling note into his hand.

'Right away, sir.'

'And remember, not a word, laddie.'

Cuthbert signed for his coffee, collected his briefcase and made for the reception area. As he adjusted his overcoat, he watched the bellboy coming back through the door from the street and acknowledged his smile with the slightest of nods and held out a sixpence for his trouble. Outside, one broken veteran would have a hostel bed and hot meals for two of the coldest weeks of the winter.

The taxi took Cuthbert from the Central Hotel to the gates of the university, by way of the crowded city centre and then the elegant terraces of the West End. As they approached the Art Gallery and Museum – an ornate red sandstone edifice nestling in the park near the university – he caught his first sight of the university itself. The thrusting spire of soot-blackened stone stood on the highest point of the hill and seemed to rise from the trees in the surrounding park.

His taxi turned into Kelvin Way, the tree-lined road through the park. The arch of the branches from both sides created a tunnel, and Cuthbert lost sight of the university buildings before emerging at the other end on University Avenue.

There, the sudden surge of undergraduates emerging from the union and making their way up the hill towards the main building meant the taxi had to slow to a stop. He watched them in their groups of two and three, all in college scarves, briefcased and laughing.

Just as the taxi found a gap and started to move, Cuthbert caught sight of two young men, tall and excited, dashing to their class. Although he could not hear, Cuthbert could see one was speaking loudly, his arms flailing and the other was rapt, his gaze fixed on his classmate as much in admiration as attention.

Cuthbert saw himself almost twenty years before, in a different city at a different university, but just as eagerly hanging on the words of a friend. The years might pass, taking with them the new harvest of youth, but new seeds would be sown, and new stalks would grow. And the faces would always be the same, running up that hill to the next class.

The letter outlining Cuthbert's itinerary for the visit had specified a tour of the university department of forensic medicine at 10.30 a.m., followed by a meeting with the dean, Professor Quinn, for lunch. The taxi driver offered to navigate the campus to take Cuthbert to the door of the department, but as it was still only ten o'clock, he chose to be dropped off at the gate and to walk.

Behind the high railings on University Avenue, there was a complex of buildings around the central tower and its adjacent quadrangles. Cuthbert joined the trains of students filing between classes and again savoured the bitter sweetness of nostalgia.

He walked past the Botany and Natural Philosophy Buildings and paused to take in the scale of the chemistry departments. The Zoology Building with its famous museum was on his right as he approached his destination, the West Medical Building.

Cuthbert paused to take it in. It looked much like all the others in terms of architecture and design, but for a pathologist, this was almost a place of pilgrimage. This was Glaister's department, where he worked and where he had written the textbook that every member of Cuthbert's profession learned almost by rote.

But it was a large building and only now did Cuthbert realise that it housed a triumvirate of medical departments – *materia medica*, forensic medicine and physiology, the last being deemed by the university as by far the most important. Despite the fact that these departments shared the same building, there was no common space and little interaction. Indeed, there were three separate entrances to ensure minimal contact or even contamination from one to the other.

The silo that was Glaister's department of forensic medicine occupied the top two floors of the building and could at least claim the best views. Cuthbert leapt the stairs three at a time and arrived at the main office, where he was expecting to be met by Herbert Henderson, a dour man even by Presbyterian standards, whom he had met professionally on a number of occasions.

As Cuthbert had also half-expected, he was not there, and he was kept waiting for twenty-five minutes while an increasingly agitated secretary offered the distinguished visitor all the excuses she could muster.

When he did arrive, Dr Henderson was unapologetic and simply offered Cuthbert a limp handshake before leading him along the corridor to commence the tour. A good decade older than his visitor, he was battle-worn and had little time for fly-ins like Cuthbert. He was a senior lecturer in the department and had been one of the police pathologists in Glasgow South and East since the Armistice.

This was the first time Cuthbert had met Henderson on his own turf, and he was interested to learn of the case load of the department, being keen to compare it with his own in London. However, the conversation with Henderson was difficult.

He was taciturn and looked distracted, but Cuthbert pressed on, and it was only when he lighted on the subject of the social problems in the city that Henderson opened up and vented his opinions. Although Glasgow born and bred, it was quickly clear that he had come to despise his fellow citizens.

'When I started, I looked for reasons. What made them the way they are? But I gave up. There are no reasons; it's just innate bestiality. It's in their nature to live and behave the way they do.'

'But the conditions these people are living in, Dr Henderson, the unemployment? Surely that has to contribute. Most of them live in filthy, cramped apartments up a common close. There are as many as ten souls living in a single room, sharing what little sanitation there is with at least two other equally large families. The health consequences alone are staggering. Do you know that the infant mortality in Glasgow is almost twice what it is in Birmingham or London? Are you telling me the people here are so different from the poor elsewhere?'

Henderson sighed. He was clearly not in the mood to be indulgent, even for the sake of a guest.

'You've read the statistics, Cuthbert, and you think you know all about it. But they're little more than animals, the way they live and the way they act. You look at those tenements and see slums they are forced to live in; I see what they've turned them into. We don't build slums, you know; the people who live there make them. And as for unemployment, some of them have never worked, even when the city was booming. They're lazy now and they were lazy then. A third of the adult population is idle in this, the second city of the Empire. And mark my words, much of it is by choice.'

Henderson opened the door to the dissection room and took Cuthbert in. The large space was brightly lit by high windows, and there were three slabs, two of which were occupied. Henderson stripped the white sheet from one, tossing it on the floor and exposing a naked male corpse, probably in his mid-thirties.

'If you want to see the way they live, look at this.'

He picked up the mottled grey hand of the corpse and turned the fingernails to Cuthbert.

'Filthy. And look at the rest of him. This one spent his life drinking and whoring. His liver is cirrhotic, and I'm sure I don't need to point out the obvious signs of venereal disease. And look at his face.'

Cuthbert leaned over to study the corpse as he would one of his own cases and saw the long, poorly healed scar running from his right eye, across his cheek to his mouth. The upper lip was puckered on the right side due to poor suturing.

'That's what they do to each other, these razor boys. Street battles, alcohol and sex, that's how they occupy themselves. As I said, they're little more than beasts.'

Cuthbert could see that Henderson was not going to change his opinion as a result of anything he might say, so he bit his tongue. As Henderson turned to leave, Cuthbert shook his head and bent to pick up the white sheet before carefully covering the corpse.

In the hallway, Henderson informed Cuthbert that regrettably he had another pressing appointment and asked if he wished to see anything else in the department. The visitor was obviously an inconvenience that Henderson would be glad to be rid of, but Cuthbert had come a long way and was still keen to learn more about the workings of such a prestigious centre and said so.

'Well, if you'll forgive me, I'll leave you in the care of my assistant, Dr Ogilvie. I'm sure he'll be able to show you whatever it is you want. Good day to you.'

He turned and walked back along the corridor, his parting unequivocal. Although he must have known that Cuthbert was at the university to look at the regius professor position in the department, it was obvious he did not expect to see him again. Cuthbert was unfazed for he had met many men like Henderson throughout his career. As he watched him go, he felt an altogether different presence at his side.

'I'm so sorry to disturb you, sir. My name is Dr Ogilvie. It would be a pleasure if I could show you around the department.'

Cuthbert had to look down to find the short, bright-faced man. Ogilvie looked unsure as to whether a smile was expected or not and managed to contort his mouth into a compromise. Cuthbert could also see that he was trembling just enough to be noticeable and was immediately concerned that he might be the reason. He took a step back so as not to tower quite as obviously over the man, and he held out his hand with the warmest of smiles.

'Such a pleasure to meet you, Dr Ogilvie. And how kind of you to take the time to act as my guide. I know you must be very busy. Dr Henderson had been showing me around, but as you see he has had to cut my tour short. Something about another, rather more important, appointment. But I am sure that you will be a much more knowledgeable, not to say more affable, locum.'

Ogilvie relaxed a little, and this time he did offer a smile in return, realising that this visitor from London already had the measure of the place. He asked if Cuthbert had already been offered coffee and was disappointed to learn he had not. Ogilvie summoned a secretary and took his visitor to the small board room in the department where they could sit in relative comfort.

Cuthbert raised an eyebrow as he noted the painting of Glaister glowering over the room. How long would it be before another, perhaps smaller, oil of his successor would join it? He discarded the thought and took a seat under the painting so he would not have to look at it.

'I must say, Dr Henderson has very fixed views on the lower echelons of society in this fine city of yours. I got the impression that he attributes none of the problems facing the poor to anything but their own doing.'

Ogilvie poured the coffee from the silver pot brought in by the secretary and said, almost casually, 'He is somewhat of a misanthrope.' As soon as the words were out of his mouth, he tried to bite them back. 'But, of course, I don't mean that as a criticism. Please don't think that.'

Cuthbert was amused at the panic rising in Ogilvie's voice and put him immediately at ease. After all, he recognised Henderson for what he was: a bully.

'Please, Dr Ogilvie, you need have no concerns over my discretion, nor over my own opinion of your boss. I think he is wrong, perhaps embittered by all that he has seen. Forensic medicine can certainly take its toll on the sensibilities of the best of us, but I rather think it is all a more complicated picture than the one Henderson paints.'

Ogilvie relaxed again and began to speak in a low whisper. 'He is bitter, Dr Cuthbert. And you're right, it is much more complex. I expect he gave you his "they're all just animals" speech. Well, they're not. They are forced to live like animals, but they're human beings. Goodness knows we have enough evidence of that here. We see their flesh and blood, their fragility, on a daily basis.

'There is violence and immorality, that's true. But their street battles and sex are the only free diversions these wretched people have in their lives. Some of them drink, when they can afford it, which isn't often. And, of course, you'll also hear the old chestnut that it's all about religion – that the razor gangs are about Catholics and Protestants. The truth is most of them have no interest in God. It has nothing to do with religion, other than it being a convenient tribal banner to fight under.'

Cuthbert listened as Ogilvie's conspiratorial whisper relaxed into conversation and almost became indignation. 'Why is he so bitter? He seems not just to view the poor in the city as a societal problem, but actually to hate them.'

'He probably didn't say this to you, but I think it was the war.'

Cuthbert nodded, without really understanding, although recognising that the war was used as a reason for most of the psychological ills of the day. He held his tongue, leaving space for Ogilvie to expand.

'Henderson was a volunteer early in the war and by all accounts had a very bloody time. He doesn't talk about it, of course, but we all know.'

'And?' Cuthbert was still puzzled.

'You see, most of the young men now in the gangs were children during the war – they never fought. But more than that, neither did their families. You see, they despise those who fought. They have no respect at all for those who voluntarily went to war, and they have nothing short of contempt for those who, in their eyes, weren't clever enough to avoid conscription.

'Money was made during the war in the shipyards and the munitions factories, but it was also made on the streets. After the war, the soldiers who returned to the slums were certainly not worshipped as heroes, and there were no white feathers for those who had stayed at home. Even the wounded, like

Henderson, were not pitied for their injuries as much as for their stupidity in putting themselves in harm's way. I think that's the root cause of it all.'

When Ogilvie had finished speaking, Cuthbert, whose own war had been just as much of a nightmare as every other soldier in the trenches, had very mixed feelings. Like Henderson, he had also volunteered to serve his country, but unlike him he had expected no adulation on his return.

In his time at the front, he had seen the most brutal inhumanity imaginable juxtaposed with the most inspirational of sacrifices. He had carried broken bodies and at other times been carried himself, both literally and metaphorically, by men whose names he would never know. And, above all, he recognised the utter futility and waste of it all.

Perhaps those young men strutting the streets of the Gorbals or Bridgeton with razors in their pockets had it right. Those who went to fight a war for a few feuding aristocrats deserved no praise, only pity. Cuthbert put his unfinished coffee aside. It was time to change the subject as much for his own sake as Ogilvie's, and he asked him to show him the laboratories.

'I would be most interested to learn something of the nature of your research here in the department. Might you show me that?'

Cuthbert spent a more than profitable hour with Ogilvie and two of his colleagues in the forensic chemistry laboratory. All three were excited to share their latest work with such a knowledgeable and enthusiastic visitor, and when he left for his lunch appointment, they quietly hoped it might not be the last time they would meet professionally. They even hoped that Cuthbert might return to lead them, but they were also reasonably certain that he would not be given that opportunity. Not as long as Professor Glaister had a say.

Cuthbert walked the short distance from the department

of forensic medicine to the medical faculty office in the east quadrangle. This time he was not only expected, but the dean was standing ready to welcome him at the door.

'Dr Cuthbert, my dear fellow, how do you do? Thank you so much for taking the time to visit us here in the frozen north. Glasgow must seem such a small affair after the bright lights of London.'

'Not a bit of it, Professor Quinn. It has already been quite an eye-opener.'

'Well, I could take that two ways. I do hope your experience has been a positive one. After all, it is my fervent hope you may wish to spend more time in this city and at this university.'

Cuthbert knew why he had been invited to Glasgow, and he also knew that Quinn was taking a bold step in even considering a candidate from London for the position. However, there was some history here.

Professor Lawrence Quinn had himself been a controversial choice as dean of the medical faculty. The prestigious position was one normally offered almost as an honorific to an ageing, if not ailing, physician or surgeon who had distinguished himself clinically rather than academically.

Quinn, however, was on the right side of 50 and although medically qualified was very much a laboratory-based researcher. Eyebrows were raised on his appointment, and nothing he did in his first year in the job allowed them to fall again. He was primarily a political operative, using promises where he thought they would work and a mixture of sanction and threats when he thought a heavier hand was required. With Cuthbert, the only leverage he could apply was charm.

'I thought we would lunch at our College Club. The food is tolerable, but more importantly it will allow you to meet some of the more senior staff. Most of them find their way to the watering hole at this time of day.'

The club turned out to be the busy university staffroom on the ground floor, off the west quadrangle. They lunched at a small corner table, and Cuthbert found himself being quizzed on his recent cases.

'The Dawson murder even made the papers up here, you know. That must have been quite an experience.'

'One of many, in fact. There is no shortage of drama when it comes to the crimes of the metropolis.'

'Is that so? I wonder how we might measure up in that respect. I do hope you wouldn't be bored here.'

'Not in the least. I would hope to pursue my research and my teaching with rather more vigour than I have been able to in these past few years working with Scotland Yard.'

'We could certainly accommodate that. Indeed, I would support you fully in bringing the department into the twentieth century. You've seen around it. They have excellent facilities, but it is my view that they are rather resting on their laurels. Fine though they may be, I think none of us can afford to sit quite that comfortably on the past. What do you say? Might you be tempted to come and win some entirely new laurels?'

Cuthbert smiled and said little. He was still quite undecided about what he thought of living and working in Glasgow. Quinn sensed his ambivalence and decided to call in reinforcements.

'Regrettably, I will have to get back to my desk, but I want to introduce you to someone first. Come with me, Cuthbert. May I introduce you to Professor Stockman?'

The elderly, bald man looked up from his seat with eager eyes and immediately rose to shake Cuthbert's hand. His handshake was firm, but Cuthbert could tell it had been stronger just as the slightly stooped man before him had once been taller.

Now 70, Ralph Stockman had held the regius chair in

— 38 —

materia medica at the university for over thirty years. He looked the imposing stranger over with a critical eye but was charmed the moment he opened his mouth to speak.

'Would that be an Edinburgh accent I detect, Dr Cuthbert?'

'Indeed it is, sir. Not unlike your own.'

'Goodness knows there's few enough of us in this place. We need to stick together. Come and join me, young man, and tell me your story.'

Cuthbert's guide could see he was in good hands and took his leave. As Cuthbert took a seat, the professor raised a finger to attract the steward and said, 'You'll take some tea with me, I hope.'

'Delighted, sir.'

'Well, Dr Cuthbert? What brings you to the wrong side of Scotland? Are you visiting, or are you looking to stay in this godless place?'

Stockman had a glint of mischief in his eyes that Cuthbert suspected was undimmed with age. He had never before met him but knew of the professor's reputation and his work.

'I'm here at the invitation of your dean, sir. It seems you are seeking to appoint a new chair of forensic medicine, and for some reason he thought I might be a possible candidate.'

'Don't be so modest, Dr Cuthbert. If you're here in that capacity, you are certainly here on merit, and as an outsider, on merit alone. What you need to know about this grand institution, young man, is that it likes its own, and outsiders are few and far between. You will find that the majority of my distinguished colleagues have been nowhere but this city and this university. They studied here, they earned their degrees here, and they have worked here ever since. That's the way they like it, but, of course, it does lead to a somewhat inward-looking point of view. And the ones they regard as the greatest outsiders of all are men like us – from Edinburgh.'

Cuthbert, who had lived and worked in London for the last seven years, had all but forgotten the rivalry between Scotland's largest city and its capital. Everything Professor Stockman said of Glasgow, Cuthbert knew to be equally true of Edinburgh, where many of the faculty were University of Edinburgh graduates.

He was happy in London and had spent his years there working hard at building connections and professional relationships. He had developed a good working partnership with his colleagues at Scotland Yard and had even found a warm companionship with his housekeeper.

Now, sitting in the high-backed leather chair in the smoky College Club that was trying hard to echo those other Pall Mall institutions, he began to wonder why he had come.

Stockman leaned over and in a conspiratorial whisper asked, 'Have you met the old buffer yet?'

'If you mean Professor Glaister, I have only met him twice and both times briefly at that. I attended the funeral of my own professor, Harvey Littlejohn, in Edinburgh a few years ago and he was there.'

'Holding court, I wouldn't wonder.'

'You don't sound like an admirer, Professor Stockman.'

'Oh, he has few admirers in this place. But I think he has always had a particular dislike for me. I am a pharmacologist, a proper one, while he dabbles somewhat in toxicology – a gifted amateur, really. We have crossed academic swords on a number of occasions over the years. We're all arrogant here, but he does rather take the trait to a new level. He does know how to be courteous though, when he's not trying to pick a fight with you.

'Anyway, you'll meet him soon enough. He's lost a little of his fire, but he's still thoroughly objectionable. And then, of course, there's the younger son. You won't meet Junior, as he's still out in Egypt, but the word is he's on his way back to take over where his father has left off. Apparently, he's keen to make a name for himself in his father's profession. I don't altogether agree that's a good path for any young man. After all, it does rather invite unfavourable comparisons, don't you think?

'That said, he does have the advantage over you, no matter who you are or what you've done, Dr Cuthbert. He has Glasgow blood and a regius professor's blood at that.'

'As I said, professor, I am somewhat bemused as to why I'm here at all. But perhaps it is simply a subterfuge to take the appearance of nepotism off the proceedings. In any case, I'm not sure I want to leave London, not yet anyway. This is the first position I have been invited to apply for, and I thought it would be an interesting and valuable experience, if nothing else.'

'And why are they not snapping you up in London or Oxbridge? Too qualified or not qualified enough?'

'I'm sure they have their reasons, sir, but I am in no hurry. I have more than enough work between my duties at St Thomas's, the university and Scotland Yard.'

'Well, do think carefully about throwing your hat in this particular ring, won't you? But you don't need an old codger like me telling you what to do.'

Cuthbert smiled graciously but did not contradict him. Stockman put his newspaper down in his lap and strained his neck to see the door at the other end of the room and tutted.

'Well, well. Speak of the Devil and he's sure to walk through the door of the College Club. Looks like you'll be getting to meet old Glaister sooner than later.'

Cuthbert turned and saw the current regius professor of forensic medicine taking off his overcoat at the door. John Glaister was 75, and although clearly failing in health and vigour, he was still a force to be reckoned with.

He was a small, lean man with a hawk-like face dominated

by a thick white moustache. He walked briskly past the tables and chairs in the smoking room and looked annoyed until he found his usual seat.

His clothes were from a different era, and he was the last of the professors at the university to wear a Victorian black silk hat, frock coat and wide Gladstone collar.

Cuthbert watched him and noted how much frailer he looked compared to the last time he had seen him at Littlejohn's funeral. Then, as Stockman had correctly surmised, he had been the centre of attention and the self-appointed director of proceedings. Now, he sat awkwardly in the oversized chair and his breathing was laboured. Not helped, Cuthbert noted, by the small black cheroot which he took from a silver case in his coat pocket, lit and drew heavily upon.

'I would be obliged, Professor Stockman, if you would kindly introduce me to Professor Glaister. As I mentioned, we have met before, but I am sure he won't remember me.'

Stockman had been enjoying Cuthbert's company, and he was quite sure that once met, even for the briefest of moments, this handsome young man would be hard to forget.

'Of course, but I won't stay with you. As I said, he doesn't like me, and I don't like him.'

Stockman struggled up from his low chair and crossed the room with Cuthbert in tow.

'I say, Glaister, I have someone I want you to meet. The name's Cuthbert, from Tommy's in London. He's one of your lot – sleuth with a scalpel. Dr Cuthbert, may I introduce you to Professor Glaister.'

Cuthbert bowed his head and held out his hand. Glaister rose awkwardly and had to look up to the younger man who was a good foot taller than him. He shook hands and invited him to sit with him.

Stockman made his excuses and left without saying

anything else, much to the delight of the old man. Cuthbert reminded Glaister that they had met when he had examined him for his Diploma in Public Health in Edinburgh and again, briefly, some years later at Professor Littlejohn's funeral.

'Littlejohn always spoke very highly of you, young man. But he was a sentimental old fool at the best of times. You are in London now, I believe. And how do you find working in that Babylon?'

'No more of a Babylon than any other large city, Professor Glaister. And I have had the opportunity to work with some remarkable people.'

Cuthbert might once have been intimidated by the great man but no longer. He was sure of both his abilities and his choices, and while he acknowledged Glaister's formidable contribution to his subject, he couldn't help but compare him with another professor he had not only admired but loved as a father figure. Glaister's shoes were undoubtedly large ones to fill, but Cuthbert knew his training at the hands of Professor Littlejohn in Edinburgh and his subsequent experience made him more than capable. However, he was still far from sure he wanted to leave his own 'Babylon'.

'And I expect you are here to take my place, young man. I'm sorry your journey has been wasted. The position has already been filled.'

'That is not my understanding, professor. Nor, it seems, is it the opinion of your dean.'

'I am the one to make the decision as to whom my successor will be, and it certainly won't be in the gift of that lab rat, Quinn. No, this fine institution will be enjoying the presence of another Glaister to carry my torch.'

'Your son is a well-qualified medical jurist, but I am unfamiliar with his research achievements. Surely they are more important than blood line?'

The conversation faltered as the old man sipped the coffee that had been poured by the steward, and he put on his glasses to take a better look at this impertinent youngster.

'Research is nothing more than play. Practical experience is everything, and that is how I have built my department and my reputation. You would do well to remember that, Cuthbert. Progress is made through hard labour and casework, not toying with testing the improbable at some laboratory bench. My son John knows how to work, and under my direction he will continue the work that I have started.'

'So you plan to retain control of your department even after you have retired. I'm sure when you took the chair, you would not have welcomed such interference from your predecessor.'

'You have an insolent tongue, my lad.'

'I ceased to be anyone's lad, sir, when I put on the King's uniform and fought for my country. Now, I will annoy you no further. Good day, Professor Glaister. I wish you a long and fruitful retirement and can only hope your son knows what he has in store.'

Cuthbert smiled at the old man's thunderous frown as he rose from his seat, bowed his head again and left. He was grateful to have the decision made for him. Having been invited to visit, he would have been duty bound to apply for the post, but everything he had seen in this city and this university made it clear that he was unwelcome.

He knew now his presence was merely to stir the political pot. The dean was clearly engaged in a power struggle with old Glaister, but Cuthbert had no doubt who would win. The post would undoubtedly go to the young Glaister, and as far as Cuthbert was concerned, he was welcome to it. He still had aspirations to pursue a more academic career, but there were other universities, and some were better than this one and had the advantage of being much closer to the people in his life who mattered.

*

He decided he needed to walk to clear his head, and he crossed the large east quadrangle and went out to the back of the main university building to take in the view across Glasgow.

Standing at the foot of the university's flagpole he could survey the River Clyde, the entire south of the city and the hills beyond. The river was thick with traffic and the pall of smoke from countless chimneys blackened the air. The Clyde and the shipyards on its banks were the main source of the city's wealth. Heavy, hard industry pounded through hammers and riveters had made Glasgow famous.

Its dense population, huddled for the most part in those dreadful overcrowded tenements, were told, as Henderson had put it, that they lived in the second city of the British Empire. Other cities made the same claim, but Glasgow did so with some justification. Here, they built the world's ships and trains. They wove the world's carpets and made its sewing machines. There was nothing, they said, that could not be built in Glasgow.

Cuthbert turned away from the panorama and looked back at the dark gothic tower of the university looming above him. The tower, not quite made of ivory but soot-stained sandstone, was already high but was built on a hill giving even greater elevation. Visible across the city, this was a symbol of another kind of industry: the manufacture of ideas and the pressing out of minds. What they were doing down there on the river, with sheet metal, hammers and welding torches, they were also doing in their own way up here in their lecture rooms.

Cuthbert knew from his time in Edinburgh, and his more recent workings with the University of London, that all universities were riven with political intrigue. He could not blame Glasgow for being just like all the rest, but at the same time he was keen to get away.

He had intended to stay the rest of the week in the city but started walking back down University Avenue and then briskly through Kelvingrove Park towards the city centre and his hotel, with the intention of rearranging his train booking. If possible, he wanted to leave that night. He had wasted enough time in the second city and was eager to return to the first.

At the hotel, he informed the staff of his change of plans and managed to secure a berth on the night train from Central Station to Euston. It would depart at eleven, and he would have plenty of time to dine and do some reading before he embarked.

He changed for dinner and arranged for his bags to be repacked. By nine o'clock, he was relaxing in the hotel lounge with a glass of whisky and his small, leather-bound copy of Juvenal.

Lost in his reading, he failed to notice the bellboy approaching him. It was the same one who had run his errand that morning, but this time he stood at Cuthbert's side waiting for him to look up. He only coughed when he could wait no longer.

He asked him to come to the house telephone as there was an urgent call for him. Cuthbert immediately thought it might be Madame Smith checking in on his progress. After all, who apart from her and the people at the university knew where he was staying? But the voice on the phone was unfamiliar with its Glaswegian accent.

'Dr Cuthbert? I'm sorry to trouble you, sir, but we need your help.'

Chapter 4

Bridgeton: 12 May 1921

The slap on the side of his head was so hard it swept him off the chair and onto the bare boards of the floor. His ear was ringing, but he instinctively rolled into a tight ball waiting for the first of the kicks. His father's heavy boot thumped into his back, and he squealed in pain as he scrambled under the table to escape further blows.

'Leave the wean, you bad bastard.'

The baby in his cot by the bed recess let out a cry, and the woman placed herself between the swaying drunk and the table. She bore her own bruises from his fists, but she would not have him hit the child again.

'Rabbie, get oot o' here and run to Mrs Clark's. Away ye go!'

There was a scurry of gangly limbs and scraped knees from under the table and a flash of short trousers as the boy made for the door to the landing. His mother held her ground and stared her man down. She knew she would now take the brunt of his drunken rage, but she could cope with that as long as her son was safe.

The boy rapped on the downstairs neighbour's door, and when Mrs Clark opened it, she saw the tear-stained face of the ten-year-old, still with the red finger marks of his father's hand across his cheek.

'Him again?'

'Aye, Mrs Clark. My maw told me to come down. Can I come in?'

Sitting at the table in the middle of the single room were three small girls, silently eating slices of bread. From behind the thin curtain screening off the recess bed there was an explosive hacking cough followed by a weary sigh. Like Rabbie's house, this one was bare, and the only warmth was from the cast iron range that served as both heater and stove.

'Sit yourself down, son, and I'll give you a piece. Would you like that?'

Rabbie was trembling. He looked up at the woman, and like a dry sponge soaked up the kindness she proffered. He found a chair beside the girls and bowed his head to hide his tears from them. He took the slice of bread spread with dripping, savouring each mouthful, but was unable now to control his sobs.

'Why's he crying, mammy?'

'Hush, Sadie. The wee boy's hurt himself. Leave him be.'

The small girl looked at the boy, some four years her senior, and reached up to put her arm about his neck. 'D'you want me to kiss it better?'

Rabbie shook his head and wriggled out of her embarrassing embrace. His chin on his chest, he sat eating his bread in the silences between their father's coughing fits.

When Bessie McDiarmid came to collect him, Mrs Clark first took her out onto the landing to talk. Rabbie could not hear what they were saying but knew that once again his mother would be on the receiving end of the advice she was always given: leave him.

As she came in, she was still thanking Mrs Clark and

apologising to everyone about the bother she had put them to.

'Mr Clark, how are you keeping the day?'

He coughed in response and then found enough breath to add, 'Ach, just the same, hen.'

Rabbie was led back upstairs, and his mother could see the fear on his face as she pushed the door open.

'It's all right, son. He's away, and he'll no be back the night.'

Inside, his little sister was still huddled in the corner near the sink from where she had watched everything that had happened. She was naturally a quiet child and was easily forgotten, which meant she saw and heard more than she ever should.

The baby was sleeping now in the basket on the floor beside the girl, and Mrs McDiarmid went to the press to get the remains of a loaf. She cut another slice of bread for Rabbie.

'Want a wee bit o' sugar on it, son?'

He came and pressed his head into her bosom, and she embraced him, trying to move his small head from where the last blow had landed.

'D'you know something, son? Tomorrow's going to be a better day.'

*

That night, instead of sharing the truckle bed with his little sister, they all slept in the bed recess, under the big blankets.

When he woke, his mother was already up tending to his baby brother. He watched her quietly from the bed before she realised he was awake and before she knew she must conceal her pain. She held the baby awkwardly, wincing as she moved, and Rabbie knew she had been kicked because he knew that was how it felt.

The hatred welled up inside him and bubbled out in the form of hot, frustrated tears. He knew he could do nothing to stop the man, and at the same time he knew he had to try.

His mother glanced over to the bed and saw that his eyes were open, and she smiled and straightened. 'C'mon, or you'll be the last one up. School's no going to wait for you.'

He splashed his face with some water from the cold tap and put his shirt on over the vest he had slept in. His grey jumper was over the back of the chair, warming in front of the range, and he grabbed that after pulling on his shorts. His socks were in his boots by the door, and in a trice he was sitting at the table, sipping the milky tea his mother had poured and eating the watery porridge she had prepared.

His little sister was already dressed when he sat down, and she was writing in her school jotter. He peered across trying to read it upside down, but sensing he was prying, she curled her left arm around the page.

'What you writin', Lizzie?'

'It's my news.'

'News?'

'Miss Mackie says we have to have some news to tell every day, and we have to write it down in our jotter.'

'So what's your news the day?'

'I'm no tellin'. You'll just laugh.'

'Naw, I won't. C'mon, what is it?'

'Well, I'm writin' about you eatin'.'

'Me?'

'Aye, you. You're always eatin'. You'd eat everything if Mammy let you.'

'I would not. Here, let me see what you're writin'. Give me it.'

Rabbie grabbed at the jotter across the table, and Lizzie fought to hold on to it. She screamed, and their mother intervened just as Rabbie drew back his hand to slap the girl.

'Don't you dare raise your hand to your sister. I've got one bully in this family; I'll no have two.'

Lizzie was now sobbing. 'You're just like my da. You'll be kicking Mammy as well soon.' She said it quietly, almost to herself, but her brother heard and was horrified.

'No, Lizzie. I'm no like him. Don't say that.'

She just looked at the boy through the same burning tears of frustration that he knew so well. She had already realised that her brother would grow into a man and be able to fight back, but that she would always be at the mercy of those with clenched fists and hard boots.

'Get yourselves to school, the pair o' you. And no more fightin'. Rabbie, be sure and see your sister to the gate.'

The children collected their coats and left together. They walked down the close stairs in silence and only in the street did Rabbie reach for Lizzie's hand and say that he was sorry.

'I would never kick my maw. I don't want you to think I would ever do that. Here.'

He searched in his pocket and pulled out a small chewy caramel in a bright red wrapper.

'I've been savin' it for special. But you can have it. Sorry.'

Lizzie took the sweet and put it in her own pocket, deciding that it was too precious to be eaten without the spice of anticipation. This way, all day long, she could think about it in its lovely red paper and imagine what it would taste like when she finally unwrapped it.

At the school gates, Lizzie went into the girls' playground and Rabbie into the boys'. He was immediately set upon by two classmates who needed a third for the game they were playing. Rabbie was dragged, though not unwillingly, to the shed where Jimmy was holding court.

'Right, is that us wi' a team? It's three-a-side kick-the-can. They chalk marks over there are the goals.'

The six boys all scrambled for possession of the battered can that was doing service as a football. The game was rough but good-natured, and even the knocks that each received were taken in their stride. When the bell rang, the score was standing at a draw and there was a tacit agreement made by six serious faces that this would need to be decided later.

Over in the girls' playground, Lizzie and her classmates were already lined up alongside the other classes waiting to be admitted. The boys were always less compliant, and Miss Watson often had to call more than once to bring some sort of order to the throng.

'It's only your own time you're wasting, boys. Jimmy Summers, would you put that tin can down this minute and get in line.'

Rabbie liked school because he liked learning. He also liked the way the school smelled, and the way that his teacher talked to them. He had heard that at the big school the teachers would punish pupils with the belt, but here there was a tenderness, and although Miss Watson could shout, he could never imagine her hitting one of them.

That morning as usual it was arithmetic. They had been thoroughly drilled in their times tables, and most of the pupils, with the exception of Jimmy Summers, were adept at multiplying and dividing in their heads. Jimmy always seemed to get his sums wrong and spent more time sitting in the corner on the seat reserved for the dunce than at his own desk. When he sat there, he always made faces behind Miss Watson's back, and it was all Rabbie and the others could do to hold in their giggles.

There was writing and reading and then there was Rabbie's favourite: geography. He loved when his teacher pulled down the large map of the world like a roller blind at the top of the blackboard and started to tell them stories about other countries. He'd decided that one day he would go travelling, maybe on a big ship from the Clyde. He knew the names of all the continents and the oceans, and in his head he was already charting his voyages.

On the way home, Rabbie and Jimmy walked side by side and Lizzie trailed behind, in sight but out of earshot. Jimmy's shirt-tail was out, and he was scuffing his boots along the pavement, trying to keep a small stone in play. All the while, he was talking about the freedom of the weekend before them and all the things he and his father would be doing.

Rabbie's father, Wullie McDiarmid, worked in the engineering sheds at Barclay's on Fielding Street. He was as unreliable as he was unskilled, but when he showed up and when he was sober, he could put in a shift. He was only kept on the books because the manager could pay him less than the rest. The man with the bowler hat knew Wullie McDiarmid would never find another job, not without any references – a fact he regularly used as a stick to keep him under his thumb.

Jimmy Summers' father also worked at Barclay's, but from the way the boy talked about him, Rabbie could not imagine anyone more different. Jimmy told tales of how his father was the best goalie in the street, and when they played with a real ball he would always be on the winning side.

The Summers family were just as poor as the McDiarmids, but Rabbie could see that they had riches he could only dream of. Jimmy's father was a big brute of a man but had never laid a finger on any of his sons. He was strict but was more likely to hoist them proudly on to his shoulders to get a better view than to drive them under a table.

When Rabbie listened to Jimmy talk about him – of the games, of the walks on the Green, of the kite he had made him – he wondered what it was he had done to make his own father the way he was. He knew somehow that it must be his fault, but in his ignorance he felt powerless to change it.

When they arrived home from school, the brother and

sister pushed on the open door of their house and tumbled in laughing. They knew their father would still be at work and that the single end was safe, at least for the time being.

Their mother had spent the day mopping the close stairs and landings. It was her turn to clean the communal areas, and she took great pride in making sure a good job was done. She had no desire to be branded in the same way as Mrs Comerford upstairs. Once, when she was mopping the close with disinfectant, she overheard a neighbour pass comment on how she was doing.

'Well, I'll say one thing for her, Mrs McDiarmid never jukes her turn. No like that slitterer upstairs on the top landin'. Stairs hardly look as if they've been washed after she's had a go. And she makes more mess than she cleans. Spatters all up the walls.'

The toilet also had to be cleaned, and that was a bigger job. The toilet on their landing served the three single-roomed homes on the floor. The plumbing was old and unreliable, and it was not uncommon for one of the toilets in the close to be in need of repairs — repairs which the factor would never get around to. The burden on the toilets became even greater then, with as many as forty people using each one.

Bessie McDiarmid had spent time that day on her hands and knees scrubbing the floor and walls of the pokey space to get rid of the grime and the smell.

She was tired when the children arrived but managed a smile of welcome. They knew that today was always a difficult one for their mother because it was Friday: pay day.

Bessie McDiarmid was anxious as usual. Her purse was empty, and there was little left to pawn. She, herself, had not eaten that day, giving what she had to the children. Now with no food at all in the press, she waited, watching from the window for her husband to come home.

Already the gaslights in the street were coming on, and she

knew he must be in some bar, preferring the company of his drinking cronies to his family. She put on her coat and steeled herself for the search. Rabbie saw her quick bony fingers fasten the buttons and then straighten her knitted beret in the small mirror hanging on the back of the door.

'I need to go and look for your da. You stay here, Rabbie, and watch the weans. I'll be back as soon as I get what's left o' his pay packet.'

As she walked along the Main Street, Bridgeton was humming with activity. It had gone six o'clock, but most of the shops were still open, with the lights in their windows reflected on the wet roads outside. The bars that seemed to be on every corner were full and customers spilled onto the pavements. A tram clanged past throwing sparks from its trolley head as it scraped along the overhead wires. And on the corner where the George was, a boy not much older than Rabbie was calling out loudly to sell the sheaf of evening papers folded over his arm.

Bessie knew this was her husband's favourite haunt, and she pushed past two of the working men who were blocking the door. Inside, the air was thick with the cigarette smoke that had yellowed every surface over the years. The place smelt rank, but none of the men drinking appeared to notice it. She pushed her way through the Friday night crowd to reach the far end of the bar where her husband was propped.

'Wullie McDiarmid, what time do you call this?'

'A man needs a drink, woman. Do you have to give me a showin' up here as well?'

'The weans need to eat, Wullie. I need oor money.'

'Ma money, you mean. I work hard all week for it, and I'll spend it how I like.' He turned to the men beside him at the bar and stretched out his arms. 'Right, gentlemen, I'm holding. What'll you have?'

'Wullie. For God's sake, what about the weans?'

He turned and swore at her and tossed some coins onto the sawdust-covered floor. She scrabbled for them between the dirty boots and counted what she had found. The three shillings would feed them but wouldn't pay the rent.

Her husband was already regaling his drinking pals with a story and there would be nothing else for her. She knew he would be spending another night in a gutter, drunk and smelling of beer and his own vomit. She pocketed the coins and spat at his feet before leaving.

As she pushed through the door of the pub, a thin woman came steaming in. She didn't cast a glance at Bessie because she was too preoccupied in scanning the busy bar for her own husband.

*

On her way home, Bessie bought the last of the day-old bread as the bakery was closing and caught the grocer, just as he was pulling down his window blinds, to get some tea, sugar, milk and butter. That would have to do for their supper, if she was to eke out the money for the week.

Already she was worrying about the rent. She needed seven shillings and eleven pence to pay the factor's man who would be calling the following Wednesday. Like clockwork he would rap on each door in the tenement, collect the payment and note it down carefully in the rent book. Little grace was afforded unless for bereavement. Simply being poor was no excuse for not paying. She dreaded the thought of eviction and knew she would have to find the money come hell or high water before Wednesday.

As she walked back to the house, she was already going through her possessions in her mind trying to think if she had anything left worth pawning. She rubbed her hands and felt for the wedding band. She wasn't sure she could get it off even if she wanted, and things had never before been so bad that she had thought to pawn it.

Now, though, it was just a reminder of her shackles rather than her marriage, and she tugged hard, sliding it a little towards her red and swollen knuckle. She resolved to try again with some butter when she got home.

At the close entry, Mrs Comerford, the slitterer from the top floor, was standing just inside out of the night air. Like the other wives she was wearing her wrap-around apron under a thin coat. She looked embarrassed to see her downstairs neighbour and folded her arms tight about her.

'Mrs Comerford, is everything all right?'

'Oh, never better. I'm just waitin' for somebody.'

'At this time o' night? You sure everything's dandy, hen?'

The neighbour relaxed her arms and knew she had to explain herself to get rid of Bessie. 'It's the debt man. I'm just waitin' for him to come and collect. I cannae see him in the hoose. I cannae let Bill know I've gone to the loaners. But how else am I supposed to get the weans clothes and shoes with what he gives us?'

Bessie knew that they were all struggling, and one way to keep the landlords at bay and the children fed and clothed was to borrow money. It was a dangerous path though, and her own mother had always warned her against ever thinking it was a solution. She also knew that many wives who took it would never let their husbands know that what they provided was not enough.

'He's got his pride. You can't rub that in a man's face.'

Bessie McDiarmid looked at the tired woman's eyes and found herself wondering what exactly men were for. She smiled at Mrs Comerford and patted her arm. 'No be long till the weather gets warmer, hen. It's always better when it's summer.'

*

Saturdays were no different for Bessie, but with no school the children could dawdle in the morning before their mother would throw them out to play in the back court. Rabbie and Lizzie would never play together, each instead gravitating towards their own peers.

Lizzie would quickly find a game of 'shops' with the three Clark girls from downstairs and would be welcomed as a new customer. Small pebbles, twigs and leaves would be arranged to delight the clientele, and much fun would be had making just the right selection for that evening's meal. Then, roles could be swapped, and there was just as much excitement in being the shopkeeper, explaining the relative merits of your fine wares to a new customer.

The games Rabbie and the boys from the close played involved very little sitting. They would climb onto the old midden roof, which would become a bastion to be defended or the deck of an ocean-going galleon. They would also swing on an old rope tied to the railings that divided the backcourts. Great flying leaps would be achieved if a good run-up could be managed.

There was little space to play football, what with all the 'shops', so the boys had long since learned that they needed to make use of the street for that. One boy up the next tenement possessed a real ball – and all the prestige and authority that went with it.

He could pick and choose his team-mates, decide when and where the game would start, and could even declare a final score that would never be questioned even if it only occasionally matched what had actually happened. Everyone accepted his word because it was his ball, and they all knew he could walk away with it at any moment should he so wish.

While playing in the street, Rabbie saw his father walking along the pavement. He had been out all night and was now returning home, penniless and hungover. The boy knew he was only dangerous when he was drunk, and now he would be irritable but meek.

All the same, he kept out of sight and watched him enter their close. He thought of his mother in the house and of his baby brother. They'd have no escape from the foul-smelling man, but Rabbie knew that all he was likely to do was fall on the recess bed and snore away the day.

Rabbie imagined what he would like to say, to do, to the man. He imagined being taller and stronger, of being able to stand up to him and forbid him from coming into the house, or even the street. He imagined the exhilaration of taking control and of having the strength to enforce his will. Then he realised that it would be a long time coming and their family had to survive his father until it did. He suddenly wanted to kick something hard, such was his frustration.

He was brought back from his thoughts when he heard his mother shout down from the open window. She was leaning out and calling his name. There was a moment of panic in his chest as he thought she might be shouting for help, but all she wanted was a message run.

She threw a piece of paper wrapped round a coin down to his feet with remarkable accuracy and told him to run to the Co-op to get their dinner. The paper that had encased the coin was also the small shopping list neatly written in pencil. He picked it up and made immediately for the shop.

The Co-operative at the corner of Main Street was an emporium like no other, and Rabbie never shirked an opportunity to enjoy its sights and smells. He especially enjoyed watching the skill with which the server could pat up a perfect quarter pound of butter with his two grooved wooden paddles and wrap it in greaseproof paper in what seemed like a single move.

The greatest joy of all was when someone with a windfall would request a quarter of boiled ham. The joint would be hoisted onto the slicing machine, pinned in place by the securing prongs and the spinning blade turned by hand to produce wafer-thin cuts of the delicious pink meat. Each slice was collected on the other side of the machine on a sheet of the same greaseproof paper and then folded and bagged.

There were pyramids of coloured tins all around the walls, every one, he thought, a potential football. There were packets of biscuits which he had never tasted, and there were large jars of exotic ingredients from some of those distant lands on Miss Watson's map. Tea, currants, raisins, sugar, and different nuts whose names he had never learned.

The whole shop was like a theatre, and Rabbie could have stood and watched its magical performance all day. In between the careful selection of the goods and their packaging, there was also the chatter. Banter as rich as the foodstuffs on sale filled the air. Listening to the housewives of Bridgeton was an education for the young boy, and for learning about all the goings-on in his world, it was better than any newspaper.

'Well, young man. What's it to be the day?'

'I've got a list, mister.'

'Hand it over, then. It's no doing me any good in your pocket, is it, son?'

The shop assistant scanned the list while simultaneously reaching for the items, almost without looking, and all too quickly the paper bag was ready.

'You've remembered your number, son? No number, no divvy.'

Everyone who shopped at the Co-op had a number for their

account that allowed them to claim some money back, their dividend, twice a year. Every penny spent counted, and that number was one of the first things his mother had drummed into him.

'Oh aye, three-four-eight-two.'

'Well, don't tell me, tell the lassie at the till. Here.' He handed the boy the bag and directed him to the teller, but Rabbie was in no rush to leave. He had noticed that the meat slicer was just about to be put into action, and he couldn't miss that.

'Move aside, son, if you're done . . . Mrs Cameron, if it's no yourself. How's it going the day? Is your man up and oot o' his bed yet?'

'Och, you're an awful man, Mr Sloane. But you know my Charlie better than he knows himself. Listen, did you hear about the couple just moved into number ten? Scandalous, so it is.'

Heads were put together across the counter, voices were lowered, and the necks of the other women in the shop queue were strained before faces blanched and mouths fell open. Rabbie could not hear the gossip but could tell it was juicy and of the highest quality, much like the ham being sliced at the other end of the glass counter.

Rabbie walked home past the Italian café just so he could smell the coffee from its open door and then past the pawnshop with its window full of glittering objects, one of which, unbeknownst to him, was his mother's wedding ring.

As he rounded the corner, he tensed when he saw the big boys from Landressy Street. They were all of 12 or 13 years old but appeared so much taller and more mature than him. He knew that he had to walk past them and that crossing to the other side of the road would be a sign of the kind of weakness they liked to exploit. There was nothing for it but to put his head down and go for it.

As he approached the group of four boys, one stepped into his path blocking his way and he was brought to a sharp halt.

'And what school do you go to, wee man?'

Rabbie knew this was the coded question to discover if he was one of them or one of the others. Catholics and Protestants were schooled separately in the city, and if his answer was to their liking, he would have safe passage; if not, he could expect to feel their fists. The trouble, of course, was not knowing which answer was required.

The truth, that he went to one of the Protestant primary schools, might or might not save him for you could never tell which tribe you were dealing with. He learned bible stories at school, and they sang hymns, but Rabbie and his family had never set foot in a church, Protestant or otherwise. Religion itself meant nothing to him, but the tribal warfare that existed at every level in his small world certainly did.

'C'mon, wee man, are you a Billy or a Dan?' As he said it, the biggest of the boys was already clenching his fist to seal the deal.

Rabbie opted for the truth, if for no other reason than it was the easiest. 'I go to London Road Primary.'

'On your way then, pal. And watch you don't drop your mammy's messages.'

From his earliest memories, he had been aware of the divide on the streets where he lived. No one looked different, no one dressed differently, but if he and his friends had to walk past the Catholic primary school, they would be pelted with stones. And he would always join in the barrage if the roles were reversed.

He knew it had something to do with God or the Church, but he wasn't sure if there was a difference between the two. He did know that he was expected to hate them as much as they hated him. He knew he was to support his football team and despise theirs. He knew he was to think he was better in some way than they were. But when he saw the children at the Catholic school playing with their skipping ropes and chasing tin cans just like Lizzie and him did, he could see no difference. So what was it really all about?

*

On Sunday, the baby had been irritable all day. He wouldn't settle in his cot, and when Bessie tried to feed him, he would twist his head this way and that. When she did manage to get him to take a mouthful of bread soaked in milk, he would choke and spit it out and cry even more. She felt his forehead. He was definitely warm, and his cheeks were flushed.

'I think the wean's teethin'. I'll need to go and get some whisky from Mrs Brown downstairs to rub on his gums. Poor wee thing's in terrible pain.'

At the mention of whisky, her husband looked up. Bessie shook her head and raised her eyebrows. 'No for you, Wullie, so don't get your hopes up. You're no the one that's teethin'.'

Throughout the night, the child never settled and kept the adults awake. Bessie walked the floor with him, trying to soothe him and keep him quiet so that her husband could get some sleep, but every time Wullie dropped off, the baby would squeal, and he would roll over and curse the child.

Bessie took him out on the landing and continued to pace with him in her arms. By the early hours, the crying had eased, but he had become limp. She felt his forehead again and he was still warm. She also noticed that his neck was starting to swell on both sides. The child's breathing was also becoming noisy like one of the old men in the street.

She shook him gently; although he was no longer crying, he wasn't asleep. His eyes were watery and half-shut and there was a blue tinge around his lips. Bessie started to panic and ran with the baby downstairs to Mrs Clark. Despite the hour, she chapped the door loudly and called for help. Mrs Clark opened the door in alarm.

'He's just hingin', Sandra. I don't know what to do.'

Sandra Clark took one look at the distraught mother and another at the child in her arms. He was perspiring and flopped over her shoulder, his breathing laboured and rasping, and the blue around his lips was spreading. She didn't need to take a second look.

'Oh my God, Bessie, it's the diphtheria. You need to get the doctor right away.'

By the time the G.P. arrived at the tenement, the child was grey and motionless. Despite his youth, the doctor had already seen too many cases of diphtheria in Bridgeton and knew there was nothing he could do for this unfortunate child.

The child had died in his mother's arms, and sitting at the Clarks' table, she was unable to put him down for the doctor to examine him. Mrs Clark did all the talking and explained that he was 18 months old and had never been a weak child.

She managed to ease Bessie's grip just enough to loosen his shawl and let the doctor listen for his heart and look in his mouth. It was as he expected: a thick grey membrane at the back of the child's throat typical of this disease. The doctor knew that if he had been called sooner, he might have been able to cut the membrane or even slit open the child's tiny windpipe to allow him to breathe, but even that might not have saved him from the inevitable blood poisoning that would follow.

He wrote out the death certificate and tried to hand it to the mother, but Mrs Clark intervened and took it from him. She looked for her purse, unsure if she had the necessary shilling. When he saw what she was doing, he stayed her hand and shook his head.

'No need – not for a wee one like this. There was nothing I could do.'

After he left, Sandra Clark held Bessie and the dead child until she was able to let him go. She took the body and wrapped it tight in his mother's shawl and laid him out of sight under the sink.

'C'mon, hen, let's get you back upstairs. Your weans will be wonderin' where their mammy is, and you've still got them to look after.'

It was already daylight when Bessie McDiarmid was helped back into her house. Mrs Clark put the kettle on and started the tea. She saw Wullie raise his head from the bed in the recess, puzzled by her presence, and she thought it best to tell him. She found the words and said them slowly and quietly, explaining all that had happened in the night. He looked at her as if he was still wondering who she was and rolled over, pulling the blanket up over his ears. All he could say was, 'Good, one less mouth to feed.'

The violence of Bessie's attack surprised everyone. She leapt at her husband in the bed and started screaming and clawing at his face, trying to rip the very eyes from his head. He writhed but found himself bound by the bedclothes and her weight upon him. Bessie was beating him hard about the head, shouting, 'Bastard, bastard, bastard,' over and over. Either he could not fight back or chose not to.

The commotion woke the children who had been sleeping on the truckle bed, and they were startled at the sight of their mother beating their father for once. Rabbie's first thought was to help her, even though he had no idea what had prompted it all. However, Bessie's punches slowed and weakened as she exhausted herself with the effort. She was sobbing uncontrollably, and Mrs Clark took her again in her arms. Rabbie looked up at the women, now both crying, and knew that something awful had happened. He felt his sister nestle into his back and could feel her fear.

Again, it was Mrs Clark who had to tell Rabbie and Lizzie that their baby brother had died.

'Your mammy's awful upset. She'll need you both to be good. Can you do that for her?'

Both children, shocked into the morning, nodded and went to their mother. They embraced her about the legs, and she in turn bent down and knelt, scooping them both into her arms. There would be no school for them today for Bessie would not let them out of her sight.

Wullie had turned away from them and soon started snoring again. Bessie ignored him and now put her mind to getting the children ready and told them she was going to take them out. They would go for a walk on the Green. It was such a lovely day, and they could even take a piece and have a picnic. Their eyes lit up at the prospect, and she was warmed by their little faces. She had been ripped apart by the loss of her baby son but decided she needed to count her blessings. And here they were smiling up at her: one, two.

The three slipped out, leaving the father asleep. He would be waking up soon for his late shift and would be looking for something to eat, but she had decided that from now on he was on his own. She had nowhere to go, but she resolved she would never cook his meals, wash his clothes or share his bed again. She knew he would lash out, but she also knew that no pain he could inflict could be greater than what she was already enduring.

Wullie woke to an empty house, and no one came when he called. He stumbled from the bed and relieved himself in the sink rather than making his way to the toilet on the landing.

He rummaged around to find something to eat and found the dregs of the quarter-bottle of the cheapest whisky that his wife had borrowed to soothe the baby's gums. She had hidden it carefully but not carefully enough to outwit a determined alcoholic like her husband.

He swallowed it in one gulp on an empty stomach and soon started to feel the effects. He looked about the shabby single room he shared with the bony little woman who was his wife and her children that just annoyed him.

He could not understand how it had all come to this for a man like him, and he was angry. He tried to drain more whisky from the empty bottle and then threw it against the range where it smashed, covering the floor with shards of glass.

He dressed and searched his pockets for any coins that might get him another drink but there was nothing. He was even angrier that he had given her his money and convinced himself that she was just bleeding him dry. They all were. They were all against him and nobody cared about him, so from now on he needed to look after number one.

He was still brooding on his misfortune when the door opened and Bessie came in with the children.

'It's up, then. Have you no got some work to go to?'

Before she was able to take in the mood he was in, he brought the back of his hand hard across her face. She fell to the floor and Rabbie rushed to her. His sister froze in the doorway.

'Leave her! Leave her! I'll fight you if you don't leave her.'

The small boy was terrified of his father, but this time he was even more terrified of doing nothing to help his mother. She was already trying to get up to save herself from the kicking she might receive when she was down.

Rabbie's defiance was enough to distract his father long enough to allow her to rise, and when she did, Rabbie could see blood streaming from her nose and cuts on her hands where she had landed on the broken glass. But there were no tears. She held up her chin and told him to hit her again, if he dared.

'You're no man, Wullie McDiarmid. You're a coward that hits women and weans. And you can hit me till I'm black and blue, but sometime you'll have to sleep, and that's when I'll come for you, with this.'

In a swift move, she produced the sharpened kitchen knife and wielded it. Wullie recoiled, staggering back towards the bed, his boots scraping on the broken glass.

'You'll never know when I'm comin' for you, you big, bad bastard. You're nothing but a bully and a coward. And I swear to God, if you ever lay a finger on these weans again . . .'

Wullie was reeling slightly, trying to avoid the slashes through the air that Bessie was making with the knife. She was a small woman and he had never seen her like this. The little drink he'd had was already starting to wear off and with it the bravado. Bessie's eyes were wild, and there was blood dripping down the blade from the cuts on her hands.

'Get oot my way, the lot o' you.'

He pushed Rabbie roughly to the floor as he made for the door. After it slammed, the room was stilled. Only Lizzie's sobs began to break the silence, and then she was joined by Bessie, who dropped the knife and sat with her head in her hands at the table, heaving with a mixture of relief and sorrow.

For the first time, Rabbie's own frustration was dry-eyed, and he promised himself, in that moment, he would never cry again. He picked up the knife and wiped his mother's blood from it. He felt the weight of it in his hand and tightened his grip on the wooden handle before slipping it into his satchel. He knew his mother would never use it in earnest, but he was sure now that he could.

Rabbie looked from his sister to his mother and said to them both, 'I'm going to look after you. You'll see, it's going to be all right.'

Chapter 5

Glasgow: 9 February 1931

Cuthbert stood inside the small, padded booth beside the entrance to the lounge bar of the Central Hotel. He still had to press the telephone receiver tightly to his ear to block out the background noise.

'This is Detective Sergeant Hogg, sir, Glasgow C.I.D. We have a very serious situation–'

'I'm sorry to interrupt you, sergeant, but what situation are you talking about?'

'Oh, I'm sorry. I thought you'd already been informed. The explosion, sir. On Glasgow Green.'

Now the sergeant had Cuthbert's full attention.

'We estimate at least twenty fatalities and over fifty injured, and the first reports are that the scene is chaos. We don't really know what we're looking at yet. All we do know is it appears to be a political attack, and as such we need to act quickly. The chief constable himself is taking personal charge of the investigation and he's asked to meet you for a briefing. I can pick you up in twenty minutes. Will you be ready then?'

Cuthbert revised his plans with the hotel reception and had his bags taken back to his room, which he realised he might now be occupying for days rather than hours. He waited in the hotel foyer for the sergeant, and when he arrived, Cuthbert was surprised to be recognised immediately. Hogg explained that he had been told to look for the tallest man in the place.

As they walked out of the hotel to the car, a young woman approached and said something that Cuthbert barely recognised as English, such was the peculiarity of her accent. Her demeanour suggested her intent, but Cuthbert did not want to make any assumption, and he looked to Sergeant Hogg for help.

Although he had been trained in Edinburgh and was familiar with the street slang of his patients at the infirmary there, Cuthbert felt like a foreigner in Glasgow. As a medical student and later junior doctor, he had acquired a good working knowledge of the words and expressions used in the poorest districts of the capital, though he had barely walked those streets, let alone lived there.

He had grown up privileged and protected but had known from an early age that there were other worlds inhabited by much less fortunate people. Any doubts that might have remained were obliterated by his war experiences.

In the trenches, he had mixed with men from all walks of life, and many who had been reared in poverty. None, however, had been from Glasgow, and he had never tuned his ear to the west coast dialect. Two cities, barely fifty miles apart, could hardly be less alike than Edinburgh and Glasgow.

Hogg, who had been brought up in Glasgow's East End tenements, had mixed feelings about this big man from London whose hand he would have to hold through the case. He was annoyed at the time being wasted and questioned what use this outsider could bring to the investigation. Of course, the sergeant did not yet know Cuthbert.

'She's offering us her services, sir, but right now I don't

have the time to take her in and charge her for soliciting, and I assume you're too busy tonight to accept. Shall we get going?'

*

The police car headed to the Central Police Headquarters on Turnbull Street in the East End. Sergeant Hogg sat with Cuthbert in the back of the car and neither looked at him nor said anything during the journey. Instead, he occupied himself with smoothing the brim of his hat, which he ran continually through his fingers, working out the creases in the felt.

With his gaze cast down, Hogg could not help noticing the pathologist's boots, which were black and polished to a mirrored shine. The last time he had seen ones like that was on a parade ground, and he had no wish to think back to that.

The journey to the police headquarters took fifteen minutes. As the car approached, Cuthbert could see it was one of those solid Edwardian buildings in red brick and blond sandstone with elaborate statuary and detailing.

The driver turned off the main street and negotiated a narrow stone archway to take Hogg and Cuthbert into the courtyard beyond. There, they were able to enter the building away from the prying eyes of the press, who were already huddling around the main entrance.

In the hallway, Hogg turned to Cuthbert and made to speak, and then thought better of it.

'What is it, sergeant? This is already proving to be a bizarre evening. I'm not sure anything you might say could make it any more so.'

'I'm sorry, sir. It really isn't my place to say, but I can tell you're confused by all this, and the truth is, so am I. I don't know why you're here or why I've been asked to escort you. Nothing about this is normal procedure.' Hogg shook his head. 'No detective chief inspector has been assigned to the case yet and the chief constable himself is leading the investigation. It makes no sense whatsoever.'

Without further speculation they climbed the stairs to the chief constable's office in silence.

'Good of you to come so quickly, Dr Cuthbert. I hope Hogg here has been looking after you.'

Harper was in his mid-forties, wiry and vigilant, and when he smiled, he did his best to hide his tobacco-stained teeth. He held out his hand to shake Cuthbert's.

'Of course, but perhaps you could enlighten me. What's all this about, sir?'

'Surely the sergeant has given you the details of what happened here tonight.'

Cuthbert made it clear that D.S. Hogg had been informative, up to a point, but that he was still at a loss as to why the local forensic services were not being used.

'I mean, what about Glaister? Why is he not here?'

'I'm afraid the esteemed Professor Glaister is more of a figurehead than anything else these days and has played no active role with the Glasgow C.I.D. for some years. All the heavy lifting has been left to his subordinates. Normally, it would be our senior police surgeon Dr Henderson who would be in charge, but of course under the circumstances—'

'What circumstances, chief constable?'

'Of course, you won't know yet. It was a political rally ahead of the forthcoming elections. The prospective parliamentary candidate for the New Party was to set out his stall, so to speak, for the people of the East End. Tragically, he was one of the victims. His name was Alistair Henderson, and he was our Dr Henderson's brother. So I'm sure you can see why we couldn't possibly ask him to oversee the investigation.'

Cuthbert nodded his agreement.

'And there is something else you should know. This evening

I received a phone call from Whitehall. As you may imagine, with all the political ramifications of this, they are taking a very keen interest, and amongst their many requirements' – Harper paused and appeared momentarily irked as he thought about the call – 'their very many requirements, they have specifically requested your involvement in the matter. I regret to say I don't know you, Dr Cuthbert, but I am instructed that you are to take charge of the forensic investigation. They were quite clear about that. M.I.5 have cleared you – apparently your file is in good order.'

'I have an M.I.5 file?'

'Goodness, man! You're a police surgeon working with Scotland Yard – of course you have an M.I.5 file. Whether you know it or not, you will have been carefully vetted before you were ever allowed to work on cases with the Met, and since then a record will have been kept of your, shall we say, movements.'

Cuthbert was reacting badly to this revelation, and he was in danger of forgetting his manners as he barked back at Harper, 'Movements?'

'Memberships of organisations, clubs, your reading matter, minor criminal offences, any indiscretions – all the usual level three scrutiny.'

Cuthbert was appalled, and was now breathing heavily through flared nostrils, but Harper had no time to offer any sort of salve.

'I don't need to tell you how sensitive this all is. Or perhaps I do. Much of the goings-on over the last year here and in Germany have been kept out of the papers. Politically, we are in a very difficult place. This couldn't have come at a worse time.' He glanced at Hogg. 'The sergeant here will take you to the scene; in fact it would be best if Hogg attached himself to you for the duration. I have to go and speak to the reporters now. One last thing – should our friends in the press approach you for comment, I would appreciate it if you would direct them to me. Much better if we speak with one voice on this, don't you think? And you'll report directly to me, of course.'

With that, the chief constable pulled on his leather gloves and collected his cap and baton. Just before he left the office, he checked himself in the small mirror hanging to the side of his door. He smoothed his carefully trimmed moustache and patted down his short hair before adjusting his cap. He stood for a moment and admired his crisp uniform replete with its double row of coloured service ribbons before turning to Cuthbert.

'You do know, doctor, that the City of Glasgow Police is the largest force in Britain outside the capital, and my position is thus second only to your Commissioner Havant at the Met. However, what my colleagues in London have doubtless failed to mention to you is that when it comes to precedence, my force is the oldest in the country, besting yours, our nearest rival, by some forty years. The word "proud" does not do justice to my feelings for my men. They work in difficult, sometimes intolerable and dangerous conditions, and always give their professional best.'

Cuthbert bristled; he felt he was being lectured and failed to see the relevance of all of Harper's hubris. Sergeant Hogg said not a word in the chief constable's presence, and Cuthbert expected this was the way it would always be.

*

As Hogg and Cuthbert were turning back out onto the street, their car was prevented from moving forward by the crowd of reporters now spilling onto the road and blocking the traffic. They saw the narrow oak doors of the main entrance opening and the familiar figure of the chief constable emerging.

He briefly tapped his baton to the peak of his cap by way of salute to the reporters, and he stood on the single step just outside the door in order for everyone to have a clear view of him. He also stood very still so as not to blur their photographs.

'Do you have a statement, chief constable?'

Flash bulbs were still popping, and only when he saw that the photographers had had their fill did he deign to reply.

'Today we have witnessed nothing short of an outrage on the streets of Glasgow. This was an act of terrorism, but the people of this fine city will not be bullied into submission, and they will not be robbed of their rights to free speech and free elections in this way. The perpetrators of this cowardly atrocity will be hunted down, they will be brought to justice, and they will be made to pay not only for the lives they have taken but also for the principles they have violated. Gentlemen, thank you for your patience, but I am sure you appreciate I must now get to work.'

Harper nodded, raised his baton again and returned inside. The reporters' pencils caught every word, and they were delighted with the copy that this chief constable could always be relied upon to provide. Their work for the morning edition had almost been done for them, and they dispersed as quickly as they had come.

Hogg had remained silent in the chief constable's office, and Cuthbert suspected that was because he had not been given leave to speak by his superior officer. However, Cuthbert was equally sure there was plenty that Hogg would like to say.

The sergeant was in his fifties and smelt strongly of cheap tobacco smoke. His braces were almost at breaking point, stretched over his considerable belly. Hogg had doubtless seen it all in this city and was not about to be impressed by some toffee-nosed pathologist from London or, worse, Edinburgh.

Again, in the backseat of the police car, Hogg was toying with his hat, constantly pressing the felt brim rather than making eye contact or conversation. Cuthbert frowned as he watched him. If they were to work together, they needed to start speaking.

'I can see you're unhappy about all this, sergeant. I certainly have my own misgivings, but it looks as if we've both been thrown into this. So perhaps it would be best if we cleared the air. I came to Glasgow yesterday for a meeting at the university, and it's entirely a coincidence that I was here while this thing happened.'

'I mean you no disrespect, doctor, but I don't believe in coincidences. I mean, who are you? It's rather convenient that the one London pathologist the security services want involved just happens to be on hand, sitting in the Central Hotel. I tell you this thing stinks.'

Cuthbert was unruffled by the sergeant's tone and even had some sympathy with it. He didn't believe in coincidences either, but he did his best to explain.

'As to who I am, I'm a pathologist specialising in forensic medicine from Edinburgh who happens to work in London. For the Edinburgh part, I apologise unreservedly. I share your feelings about coincidence, but I regret to say, I think that is all we are dealing with here. I intend to visit the scene, appraise it, organise it and do my job. If there is physical evidence there that might help solve the questions of who, how and perhaps even why in all this, then I will find it and pass it to you. Now, you know what I'm about, so it's your turn, sergeant. Why all the brooding silence?'

Hogg almost smiled at the Edinburgh remark, but he had all but forgotten how to. He was unused to this kind of candour from senior staff, and as a detective sergeant he had little direct contact with the police surgeons, but as Cuthbert had rightly observed, they had been thrown into the case together. He stopped fiddling with his hat and looked directly at Cuthbert.

'I apologise for my rudeness just now, sir. Uncalled for. It's just that after thirty-five years, you get a nose for these things, and this one just doesn't smell right. I don't know what it is yet, but it's something and it's going to bite us. The fact of the matter is, I don't think either of us should be here. I was supposed to be retiring, next week in fact, and all my current cases were being taken over by Mackintosh. Calum was my detective constable and he's just been made up – a new, young sergeant. They all expect big things of him – chief inspector material they say, maybe even higher. Not like me. I've been a sergeant for nearly thirty years. It's the face, you see; it doesn't quite fit. Never did. So, by rights, I shouldn't be on this case, so why am I?'

'I can't answer that, sergeant, but I'm glad you are. I think this is going to need all the experience we can muster. Tell me one thing, though. How did you know I was here in Glasgow?'

'It was a Dr Ogilvie who told us. He seemed quite keen that you should be involved. Looks as if your fan club extends beyond the corridors of power down south.'

This time it was Cuthbert's turn to be silent while he digested everything that had happened in the last hour.

*

As they approached the perimeter of Glasgow Green – public park and popular meeting place – the traffic became more congested and Hogg instructed the driver to take a short cut through a back alley. This detour took them to the other side of the park, opposite the crime scene.

'We won't get any closer, sir. I suggest we walk.'

The two men got out of the car, and as soon as the cold evening air hit them, they could smell it. Cuthbert was instantly transported back to the dawn after a shelling. The cordite and burnt wood, the nauseatingly sweeter smell of burnt flesh.

Hogg froze, apparently reliving his own memory of the war. Different trenches, different fronts, but the same stench of violent, catastrophic death. Neither man spoke but each could see the fear in the other's face and silently acknowledged the other's pain.

As they moved off in the direction of the monument, where the rally had been held, the smell intensified, and Hogg stopped. Cuthbert could see he was sweating despite the chill in the night air and paused to allow the sergeant to gather himself.

'I'm sorry, sir. This is going to be harder than I thought.'

'The shooting has stopped, sergeant. We're safe. It's just the aftermath of the fire, the charred wood.'

Cuthbert spoke quietly but firmly, the way he had done with the wounded men at the dressing station. The nights were the worst, and of all the senses, it was smell that always evoked the most vivid and terrifying of memories. Hogg nodded and followed Cuthbert to the perimeter, where they were admitted to the site by a uniformed constable.

Away from the onlookers, there was a stillness to the scene, as there always was in the aftermath of violence. What had been ripped apart and thrown into the air now lay unmoving where it had landed. What had erupted had been silenced, for death is quiet. Life itself had been stilled here. Cuthbert had already seen too much death and endured its silence, but not since the war had he witnessed anything on this scale.

In front of the obelisk where the rally had been due to take place was a tangled mass of shattered timbers and smoking remains. There were still fires burning in pockets between the debris, and the stench of charred flesh became almost unbearable as Cuthbert and Hogg drew near.

Any survivors had already been taken to the infirmary and all that remained were the witnesses who could no longer speak but whose very injuries might reveal what had happened. The centre of the blast was obvious. Close to what had been a cast-iron railing, where the stage had been built for the speakers, there was now a shallow crater of scorched earth.

The railing behind was badly buckled, a park gate was blown off its hinges, and all that remained of the stage had been thrown yards away in every direction. There was nothing else to be seen in that crater save human remains. What flesh and bone there was of the victims was now lying amongst the debris.

As Cuthbert surveyed the scene, he knew it was going to be a monumental task to provide any kind of identity to these body parts. The sergeant heaved at Cuthbert's side as he saw half a head between broken timbers.

'Sergeant, touch nothing and get yourself out of here. Have uniform cordon the area off properly, get rid of the press photographers and put in a call to the forensic medicine department at the university. I want whoever they can spare. We're going to need a lot of experienced hands here, but I need you to co-ordinate things. Can you do that for me?'

Cuthbert's tone had changed, and Hogg immediately realised he was dealing with someone who knew exactly what he was doing in such a situation. He had not been sure about the big man with the posh voice who seemed to care more about his boots than the police work, but now he could see the reason for his reputation. He kept his eyes on the pathologist, for no other reason than to save himself from having to look at anything else, and nodded vigorously.

'Consider it done, sir.'

Hogg picked his way back out over the debris field and made the arrangements. Within minutes the uniformed constables had been mobilised and a double rope was being staked at a proper distance. The crowds were pushed well back, and the camera flash bulbs stopped.

Cuthbert was alone at the scene for some time before he was joined by the others. In the stillness, he stood motionless, but his eyes and his mind were working. Observation was always where every investigation had to start.

Many of his juniors over the years had been too keen to do rather than to look, and Cuthbert knew that once he started to dismantle this chaos many of the clues would be lost. Now was the time to gather as much of that elusive evidence as possible. And although he could not provide any rational scientific explanation for it, he was always aware of the importance of those first, fleeting impressions at a crime scene.

The things you saw from the corner of your eye, the things that you only half-noticed, the sounds and smells: all of it could help to rebuild the picture of what had taken place. But it was late, and all he had to work with was the illumination from the gas streetlights and the flickering fires. Even the bright moon was receding behind a heavy pall of cloud. Dawn would not be for another six hours, and the real work could only start in daylight. Now, his main concern was preserving the scene and doing whatever preliminary assessments he could.

He stepped carefully between the wreckage, taking care not to move anything. He touched nothing but made notes of everything he saw. There were mutilated corpses and obvious body parts scattered around. He could not be certain as to the number of dead, but it was certainly in the tens.

He tried to get a sense of how the blast had happened. The crater was obvious, but on closer inspection it was not circular. The force of the explosion had been directed forwards from the bomb in a fan-shaped pattern as evidenced by the debris field, with relatively little back-blast.

As he walked back to the perimeter, beyond the zone containing most of the dead, Cuthbert also noticed the glint of shining metal on the ground. The light was poor, but it was unmistakably a knife. The blade was about seven inches long and it looked sharp. Nearby was another, but this time it was a small folding knife that had been opened, and another few yards on there was what looked like a short makeshift spear made of a knife blade bound tightly with twine to a wooden shaft. Finally, lying on the grass, there was a cut-throat razor not dissimilar to the one he used himself every morning to shave.

Without touching or disturbing any of these weapons, he recorded the finds in his notebook. On the drive back to the hotel, he asked Hogg about the knives he had spotted at the scene.

'Just the Brigton Boys, sir.'

'Enlighten me, sergeant. Who are they?'

'One of the East End gangs, sir — a vicious bunch. They were there at the rally as Henderson's bodyguards. Whenever they get caught out, they dump their weapons. Usually, it's when the police outnumber them at one of their street battles and they have to scarper. They don't want to get caught carrying a knife, see, so they chuck them. I suppose it's just a reflex with them — when they have to run, they ditch their blades.'

*

As he was finishing breakfast the next morning, Cuthbert realised that in all of yesterday's commotion, he had failed to inform anyone that he would be detained in Glasgow for some time. As it was still very early, he called home first, knowing that his housekeeper would already be up.

'Madame Smith, I'm sorry to disturb you, but I have to tell you that I won't be returning to London as planned. There have been some developments here in Glasgow.'

She stiffened, pursing her lips to suppress the sadness that suddenly welled up inside her. She recovered her composure and asked as casually as she could, 'Concerning the position at the university, Dr Cuthbert?'

'No, no. I'm afraid there has been an incident at a political rally with considerable loss of life. You will doubtless read about it in the morning papers. I have been asked to assist and will be staying here for a few more days.'

'Please do not worry. Everything is in order here and you must concern yourself only with your work.' She hesitated a little before asking, 'And the position? Will you be moving from London, monsieur?'

'Oh, that. No, I don't think that is right for me. Besides, there is still much work to be done in London.'

She closed her eyes with relief as she held the receiver tightly with both hands to her ear. 'I understand, monsieur. Please make sure that you look after yourself in that city. Eat properly.'

He was always touched by the concern for his wellbeing that lay beneath her rather cold exterior.

'I will, madame. And I will call again as soon as I am able. I might need a friendly voice.'

'I will always be here when you need me. À bientôt, monsieur.'

He called Morgenthal at St Thomas's as soon as he thought he might be in the department. His assistant was startled to hear the phone ringing just as he was hanging up his hat and coat. He answered formally and was surprised to hear Cuthbert's voice.

'Sir, is everything all right? We didn't expect to hear from you for a few more days. I hope you're not worried about the department. Everything is exactly as it should be here. I can assure you nothing has been missed. Except, of course, yourself. We all miss your guiding hand. Although that's not to say we've been . . .'

'Good morning, Simon. Perhaps a little less talking and a little more listening would make this expensive telephone call go quicker.'

'Forgive me, sir.'

'I will be detained in Glasgow on police business, and I need you to hold the fort in London. Can you do that?'

'Of course, Dr Cuthbert.' And a little more hesitantly, 'Is there anything we can do to assist you?'

'There might be, and we'll talk again when I know more. You will find the story in this morning's *Times*. Or at least part of the story. I intend to find out what has really happened here. My driver is waiting, but I will call again.'

*

When he arrived at Glasgow Green, Cuthbert made his way through the crowd milling around the crime scene. The previous night there had been a noisy throng of reporters and press photographers, but this morning there was an altogether more sombre mood.

Perhaps some of these people were still waiting for news of loved ones who had not come home. Cuthbert certainly saw many worn-out, tear-stained faces. As he approached the perimeter, he was met by a uniformed constable who initially made to stop him going any further before noticing who he was and apologising.

'Nonsense, constable. You're doing exactly what you should be doing – keeping this site safe. Now, I was expecting to meet D.S. Hogg and some of the team from the forensics department. Would you be so good as to direct me?'

Before the constable could offer his help, there was a tug on Cuthbert's trouser leg.

'Aw, mister. You've got awfy shiny boots.'

Cuthbert looked about to see who had said this and found

his eyes drawn down to a small girl at the front of the crowd. Her large blue eyes beamed from a dirty face. She was clutching a clear glass bottle half-filled with a dark liquid. Cuthbert crouched down to the girl's eye level and asked, 'And what's your name, miss?'

Unperturbed by the close attention, the child raised her chin and said, 'Margaret Brown Allan. What's yours?'

'As we're being formal, I'm John Archibald Cuthbert, how do you do? And I'm glad you like my boots.'

'I didn't say I liked them, just that they were shiny.'

'Indeed, you did. My apologies. Tell me, what's in the bottle. Are you a rum drinker, miss?'

She laughed. 'Naw, don't be daft. It's sugar-ally water.'

The constable, who had been watching the scene, could see Cuthbert's puzzlement and whispered in his ear that it was a sweet drink of liquorice in water that the children loved.

'Sounds delicious. May I try some?'

The girl turned away from him, protecting her prized bottle, and after frowning at his request, mellowed and sang him the rhyme all the children sang.

'Sugar-ally water, as black as the lum. If you gather up pins, I'll give you some.'

She hooted with laughter and ran back into the crowd and was off. Cuthbert smiled, glad of the distraction from the work in hand; the constable caught his eye and indicated that they should proceed.

As Cuthbert was escorted over to the perimeter line, he saw Sergeant Hogg approach and deduced that the detective had had barely any sleep.

'Good morning, sergeant. Do we have a weather report?'

'Good morning, sir. Well, the good news is that it will be cold but dry all day.'

'And the bad news?'

'Sir?'

'It's never all good news in cases like this, is it, sergeant?'

Hogg was warming to this one, the more he got to know him. He threw a glance at the young constable and shook his head only enough for Cuthbert to see. 'Nothing that need concern you for the moment, sir. I'll give you a full report later. Your colleagues are ready for you.'

Hogg gestured to three men standing by the perimeter rope before going back to check on the control of the onlookers.

'Dr Ogilvie, good morning. And I see we also have Doctors Currie and Mathieson. It's very good to have you all – thank you for coming.'

'Dr Cuthbert, I had hoped we might be able to work together, but I certainly did not expect it to be so soon.'

Ogilvie was standing at the perimeter along with his two colleagues whom Cuthbert had met in the research laboratory at the department the day before. All three were young, and clearly excited by the prospect of such an important case, and Cuthbert could tell that none of them were inconvenienced by any memory of the trenches.

'We thought it best to await your instructions, sir. We understand you have very particular requirements when it comes to preservation of the scene.'

Cuthbert felt Ogilvie's tone was just a little too light for his liking, given where they were standing and what they were about to do, but he said nothing. His face, however, could not hide his disquiet, and Ogilvie, who realised immediately he had done something wrong, chose to stop talking lest he should further antagonise the man now in charge.

'I am quite sure you are familiar with standard procedures, gentlemen. I am viewing this as a crime scene until we have any proof to the contrary. As such, we proceed as we would in any murder investigation. First and foremost is preservation of the integrity of the evidence, and, remember, everything you see or touch is potentially a crucial piece of evidence. I expect care, diligence and meticulous attention to detail. I expect you to observe first, to record second and only third to touch. What I do not expect is speed. This is not a race, gentlemen; this is a mass murder inquiry. And what we do beyond this cordon may mean the difference between discovering the truth of what happened to these unfortunate souls or denying them any chance of justice.'

The three young pathologists from the university stood transfixed by the man towering over them. They were left in no doubt as to the importance of the task in hand and the high standards that were expected of them. Cuthbert had already left a request for Ogilvie to bring him an investigation case and appropriate footwear, and these he now produced.

'As you requested, sir, I have your wellington boots, size thirteen, and your murder bag.'

Cuthbert winced, and Ogilvie again fell silent, fearful that he had committed a further blunder. While police forces up and down the country referred to the field case that contained all the necessary paraphernalia for examination and sample collection at the scene of a homicide as a 'murder bag', Cuthbert abhorred the term.

He found it grossly insensitive both to the victims and to his profession. Again, he said nothing out loud because Ogilvie was not to know his feelings, but Cuthbert was disappointed. He had quietly hoped the young man might have been of a different calibre to the others.

He carefully removed the immaculately polished boots that had attracted such admiration from the little girl, placed them in the case and pulled on the ugly rubber boots. He looked down at his feet, now appropriately shod for the site, but felt an almost physical disgust. There was a sharp metallic taste in his mouth, and he was unsure if he was going to be able to keep his breakfast down. He raised his chin sharply and breathed as deeply as he could and found that as long as he wasn't looking at the boots he could carry on.

None of this anxiety was apparent to the three men, for Cuthbert had long learned to hide much of what he was feeling from those around him. He raised the rope of the cordon and ushered the doctors onto the site for the work to begin.

Cuthbert divided the area into four approximately equal sectors and assigned one to each of the three pathologists and took the last himself. He had instructed them to take detailed notes of the position, orientation and state of all human remains, and only once this information was fully documented, were they to prepare the bodies and body parts for removal.

He could tell by their faces that the three were eager to get started and for the opportunity to impress him. Although he now knew that he would certainly not be returning to Glasgow as their head of department, he thought it best, for the time being, to allow them to continue thinking that he might.

Compared with the previous night, when he had only been able to view the site by the dim light of the streetlamps, the stark morning sun now made the place appear like a black-and-white photograph of a battlefield. Strangely, there was no colour in the ground. The grass around the area was black from the dark earth and mud that had been thrown up by the explosion, and everywhere there were grey, shattered pieces of wood. And between them everything was dusted white by the ash from the fires which had now all burned out.

He noted charred masses that he initially took to be wood, only to see that one was a human torso and another a head. As he looked over the scene, there was no blood, no flash of gore that would signal the kind of violence that had erupted there the night before. Everything was monochrome, and as his eyes flitted from broken plank and charred post to shattered limb, it was difficult to tell one from the other.

The pathologists began their work, noting the position of each body or body part and tying small, numbered tags to each to give it a unique identification. This preliminary work, although slow and tedious, would be essential when it came later to the task of reconstituting and, if possible, identifying the victims. Fragments of clothing still attached to the remains were also carefully tagged in case they should become detached when they were moved.

*

A few hours of being doubled over meant Cuthbert needed to stand and stretch. As he did so, he saw Sergeant Hogg alone at the perimeter and thought this might be a good moment to find out what was happening.

'How's it going, sir?'

'Slowly but surely, sergeant. Tell me, what was it you couldn't say in front of the young constable?'

'Oh, you mean the bad news. Well, it looks as if we have a chief inspector on the case after all. It makes sense because the chief constable wouldn't have known his arse from his elbow in a case like this.'

'But? I'm sensing a "but", sergeant.'

'But they've assigned D.C.I. Black to the case. You don't know him, sir, and frankly you don't want to. Let's just say he's not quite in your league. Hell, he's not even in my league. The truth is, he's a slacker of the first order, and Christ alone knows how he swung this.'

'You've worked with him before?'

'Oh yes, sir. I knew him when he was in uniform, and I've watched him rise up the greasy pole ever since. We all have. People have lots of theories about his success, some of them worse than others, but nothing has ever stuck. Anyway, I have to report to him, and I expect he'll be the one you'll have to deal with now.'

'But I need you working with me on this.'

'Well, you'll only have me if he says so. That's the way it works here, sir.'

'We'll see about that. I haven't been told anything officially, and I'm scheduled to give an interim report to the chief constable at five o'clock. I expect you to accompany me there.'

Without waiting for an argument, Cuthbert returned to the scene and resolved to deal with this development later in the afternoon, as soon as he lost the light.

*

Cuthbert's driver was waiting at half past four as arranged to take him to police headquarters. He got in the back seat without waiting for her to open the door for him and told her that such niceties would not be necessary. She had better things to do and besides, he was, after all, only the pathologist.

'But if you don't mind waiting a few moments, I'm expecting Sergeant Hogg to join me.'

'Certainly, sir.'

'So what's your story, constable? I expect you already know all about me. I'm sure word travels as fast in the force here as it does at the Met.'

W.P.C. Anderson was taken aback by the directness of Cuthbert's question. She was frequently ignored by the officers she had to ferry from place to place, and she was unsure what he expected of her. She only managed the most perfunctory of replies.

Cuthbert was accustomed to the effect he had on people and tried to put the young woman at ease. 'No need to be shy with me. I'm just a visitor trying to help out, and I very much regard all my conversations as confidential. I'm good at keeping secrets – it's part of my job.'

Anderson was still uneasy, but she explained that she was from the West End of the city and that she had joined the police a year ago. She had hoped to be working much more on the front line but had found herself, like many women on the force, consigned to making the tea, driving and, if she was lucky, some paperwork.

'I can understand that must be frustrating. Will things change for you, or will you need to change direction, do you think?'

Again, Cuthbert's probing made her nervous. Was she being tested? She chose to say what she thought was expected rather than the truth. She assured her passenger that she was gaining valuable experience and that she was happy to serve the police force in any way she was asked.

Cuthbert nodded, realising he had reached that brick wall he often did when speaking to junior staff. He could not think of himself as intimidating, but then he was the only one who knew what was going on inside his head.

*

'Dr Cuthbert to see the chief constable.'

The uniformed officer on reception at police headquarters stood immediately to attention and explained that the chief constable was not available but that D.C.I. Black had asked to see him. He offered to escort Cuthbert to his office, but Hogg interrupted. 'No need, son, I know the way.'

'What did I tell you?' whispered Hogg as they went up to the first floor.

*

'Good afternoon, Dr Cuthbert. Thank you, sergeant, that'll be all.'

'How do you do, chief inspector? If you'll forgive me, I think Sergeant Hogg should stay. He has been instrumental in the logistics of this case, and my report, which is why I suppose I'm here, would be woefully incomplete without his contribution.'

Hogg stood mute by the office door while Black took the measure of the tall, well-dressed pathologist from London. He decided that it would do him no favours to get off on the wrong foot with this one.

'As you see fit, doctor. Now, I know Chief Constable Harper said you were to report to him personally, but there has been a change of plan. I am now in charge of all this.'

'Excuse me, chief inspector, but not all of it, surely. I was led to understand that our friends in Whitehall had specifically requested that I take charge of the forensic investigation. Is that not so?'

'Yes. Yes, I suppose so. That is also my understanding, but everything else is in my remit.'

'Except, of course, Sergeant Hogg here, who has been assigned as my points person and primary contact with C.I.D. Or do you plan to override the chief constable on that matter too?'

'No, if that's what you want, I'm happy for you still to work with Hogg, but I do need to be kept fully briefed. You must understand that.'

'Of course, chief inspector. Now, how often do you want my reports? Do you require them all to be written or would you prefer oral interim reports, say on a daily basis? As I'm sure you are aware, with an investigation on this scale, there will also be a requirement to utilise the services of outside forensic laboratory services in order to deal with the number of analyses that will be needed. I assume you have already established appropriate budgetary centres for these to be charged to. Perhaps you could let me have the details as soon as you have them. And I expect you will be attending the post mortem examinations of all the victims. I assume that is standard practice here, as it is in London?'

Cuthbert never blinked as he was speaking, and the chief inspector was left a little dazed.

'Just come and see me when you've something to report, and I'm happy to leave all the day-to-day this and that with the sergeant here. Now, if you'll excuse me, I'm very busy.'

*

Outside the office, Hogg laughed out loud, and Cuthbert hushed him with a mock frown.

'Sir, it was worth getting up this morning just to see that. Can I stand you a tea in the canteen?'

'Oh, let's not get ahead of ourselves, sergeant. We don't want to have all our fun in one place. Drive back with me to the Central Hotel. They have a good dining room, and we can eat there. "Outside forensic laboratory services" are paying, and we can plan this out properly. After all, it doesn't look as if we're going to get any help from this place. When you said before that you didn't know why we both ended up on this case, I think I know the answer now, sergeant – it's so it gets solved.'

Chapter 6

Glasgow: 11 February 1931

As the sun rose over the bombsite for a second time, little had changed. Doctors Currie and Mathieson were already at work when Cuthbert arrived, and he was pleased to see they were working in their designated sectors in a methodical way. Both were wearing white coats over their suits and had swapped their shoes for heavy wellington boots. They were also both sporting thick knitted hats in deference to the winter chill in the air.

From the perimeter, he watched as Mathieson identified a new find. From Cuthbert's distance it appeared to be a limb, probably a leg or at least a part of one.

He noted how the pathologist took care to study the body part, note its position, mark its grid location on the site map he was carrying and then tie a numbered label to it. Mathieson then gently brushed the ash and soil from the limb and noted any remnants of clothing still attached. Only then did he stand up from his crouched position and call over to the police photographer to let him know that he had another one for him.

The site was in good hands, thought Cuthbert, and if there was a story to be told about what had happened here, he was sure they would unravel it between them. He quickly changed into the wellingtons he found so distasteful and wrapped his own boots in a soft flannel before placing them in his bag. As he folded the cloth, he could see his own face in the polished toe caps, and he held that thought as he lifted the cordon and went to work.

His morning was spent much as the day before had been, with the meticulous survey of the site and the cataloguing of all human remains. There was a stiff breeze blowing from the east, but mercifully the rain had stayed off. Cuthbert was keen to complete the fieldwork as quickly as possible, for he was sure their luck would not last. The job was difficult enough in these conditions; it would be all but impossible if the weather turned.

Cuthbert moved to a new area within his sector, slightly further away from the bomb crater, having completed his work there. He looked about him carefully and was suddenly forced to close his eyes when he saw the small hand jutting out from under a plank of wood.

He had been a doctor for some fourteen years, and for twelve of those he had been a pathologist. Despite his exposure to death on a daily basis during that time, he had never got used to dealing with the body of a child.

He steeled himself and gently lifted the wood. Underneath, a boy about 3 years old was lying face down in the earth. His body appeared intact, but his legs, having been in contact with the charred plank, were badly burned. Mechanically, Cuthbert took note of the details and prepared to tag the body.

He was thankful for the rigour of procedure at times like these and did his best not to ask the questions that were starting to race through his mind. What was a young child doing at a nighttime political rally? Why had he been allowed to come? What could an innocent child possibly have done to deserve this? And how could any God allow a child to die in the dirt like this?

The moment only served to remind him of his difficult relationship with the God he had been taught to love as well as fear in his own childhood. It had become so hard for Cuthbert to equate the love he was told this God imparted with the utter indifference to suffering that He seemed to display. Where was God in the trenches, in no man's land, in the operating theatres of the field hospitals, in the clouds of poison gas? Where was He when the innocents were raped and murdered, when they were tortured, when their bodies were ripped apart? Where was He when this small child, now lying at Cuthbert's feet, was caught by the hot, terrifying blast of the bomb?

He placed his hand ever so gently on the back of the child's head and smoothed his hair. He sighed heavily and whispered, half to the child, half to himself, 'Don't worry, laddie, we'll find out who you are.'

Cuthbert rose and walked back to where he had left his bag, to collect some more tags. As he did so, he stubbed the toe of his wellington on a sharp piece of metal in the ground at the edge of the bomb crater. He bent to take a closer look and saw that it appeared to be a metal plate about half an inch thick. When he tried to dislodge it, he found it wouldn't move. He scraped away the soil and ash from around its edges and saw that it was in fact not flat but gently curved with a sharp edge and that most of it was buried deep in the ground. He looked around but could see no other similar fragments. It was a large area and there was still so much work to do.

He and Ogilvie and the other junior pathologists from the university could deal with the human remains, but there was a lot of detailed forensic evaluation of the site to be completed, especially the bomb crater. And time was not on their side. So far, the weather had been dry, but this was Glasgow in

February and that would change. Winter rains or even snow would make the job impossible.

He realised, if he was going to solve this, he needed more manpower to recover what physical evidence there was. But where was he going to find people who had the necessary ability for such painstaking work and the understanding of the importance of careful procedure and documentation? As he was brushing some more soil away from the metal fragment, he had an idea. He called Ogilvie over and asked him a single question: 'Tell me, does the University of Glasgow have an archaeology department?'

A phone call later, and all was arranged. Within the hour, Professor Gordon Baxter and four postgraduate students arrived suitably shod and ready to undertake the work. Baxter was a man in his late sixties, dressed as if he had just stepped from the pages of *The Lost World*. All that was missing, Cuthbert mused, was the pith helmet.

The students were altogether more conventional – all in their twenties, there were two men and two women. They all looked very serious, and Cuthbert was pleased to see that they were aware of the importance of the task in hand. He found that he had only to offer them the briefest of instructions about maintaining the integrity of the site as such an approach was already second nature to them. His last concern was that they may glimpse some of the human body parts, but again he was reassured by their professionalism when they reminded him that they too often dealt in human remains, although theirs were admittedly less recent.

Baxter greeted Cuthbert warmly and thanked him for giving his students such 'a golden opportunity'.

'We are a small department, Dr Cuthbert, but we are keen to put our expertise to use when needed. We will not disappoint.'

Cuthbert did not doubt it.

*

The following afternoon, Baxter arranged to come to the city mortuary to present the archaeological team's findings. On the wooden laboratory bench, the professor, now more conventionally dressed in his academic tweeds, had laid out everything his team had excavated from the crater site.

There were numerous pieces of curved, blackened metal about half an inch thick, along with a number of what appeared to be small, discoloured brass objects. All the objects had been brushed clean of soil and debris but not washed, and each one had been numbered and tagged to identify it. Beside them on the bench he placed a large map of the site divided into sectors of one square yard, with the position of every find marked in red along with its identification number.

Cuthbert was impressed with the work and said as much.

'Robust record-keeping is the basis of all good archaeology, Dr Cuthbert, and I expect it comes in rather handy in your field too.'

'Indeed, but I have to work hard to get my junior staff to understand that it's often the record-keeping that matters as much as the more glamorous parts of the job.'

'Yes, it's the same across the board. I only hope we have been able to offer you some assistance. Shall I talk you through our findings?'

Cuthbert and Ogilvie took their seats beside the bench, notebooks at the ready.

'Gentlemen, let us begin with these fragments. They appear to be cast iron, and the curvature would suggest they are part of something cylindrical with an internal diameter of approximately six inches. They appear to be consistent with a metal pipe. We speculated that it might simply be an underground drain damaged in the blast. But Caroline, my

Ph.D. student, has checked with the City Surveyor's office and there are no water or gas pipes running underneath that area of the park. She and Charles, my other student, have also attempted a partial reconstruction. We do not have all the fragments as some will have been irretrievably lost in the explosion, but from what we have it looks as if the section of pipe was about two feet long.'

Cuthbert nodded, and Ogilvie knew what he was thinking. 'I think you have found the bomb casing, Professor Baxter. There are several similar instances in the literature of short lengths of pipe being packed full of explosive and fitted with detonators.'

Ogilvie eagerly chipped in, 'Yes, the San Francisco bombing in 1916 – if I remember correctly, that was a pipe bomb.'

'Indeed, and it's a technique that has been used by more than one anarchist group. But tell me, professor, in all the instances I can recall, the pipes have also been packed with metal objects and fragments, such as lead weights, screws, pieces of broken blade. Did you also find any such metal projectiles amongst the pipe fragments?'

Professor Baxter did not like to answer any question without first carefully consulting his field notes and Cuthbert was happy to wait while he did so.

'No, we did not. There were, as I will show you in a moment, several small brass objects, but nothing as you describe. Do you think that's important?'

'Anarchists want to create terror by killing and maiming as many people as possible, professor. That wasn't the case here. Given the size of the crowd, the death toll, although terrible, is remarkably low, as are the number of casualties. Most of them were caught in the immediate blast or were hit by fragments of the wooden platform. No building was destroyed, there was no flying masonry and glass, and, importantly, there was no shrapnel. So far, we have seen nothing like that from the bodies either. If this had been an anarchist attack, there would have been even more casualties. Please go on, Professor Baxter – what of the brass objects you found?'

'As you can see on the map, these were found scattered some distance from where we believe the bomb went off. At least one item is identifiable as the brass fastener from a suitcase. The others are seriously damaged and some look to consist of several different components fused together, perhaps because of the heat of the blast. If you look closely, however, I think you will see that there are what appear to be small gear wheels or cogs. Perhaps some form of mechanism or even a clock?'

'I think that's exactly what it is, professor. This was a time bomb consisting of a cast-iron pipe packed with dynamite or T.N.T., with the detonator wired to a clockwork mechanism. It was surely timed to go off when the candidate was giving his speech. He arrived on time – had he been ten minutes late, he might still be alive. There was no packing of the pipe with nails or lead fishing weights or the like. They weren't trying to kill a lot of people with a wave of shrapnel. As I mentioned, there is precedent in other acts of terrorism where that was exactly the bombers' objective. This time it looks like they were only trying to kill the man standing above the bomb – the candidate, Alistair Henderson. Put simply, this was an assassination, and the other victims were collateral damage.'

Cuthbert began to thank Baxter for the work and for the crucial clues he and his team had uncovered when he was interrupted.

'There is just one other thing, Dr Cuthbert. At the edge of the crater, we also found this.' Baxter held up a small brass cylinder between his gloved finger and thumb. 'I'd say this was a bullet cartridge. There was just the one, and it could of course be an entirely incidental finding, something buried in the ground for years and just thrown up by the explosion, but' – he held it to his nose – 'it does smell fresh to me.'

Cuthbert took the cartridge, studied it and also smelled it before handing it to Ogilvie. There was no doubt it was a spent bullet cartridge. Cuthbert was thinking several thoughts at once and knew that this would take some explaining. Again, he thanked Professor Baxter.

'We deal in the past, Dr Cuthbert, and I'm not sure it matters if that past was a millennium ago or a day ago. Our work is still about piecing together what happened then from what little physical remains we can find today. The students enjoyed this challenge, and it has certainly given them all invaluable practical experience as well as a rather good story to tell. But, young man, I will be cross with you if I find they take up forensics rather than the altogether more noble calling of archaeology.'

They both smiled as they shook hands, and Cuthbert assured him he was more gamekeeper than poacher.

When they left, Cuthbert and Ogilvie carefully bagged up the fragments and recorded them in their evidence book. Currie and Mathieson were still at the scene of the bombing continuing the laborious task of logging the position and numbering of all the human remains. Before Ogilvie left to join them, Cuthbert asked him how he thought it was going.

'We're making excellent progress, sir. I would estimate that about two thirds of the site have been covered, and we should have the rest completed by lunchtime tomorrow. There's quite a cold front coming in, but we should get everything back before any snow.'

'Excellent. I will stay here this afternoon and complete the preparations for the receipt of the remains. When you have finished the logging at site, I want you to be in charge of boxing everything up. It all needs to come here in the first instance and then we can start with the next stage.'

*

Cuthbert had already been mulling over what that next stage would be. He knew that the usual methods of identification were not going to be possible for the majority of the dead. There were eight largely intact corpses, and these could be shown to relatives for formal identification after their post mortem examinations. But showing the collections of body parts even if reassembled would be highly inappropriate. What he needed were details and, if possible, photographs of the missing, and for that he needed Hogg.

He phoned and asked the sergeant to come to the mortuary that afternoon to discuss progress in the case. When he arrived, Cuthbert thought Hogg looked just as uneasy as every other police officer he'd seen in a mortuary.

'I'm sorry we have to meet here, sergeant. It was really for my convenience and was a little selfish of me.'

'No need to apologise, sir. I understand perfectly what you have to do. What is it you need from me?'

Cuthbert explained the difficulties with identification and how a detailed list of names, ages, and any physical characteristics of those missing and presumed to have been lost in the bombing would be of the greatest help. 'And, of course, photographs, if any exist. I know it's asking a lot of you and the men, sergeant.'

'Not at all, sir. In fact, I already have it. I assumed you would need such a file and I've had everyone working on it since the morning after the bombing. I have it here.'

Cuthbert took the thick file that was proffered and was speechless. He opened it and saw that each page consisted of a neatly completed form for each missing person arranged in alphabetical order. Listed were the full name, sex, age, height and approximate weight of the missing person along with a description of their clothing, any scars, distinguishing marks and tattoos, and for about half of the victims there were small photographs pinned to the pages. All in all, there were twenty-four sheets, corresponding to twenty-four men, women and children who had gone out that Monday night and never come home.

'This is remarkably good work, sergeant. I can't tell you how much this will speed up our work here. You must thank the men from me.'

'Men and one woman, sir. W.P.C. Anderson asked if she could help as you needed no driver during the day while you were working on site or here. I didn't think you'd mind her being redeployed, as it were. She's proved a real asset, I can tell you. She probably tracked down and interviewed more relatives than any of the men.'

'Well, give my thanks to them all, sergeant. I really am very impressed, and your contribution here will not go unacknowledged.'

'It's just part of the job, sir, and we both know it needs to be done well or not at all. Is there anything else?'

Cuthbert was interrupted by the phone on his desk. It was the first time he had heard it ring and it startled him. He took the call, and, stern-faced, hung up after a brief conversation.

'I'm afraid we've been summoned by our friend at headquarters. D.C.I. Black wants an urgent update because of new developments. He didn't elaborate as to what those were.'

Cuthbert collected his coat and hat and said that he would take the opportunity to walk as he needed the air. As he was going, Hogg remembered the newspaper in his pocket.

'I expect you've seen the papers, sir.' Hogg handed Cuthbert that morning's edition of the *Daily Mirror*. 'It's Mosley up to his old tricks again. He gave a speech last night at a big meeting in London claiming it was an assassination here in Glasgow.'

Cuthbert took the paper and looked at the front-page photograph of the dark-haired orator with his hand raised in moral outrage, clawing at the air for revenge.

'I can honestly say I have never before agreed with a single word that man says, but I have to this time – it was an assassination.'

'And look at the headline, sir. He says the Jews were responsible.'

'Well, of course he does. The man's an out-and-out fascist and an anti-Semite. He'll do everything he can to politicise this, and I expect that's exactly what everyone was frightened he might do.'

Cuthbert read the column that reported the speech. There were all the words he expected to see when he read of Mosley and his antics, replete with exclamation marks. 'Action!', 'Into battle!', 'The crisis of 1931!'.

The reporter painted the scene of a man with aristocratic looks and a powerful, harsh voice more suited to the parade ground taking to the stage 'after the audience rose and swept a storm of applause towards the platform'. And, as in every report of Mosley, there was mention of his bodyguards, in this case his 'husky prize fighters that surrounded him'.

Hogg watched Cuthbert shake his head as he read the article, and he offered some further thoughts.

'I think what's more worrying is what he or, more accurately, his supporters will do next. Mosley and his gang of thugs have never been as popular here as in the south, but there's enough to cause trouble.'

'What sort of trouble, sergeant?'

'Retaliation, revenge, retribution – call it what you like. They set themselves up as judge and jury and even executioner. I expect Black's under a lot of pressure to put all this to bed. And as you know, he wouldn't know how to make a bed, that one. I reckon that's why you're being summoned, sir.'

*

The meeting with D.C.I. Black was brief. As Hogg had anticipated, it had been prompted by Mosley's speech and the subsequent high alert the police force in Glasgow had been placed on.

Black was visibly anxious but did not ask Cuthbert anything about the progress of the case. He merely used the meeting to vent his frustration at the pace of the investigation. Cuthbert suspected that the chief inspector's mood was second-hand, and that Black had been on the receiving end of a similar tirade.

He told Cuthbert he wanted answers and he wanted them now. The chief constable, he was informed, was away on police business and had left the chief inspector to carry the case – and doubtless also the can, if things went wrong.

Cuthbert left the office none the wiser as to what more was expected of him, but he was already getting used to Black's ineffectual bluster. It had little effect on him. Cuthbert had no time for those who merely went through the motions of their outrage.

He returned to the mortuary to start work on what he regarded as the most difficult of the identifications. He consulted Hogg's file and looked for a page under the letter 'H'. There it was: *Henderson, Alistair*. Cuthbert studied the physical characteristics outlined on the form. At five foot ten inches, he would have been regarded as a tall man in Glasgow, and there was mention of an old appendicectomy scar, and a mole on his left ear lobe.

It wasn't much to go on, but it was a start. This would likely be more a process of elimination than anything else; whatever was left after everything else had been accounted for might reasonably be Henderson. Cuthbert, however, was never happy with that kind of approach for he considered it to be fundamentally disrespectful. There had to be something else.

He noted in the description of the candidate's clothing that he had been wearing a very light grey flannel suit, not at all typical of men's attire for that time of year. A summer fashion, yes, but not in winter. If any very light grey fabric survived adhering to the various male body parts they had collected, that might help.

Cuthbert also noted that he had been wearing a distinctive striped tie and rosette in the party colours of amber and black. Again, if any matching fragments were found, they might provide a positive identification.

He consulted the running inventory Dr Currie had been compiling of all the body fragments. This described the anatomy and state of each of the parts that had been identified thus far. Cuthbert scanned down the column headed up 'Clothing'. Where there was a tick there was a brief description of what had been found.

On the first page he found a right adult foot and ankle associated with a torn shred of light grey material. He realised he would have to see it when it was brought to the mortuary to be sure, but it might be a match.

*

Cuthbert spent the rest of the day alone at the mortuary setting up the office and assessing the facilities in the dissection room and laboratory area.

The city mortuary was a single-storey red-brick and sandstone building. When Cuthbert first saw it, it immediately reminded him of the police headquarters building, only half a mile away, that had doubtless been built at roughly the same time and in a similar style.

The mortuary stood conveniently next to the Glasgow

High Court on Saltmarket, one of the old thoroughfares that led up from the river to Glasgow Cross and continued on up the hill to the Cathedral as the High Street. This was the old heart of Glasgow and for centuries it had seen more than its fair share of violence as well as both its medical and judicial consequences.

One of the main entrances to Glasgow Green stood opposite the mortuary, and from the doorway Cuthbert could look across, his eyes drawn by the towering obelisk of Nelson's Monument, to the scene of the bombing. Indeed, it was the proximity of the mortuary to both the site and to the police headquarters that had made Cuthbert decide on it as a centre for the forensic investigation. It certainly was not the facilities the small department offered or the willingness of its staff.

There were only two men who serviced the mortuary. One was a technician, while the other was little more than a doorman-cum-janitor. As far as Cuthbert could tell, they had been hiding from him since he first arrived. Admittedly, they had got off to a poor start and for that Cuthbert blamed himself.

It had been the evening of the bombing; he was tired, and had just been handed the news that his life, whose privacy he always defended, was on file at M.I.5 and that he now had to lead a major investigation in a strange city with no staff.

When he encountered the two mortuary employees, he was unimpressed to the point of rudeness and they, for their part, took fright at the force of Cuthbert's demands. He resolved to apologise when he next saw them but was unsure when that might be.

Now, in the office adjacent to the dissection room, in a silence that was only broken by the loud, insistent tick of a Victorian wall clock, Cuthbert was starting to feel the weight of it all. He missed the familiarity of his own department, his own staff and most of all his home. He had no idea how long he would have to stay on in Glasgow, but he did know that he would be there until the job was done.

*

That evening, Cuthbert was lost in his thoughts as he sat polishing his boots in his hotel room when the bedside telephone rang. It was late and he was avoiding sleep as he often did.

When he was in his normal environment, he would close his office door at the hospital and spend his lunch hour on his polishing ritual, swirling the oily black polish in small circles into the leather and spitting lightly on the cloth when he felt the polish become gritty.

His need for clean boots with a mirror sheen was nothing short of pathological, and he knew it. However, he could see no way of healing whatever part of his damaged psyche was the cause. Instead, he had turned the daily obsession into a form of meditation which he told himself was in fact a healthy thing to do. Such are the delusions that help us live.

Now the phone was on its fourth ring, and he was shaken out of his reverie. Annoyed, he put his boot and cloth aside and carefully picked up the receiver so as not to smudge it with polish.

'Dr Cuthbert. This is the hotel switchboard. I am sorry to disturb you, sir, but I have a trunk call for you. The gentlemen would not give his name, but says it is of the utmost importance. Do you wish to take the call?'

'Do you know where the call is from?'

'It's the Central London exchange, but I am afraid I cannot be more precise than that. Shall I say you are unavailable?'

Cuthbert paused, thinking that it might be Morgenthal or even Mowbray trying to get in touch, but he couldn't fathom why either of them would withhold their names.

'No, better put it through.'

There was a click on the line and the hiss of some distant static, but nothing more. Cuthbert held the receiver and chose not to speak until he was spoken to. Finally, there was a male voice, muffled and not one he recognised.

'Dr John Cuthbert?'

'Speaking. Who is this?'

'That is not important. What is, is that I am calling from the Ministry, and we need your assistance.'

Cuthbert was immediately on his guard and considered hanging up then and there, but before he could decide the man on the line continued.

'You are conducting the forensic investigation of the crime committed in Glasgow. What you must understand is that we are viewing this as a political assassination, and we require a speedy resolution to avoid any further bloodshed.'

'We are working as fast as is appropriate, and if there is evidence to indicate who the perpetrators were, we will find it.'

'Oh, Dr Cuthbert, we know who the perpetrators were. They were members of the Jewish Socialist League.'

'I've never heard of them, and we have certainly come to no such conclusion as yet. There is a great deal of work still to be done.'

'I do not think you understand me, Dr Cuthbert. It was the Jewish Socialist League and that is what your report will reflect. Are we quite clear?'

'Am I to understand that you are asking me to report a conclusion before I have done the investigation?'

'Not at all. I am not asking you to do anything, I am ordering it. The local leader of those Jewish rabble-rousers is the one who planted this bomb and his swift arrest and conviction based on your evidence is what we need right now.

Anything less, and we'll have a bloodbath on our hands. I'm sure we understand each other.'

'Who is this?'

'Just think of me as a friend.'

There was another click and the silence of empty air. Cuthbert was furious and rang the hotel switchboard, but they were unable to tell him any more about the origin of the call. All they could say again was that it was from the Central London exchange. He made a note of the time and wrote down exactly what the mystery caller had said. He was not sure what he would do with it, but instinct told him to record the evidence.

*

Cuthbert slept badly. Early the next morning, he telephoned the police headquarters and left a message for Sergeant Hogg to call him at his hotel as soon as he arrived. Cuthbert had just started his breakfast when the call came through.

Without explaining, Cuthbert asked Hogg what he knew of the Jewish Socialist League. The sergeant was surprised by the request but expected that Cuthbert had a good reason.

'I'll dig out what we have on them, sir. I can be at the mortuary in an hour. Shall I meet you there?'

Cuthbert had lost his appetite, and he was missing the quiet and simplicity of his breakfasts at home served by Madame Smith. There were no hot croissants wrapped in white linen to be had in this hotel dining room, and while he had been excited to enjoy bacon and eggs for the first time in years, the novelty had quickly worn off.

Outside, W.P.C. Anderson was already parked and waiting to take him to the city mortuary. He greeted her warmly despite being distracted by the call from the Ministry that was still swirling in his mind.

On the way, he tried to shake himself out of his thoughts. He needed a new subject to occupy him. His gaze alighted on the badge on the constable's police cap. It was the same civic crest he had seen around the city. The Edinburgh City coat of arms not surprisingly boasted a castle, but Glasgow's was more difficult to understand. When he asked the constable about it, she treated him to some poetry by way of explanation.

'Do you not know the rhyme, sir? We all learnt it at school.'

With an unexpected lilt in her voice, she proceeded to chant the verse.

Here's the tree that never grew,
Here's the bird that never flew,
Here's the fish that never swam,
Here's the bell that never rang.

'I'm afraid I'm none the wiser, constable.'

'They're all connected to our patron saint, St Mungo. I don't remember about the tree, or the bell for that matter, but I was always intrigued by the bird, and the fish is the best one of all.'

Cuthbert wondered if she was being serious, and he waited to see if any more illumination might be forthcoming. Finally, he had to ask. 'Well, do tell, constable, unless of course it's only a story for native Glaswegians.'

'Not at all, sir. The bird that sits in the tree on the coat of arms is a wee robin, and I think we say it "never flew" because when it died, St Mungo took it in his hands and prayed over it so that it came back to life. It was one of his miracles.'

'And the fish? Are you saving the best till last?'

'The fish, sir, is at the centre of a love triangle, no less.'

'Am I to understand that someone was in love with the fish?'

Anderson laughed. 'No, sir! There was a king who gave his beloved queen the gift of a special ring. But she gave it away.

I always thought that was ungrateful, especially as she gave it to her boyfriend, a knight. He, the hapless knight that he was, promptly lost it. Of course, the king expected to see his queen wearing the ring and made quite a fuss when she wasn't.

'The knight was frightened for the queen's life, and he went to St Mungo and confessed all. The saint took pity on him and sent a monk to fish in the River Clyde. He brought back a prize salmon, and when the fish was cut open, what do you think they found inside?'

'The bird?'

'No, sir, the ring. But you're teasing me, aren't you?'

'Just a little, constable. But you're right it makes a good story. We all need stories to remind us where we came from.'

*

When they arrived at the mortuary, Hogg was already there, standing outside the main door.

'My apologies, sergeant, I didn't mean to keep you waiting. Let's get out of this chill.'

Hogg, who had arrived early, could have gone inside to wait, but he had resolved to spend as little time as possible inside that charnel house. Cuthbert offered him a seat in his office and asked again about the Jewish Socialist League.

'They're one of the political groups in the city. Young hotheads from the Southside – Govanhill mostly. And, obviously, they're Jewish. There's quite a tradition of left-wing politics in that community, and what with the current swing to the right, they're getting more vocal and more active.

'They're idealists, of course, but they certainly haven't been involved in any real violence. We've arrested a few over the last year, but mainly for public order offences. Nothing like what we're dealing with now. We do, however, have witnesses that place a group of them at the scene.

'They were mostly in the trees at the edge of the rally and seemed more interested in waving their flags and making a racket than anything else. That's really what they do. They shout down the fascists when they're trying to speak, and they draw attention away from the platform. Not much more than high jinks, if you ask me, sir.'

'Who's their leader? Has anything changed there recently? Perhaps there's been a change in strategy.'

'According to our file on them, it's a young lad by the name of David Goldberg. Nothing much about him, to be honest. He's twenty-three and seems to have lived in the Gorbals his whole life. No police record until last year when he was picked up with a few others at a militant Protestant march. They chucked a few stones and made a lot of noise. Goldberg was cautioned and released. Nothing else.'

'Hardly a criminal mastermind, then.'

'Doesn't look like it. But maybe the real masterminds don't get themselves caught. Why such an interest in the Socialist League, sir? There are other groups who might be a better fit.'

Cuthbert almost told Hogg about the phone call he had received the night before, but at the last moment he chose to keep it to himself.

'No reason, sergeant. It's just that I heard them mentioned, and since they were actually present at the bombing, I think we have to consider them as suspects.'

Hogg could read people, and he knew Cuthbert was lying to him. Nevertheless, he was in no position to challenge him on it. He also had to concede that the presence of some of the young Jewish activists at the scene could not be overlooked.

'I can look into them further if you think it might be useful, sir.'

'Please. I do think it would help answer some questions.'

Chapter 7

Glasgow: 13 February 1931

At the city mortuary in Saltmarket, Cuthbert started making the final preparations for the arrival of the human remains. He had left Ogilvie and Currie at the scene that morning and had brought Mathieson back with him to help.

The young man was the quiet one of the three, and that was the main reason Cuthbert chose him. Without speaking, Iain Mathieson just got on with it, quickly and efficiently. He was about the same age as Simon Morgenthal, but he had much less to say for himself.

Cuthbert had observed him at the site and found his work to be meticulous, and when he had perused his field notes, he was equally impressed by his succinct style and close attention to relevant detail. He also liked his grammar. There was only one thing Cuthbert believed to be more important than good English grammar and that was good Latin grammar.

Now, he watched as the young man cleared the bench space and washed down the slabs. There was still little or no technical assistance available in the mortuary, which had never been built or staffed with what was about to happen in mind. And Cuthbert kept watching him work, wondering what he was truly thinking about the good-looking young man and questioning himself on his real motives for choosing him to help.

He knew from long experience that he could not completely control his feelings, but he could consciously put them to one side, especially if they might interfere with his work. And that was certainly the case here.

'Dr Mathieson, thank you for that. Sterling work. Perhaps you would like to take your lunch break now, and when you get back, I'll take mine. I think it best if one of us is here in case our colleagues at the site need anything.'

Alone in the mortuary, Cuthbert unpacked some books he'd had delivered from the university department and took one of the two desks in the small office adjacent to the dissection room. He looked down at his boots, which to anyone else would have appeared pristine, but he could see the smallest of scuffs.

He took his polishing kit from his briefcase and proceeded to do his daily ritual. He needed to free himself from the present and revisit his past, and as he rubbed the polish in small deliberate circles on the leather he wondered when, if ever, he might stop feeling like this.

*

That afternoon, when the boxes started to arrive, the calm of the empty mortuary was broken. Now collected in the confined space of two rooms, the human remains that had been spread over a third of an acre of ground looked overwhelming.

The best estimates so far were that there were twelve adult male and six adult female victims along with at least four children. The figures were almost certainly an underestimation, as some of the bodies would never be recovered because of the fires that had consumed them afterwards.

Cuthbert surveyed the mortuary dissection room and was again troubled by the scale of the task ahead. The three junior pathologists were, however, working diligently and in a highly systematic way. Each box was checked against a master list and the numbered tags on each of its contents were read out by one doctor and cross-checked by another before it was unloaded. It took most of the afternoon to arrange and catalogue the remains, after which the real work could begin.

Cuthbert again broke the work into four roughly equal sections; he and Ogilvie would work in the dissection room while Currie and Mathieson would take the adjoining laboratory. Those bodies that were intact, or largely so, would be the first order of business, and the first three had already been laid on the mortuary slabs awaiting examination.

Three others had been placed in the mortuary fridges and two had been stored as respectfully as possible on the floor. All the others were nothing more than a massive jigsaw puzzle of body parts, and Cuthbert had assigned the two working in the laboratory area to making a start on trying to piece these together. He knew this would be essential to aid identification, but more than that, he also knew that he had to return as intact a corpse as possible to each family for burial.

The first of the bodies that Cuthbert examined on the slab was that of a young woman. She was likely 20 to 25 years of age, and a lot of her clothing was still in place. Cuthbert carefully cut these pieces away and bagged them. He also checked the surface of her body for any marks or scars that might aid identification, as well as for physical evidence of the trauma that had killed her.

The thing that struck him was just how untouched she was as she lay naked on the slab. Her limbs were intact, there was no blood, no fatal gash, no ragged wound, indeed nothing at all to indicate how she might have died at first glance. The post mortem staining resulting from the blood falling through gravity to the lowest portions of the body after death indicated conclusively that she had died lying flat on her back, doubtless after being thrown to the ground by the blast.

Like all pathologists, Cuthbert knew that blast injuries were of three sorts. First, the massive pressure wave produced by the bomb often caused major internal trauma, especially of those organs that contained air – the middle ear, the gut and most importantly the lungs. If that did not kill you, projectiles hurled through the air might cause fatal penetrating wounds. And, finally, the blast might throw the victim against a hard object or surface again resulting in fatal trauma.

This woman had no signs of any penetrating injury and had clearly not been hit by any of the flying fragments of wood from the platform. She had no blast burns to her face or hands, suggesting she was not that close to the bomb when it detonated, but the pressure wave could still have caused serious lung damage – collapsed lungs associated with severe pulmonary contusions or bruising and bleeding.

That might have been enough to kill her, but Cuthbert noted there was also a serious head wound to the back of her skull. Mathieson had found her body at the scene, and when Cuthbert consulted his field notes, he saw that her head had forcibly struck a sharp rock lying on the ground. Before Cuthbert completed the examination, he was all but certain that traumatic brain injury would be the cause of death.

While he performed the post mortem examination of the young woman, Ogilvie was working closely on an elderly man on the adjacent slab. As the two pathologists worked, neither spoke but focused all their attention on the bodies before them, both men intent on defining the cause of death and gathering any clues that might aid identification.

Only when they had both completed the internal examinations of the bodies, reconstituted them and covered them in white sheets was there any exchange.

'Secondary blast injuries from penetrating wood fragments and subsequent massive haemorrhage, sir.'

Cuthbert nodded and confirmed that he had found internal evidence of pulmonary haemorrhage consistent with a primary blast injury as well as a fatal head injury.

Ogilvie sighed and removed his gloves and said, 'Well, two down, another goodness knows how many to go.' But as he said it, he could almost feel Cuthbert's chilling stare.

'Dr Ogilvie, if you wish to continue working on this case, please do not let me hear you speak like that again. These are not boxes to be ticked off – they are people who should be respected even in death. Am I understood?'

'Of course, sir. Please forgive me. I did not mean to show disrespect. I think tiredness has got the better of me.'

'We're all tired, laddie. It's been a long day and there's another waiting for us tomorrow. Please write up your report and get yourself home. But be back here in the morning at eight o'clock sharp. I want to release as many of the intact bodies to their families as possible, if we can get their post mortems done, their identities confirmed and their death certificates issued.'

Soon afterwards, he also sent Currie and Mathieson home. When he had the mortuary to himself again, Cuthbert took the opportunity to phone London.

'Detective Chief Inspector Mowbray, please. Dr Cuthbert calling from Glasgow.'

The switchboard operator at Scotland Yard sat up when she heard Cuthbert's familiar voice and immediately put him through.

'Jack, how's the old country?'

'I'd forgotten we were on first-name terms. I told you it was going to take me a while, Jim. But, there, I've managed it.'

'Proud of you. Now, to what do I owe the honour?'

Cuthbert explained that he had a problem, in fact two

problems, and he needed Mowbray's help. He asked first about M.I.5.

'Did you know I had an M.I.5 file? Do you have one?'

'Don't get your kilt in a twist over that. We've all got security service files. This is the Met. We might have to investigate a fraud or even a murder at the heart of government. You don't think they take chances on that. And you, well, you could be a Scottish infiltrator. They especially don't want to take a punt on the likes of you.'

Cuthbert was not as amused as Mowbray had hoped and was still surprised and disappointed in himself that he had not known about this.

'What's the other problem? You rusting in the rain up there?'

'Do you know a D.C.I. Morrison Black?'

'Can't say the name rings a bell. Is he leading the case?'

'Yes, and no. The chief constable took charge initially, but now it seems this man has taken over. By all accounts, he's not up to the job.'

'Well, you don't expect every D.C.I. to be as good as the one you're used to in London, do you, Jack?'

Cuthbert was still not in the mood for levity, and the impatient sigh that Mowbray heard on the end of the line made that clear.

'What is it you want to know?'

'Anything about him. He seems wholly unsuited to lead this investigation and by all accounts has never shown any aptitude for serious police work, so how does someone like that rise to be a D.C.I?'

'I don't know him, but I can check him out for you, and as for your second question, did you never meet a senior officer during the war that you thought was a halfwit? Incompetence is everywhere. I'm just as astonished as you when I see it rewarded. But in the force, there are all sorts of things that help get you promoted apart from skill and hard work. Your D.C.I. Black might not know much, but I bet a pound to a penny he knows how to give a funny handshake.'

Cuthbert was exasperated at the thought of such corruption and favouritism, but he thanked Mowbray for listening to him let off steam. He thought about asking Mowbray what he thought of the anonymous call he had received from London, but decided, just as he had when speaking with Sergeant Hogg, that it was best kept a secret for the time being.

'Look, Jack, your D.C.I. doesn't know what he's got with you running the forensic investigation. Why would he? He'll never have had the opportunity to work with the kind of intellectual ally you are. Do what you do best and solve it for him. This time you'll need to be more than a pathologist. But, if my experience of you is anything to go by, you can't help yourself in that department. Who have you got who you can rely on?'

'The sergeant is working well with me, and I've got good support from the young pathologists here. I'm sorry to be phoning you like this. I don't know what you can be thinking of me.'

'I'm just thinking you're worried about doing the best job you can, and I know you will. I'll look into Black for you but go with your gut about everything else.'

*

That evening in his hotel room, he went over everything on his mind. He had some experience of this kind of carnage and was no stranger to the hard work involved in putting it all together, but this case had some odd quirks that he could not resolve.

In particular, he was still puzzled by his involvement in the case and by Glaister's absence from it. He understood that the professor was old and about to retire, but he was the most senior forensic specialist not just in the city but in the country, and here was a forensic jigsaw that needed all the expertise that could be gathered. Where was he and why was he not working on it?

*

The next morning, Ogilvie arrived at the city mortuary shortly after Cuthbert. Before he started his work, Cuthbert took the opportunity to quiz him.

'Tell me, Dr Ogilvie, have you heard from Professor Glaister lately? I expect he's taking an interest in this investigation.'

'Oh, I don't know about that, sir. I think he's abroad at the moment. A conference in Paris, I believe, or maybe Geneva?'

'But he does know about this and about me?'

'I couldn't say, sir. He left in the afternoon, before the bombing, and by the time I was contacted about it, he was already well on his way to Southampton. I thought it best not to trouble him. After all, I knew you were still here.'

'Do you mean to tell me that Professor Glaister knows nothing of this?'

'I'm sure he'll read about it in the papers, but we don't expect him back for another three weeks, maybe four. I believe he's examining in Berlin after the conference, and these days he likes to travel at a more leisurely pace. And everyone, even Dr Henderson, encourages it.'

'You've deliberately excluded him from all this, haven't you?'

'Please, it's not like that at all. He would never have done any of the practical work. He hasn't for years. All he would have done was make life difficult for everyone and then waltz off with all the credit. He still expects to be the most important person in any room he enters, but the truth is he's no longer the force he once was. Trust me, this way is so much easier.'

Cuthbert was dumbfounded and only hoped that when the time came, he would not be treated with the same kind of disrespect and deception by his junior staff.

*

Late that afternoon, Cuthbert took Sergeant Hogg with him when he went back to see D.C.I. Black at police headquarters. The pathologist now had a story to report and was not about to be seen as the weak link in the investigation.

When they arrived, the chief inspector kept them both waiting at reception, doubtless, thought Cuthbert, as a gentle reminder of who was in charge. After twenty minutes of their time had been wasted, Black summoned them to his office.

Cuthbert greeted him warmly and betrayed not a trace of his annoyance. He asked about the chief constable only to be reminded that Black would be the one now receiving his reports and, in any case, Harper was currently unavailable.

Cuthbert wasted no more time and immediately gave Black a summary of their findings including those relating to the recovery of the bomb fragments.

'The explosive could have been dynamite or T.N.T., but dynamite would have been safer as they would have had to transport it on the day to the area under the stage. It was probably brought in a bag or a box. One man could have carried it – it probably weighed twenty-five to thirty pounds all in.'

'Who would have made it?'

'Someone with a degree of technical skill would have had to put it together, chief inspector, but it's not complicated for anyone with the right training. Plenty of them around, I'm afraid. We did a good job teaching men how to kill in the war. If this was London, the dynamite would probably be ex-army. There have been a number of thefts from ordnance stores in the Southeast in recent years and we know there are explosives out there. It's just a case of knowing the right people. I expect it's no different here in Glasgow.'

Cuthbert also presented an update on the identification of the victims. He went through the list that had been compiled by Hogg and the constables and that had now been annotated by the pathology team. He was able to offer positive identification on five of the intact corpses and tentative identification on some six others. While he went through the names, Cuthbert watched Black's attention wander. The chief inspector was finding some dirt under his fingernails considerably more interesting than Cuthbert's report, and the pathologist chose to fall silent almost mid-sentence to allow the senior officer a chance to respond.

'Very good. So what about Alistair Henderson, have you managed to piece the candidate back together yet?'

'As I was just saying, chief inspector, it's not quite as simple as that.'

'Yes, just run that by me again.'

'I believe the bomb was intended primarily for him, and it would have been placed directly under the point where he was standing on the platform. The bombers knew exactly where he would be because of the microphone of the public address system. He was probably only a few feet from it when it went off under him. Of all the victims, he will have taken the greatest force of the blast.'

'What is it you're saying, doctor? That there won't be much of him left?'

Cuthbert frowned by way of acknowledgement.

'So what do we know about this man? Why would anyone want him dead?'

Cuthbert turned to Hogg, who had been standing all this time while the others were seated, and invited him to contribute. The sergeant, however, was acutely aware of the pecking order in the room and looked to Black for permission to speak.

The chief inspector now looked impatient as well as distracted, as if he had already forgotten his question and at the same time wanted them both out of his office. He turned up his palms, shrugged and uttered a barely discernible, 'Well?' Hogg looked back at Cuthbert and took the opening.

'Alistair Melrose Henderson was forty-nine years old, born in Ayrshire and had been living for the past twenty years in the West End of Glasgow. He has family money and also a major interest in two companies – he is a three-quarters owner of one and a fifty per cent shareholder of the other. He's dabbled in politics for years but has never before stood for any office.

'He's on close terms with several of those high up in Oswald Mosley's New Party, including Mosley himself. He and his wife socialise with the Mosleys and that set in London.'

'What's this about a New Party? Is that what they're calling themselves?'

'Yes, sir. As I'm sure you know, Mosley has been affiliated at one time or another with both the Conservative and Labour Parties, but neither have suited his political agenda. He has now decided to set up his own so-called New Party, and by all accounts he has a lot of high-profile support. Their platform is very right-wing, and they are already aligning themselves with the European fascist movements.

'They're busy preparing for the General Election later this year. Henderson was to stand in the Shettleston constituency here in Glasgow. The rally on the Green was his first foray into speaking directly to those he hoped would vote for him.'

Black snorted in derision. 'I wouldn't get too excited about their politics, if I were you, sergeant. It's not been my experience that anyone was ever killed over a ballot box.'

Cuthbert did not regard himself as a political animal.

However, he could not contain his disgust for the extreme and, as he saw it, inhuman views of the fascists, or his shock that Black could be so ignorant of history.

'I have to disagree with you, chief inspector, in the strongest terms. More men have died over politics of one form or another than anything else, in recent years. Have you forgotten why we fought a war? And it would be a grave error of judgement to minimise the influence of these fascists. They are small-time thugs just now, but what do you imagine the world might be like if they were to gain any real power?'

'That will never happen – not in this country or anywhere else for that matter. And even if it did, would it be so bad? A little law and order and the streets cleaned of all the undesirables.'

Cuthbert got to his feet and loomed over Black, who leant back in his chair, recognising the force in Cuthbert's voice and realising that he had crossed some sort of line.

'Chief inspector, this case *is* about politics. This was a political assassination. I abhor this man's politics, but I will do everything I can to scrape his shattered body from the ground because the dead, no matter who they are, deserve that level of respect.

'It is the living, however, who have to endure the consequences of these men's actions, and I urge you to think carefully about your use of the term "undesirable". When you say it, you use it as a shorthand to mean Jew, Pole, foreigner, someone who is different from you. You would do well to remember that, to a man like Mosley and his gang of brutes, you are the one who's different. A Scot, a commoner, working class – you don't talk like him, you didn't go to his kind of school, you don't go to his clubs or move with his set. What makes you think you won't be classed as one of his undesirables when the time comes?'

Black said nothing. He was unused to be spoken to in

such a forthright manner, especially in his own office. None of his junior officers would have dared to challenge him, but Cuthbert didn't work for him or anyone else in Glasgow. The man had the blessing of Whitehall and that was the most important factor determining his next move.

Black smiled and shook his head, saying how Cuthbert had misunderstood him, how well he thought his investigation was going and how right he had been to involve Hogg. He did everything but kneel before him and kiss his hand in gratitude in an attempt to turn the situation around.

Cuthbert was now disgusted with him even more. He remained standing and explained that he and Hogg still had much work to do and that he would report further when a little more 'piecing together' had been done.

Without waiting to be dismissed he opened the office door and ushered Hogg into the outer office and then quickly down the stairs.

'Get me out of here, sergeant, before I resort to violence.'

From anyone else, Hogg would have taken the words as just an idle expression, but he could see Cuthbert's eyes, and as he assessed the strength of the man, he thought it best to do exactly as instructed.

In the car, Cuthbert calmed down and apologised to Hogg. He rarely lost control but knew that a moment longer with Black might have been the tipping point.

'I need to talk through all this in some more detail. Constable Anderson, would you be kind enough to pull over and switch off the engine?'

She complied immediately and Hogg wondered what was coming.

'I would like to propose a rather unorthodox approach to this case. From what we have just witnessed, I am forced to conclude that D.C.I. Black is at best stupid and incompetent or, at worst, he is part of the underlying problem. Either way, he is a hindrance to this investigation.

'This was a politically motivated assassination, and I am required to provide him with reports, which I shall continue to do on my own, but I want to form an alternative investigative team consisting of we three.

'I understand the delicate nature of this request, but I reassure you that I am not asking you to do anything wrong, simply to do what should be done a little differently. In practice, I would like to meet you both at my office at the city mortuary each day so we can share intelligence and the results of any further investigations. In parallel, Black will doubtless be putting his oar in all the wrong places, but with my regular meetings with him, I'll be able to keep us abreast of that. Thoughts?'

W.P.C. Anderson said nothing, deferring to the seniority of Sergeant Hogg who spoke up.

'We were always going to have to do this on our own anyway. First with the chief constable and now with Black. Neither of them were ever going to make any serious contribution. Daily meetings and updates would give the investigation the structure it badly needs. And as you said, it's only what should be happening anyway if the investigation wasn't as half-arsed as it is.'

Still W.P.C. Anderson said nothing, and Hogg knew she would maintain her silence until he gave her leave to speak. When he did so she asked why Cuthbert thought she would be needed.

'Because, constable, you have a fine head on your shoulders, and it will be brains that will solve this – it always is. Can I count on you?'

'My job is to be at your disposal during the investigation, Dr Cuthbert, so, yes, I'll do anything you ask. Shall I take us to the mortuary now so we can make a start?'

*

At his office, Cuthbert cleared the wall behind his desk and moved a large cork pinboard from the hallway and put it up.

'This can serve as our working board for the investigation. It's a method used by my colleagues at the Met, and it works very well, I find. All relevant information will be summarised here, along with photographs of the main victim and any suspects as and when we have identified them. We are looking for connections to unravel this. So let's summarise where we are. Sergeant Hogg, would you be so kind?'

The sergeant, unused to this level of organisation, nevertheless welcomed it. He wasn't too old to learn some new tricks and was willing to try anything once. Likewise, Anderson looked on eagerly, a fresh notebook in her lap. From the sheaf of papers he had with him, Hogg retrieved a black-and-white photograph and pinned it to the centre of the board.

'Alistair Henderson, one of the twenty-odd fatalities of the bombing on the night of ninth February but who we believe to be the main target of the attack. He was scheduled to give a speech on Glasgow Green, and the event was well publicised. Anyone who wanted to cause him harm would have known exactly where and when to find him.'

'Motives?' The question had come from Anderson as she chewed on her pencil and prompted Hogg to enumerate the possibilities.

'Henderson was politically right-wing, in fact extremely so. There are a number of groups and individuals in the city who would have taken great exception to his platform. He preached a cleansing of the streets of "undesirables" and targeted the Jews in particular. So one motive would be a response to his anti-Semitism – and the slightly bigger picture of what he and Mosley's New Party stand for. Henderson may not have been attacked for who he was rather than what he represented. Sending a political message loud and clear.

'However, I'm also looking into Henderson's private life to eliminate any motives connected to his business affairs. There's also a rumour of adultery – a young secretary – but nothing concrete on that yet.'

Anderson shook her head and remarked that wives don't blow their husbands to smithereens when they find out they've been unfaithful. 'Far too quick. And I think the business angle is a non-starter. That's not how any kind of dispute's going to be solved. They'd want his money, his assets, not his martyrdom. No, I believe this is about politics – as you said in the car, Dr Cuthbert.'

This was the most Cuthbert and Hogg had ever heard the young woman say, and Hogg smiled at the pathologist as if to say, I told you so.

Cuthbert looked closely at Henderson's photograph. He had never met the man, but there was a marked family resemblance to his brother. The man in the photograph was smiling and very much alive, but Cuthbert knew that some of him at least was now in the boxes of tagged remains in the next room.

He turned to Anderson and followed up on her argument. 'In that case, who should we suspect?'

'There are a number of Jewish groups in the city, especially on the Southside – Govanhill and the Gorbals – but this doesn't fit with any of them. Some have been vocal at previous fascist meetings, but the extent of it has been to shout the speakers down. There have been a few scuffles, but there's never been anything on this scale – premeditated or violent – at least not to my knowledge.' She looked at the sergeant for confirmation and he nodded.

'Could that have changed?' asked Cuthbert. 'I mean, all it might take is for a member of one of those organisations to take matters into their own hands, to seek an altogether more radical solution. Take, for example, the Jewish Socialist League. You were looking into their leader, sergeant. Anything to report there?'

Hogg was puzzled and looked across at Anderson. 'Why the J.S.L., sir? I mean, all they do is make a noise. This isn't their style at all.'

'All the same, I think it's important we pursue this. Have you tracked him down yet, sergeant?'

Hogg shook his head. 'Not yet, sir, but the constable and I will start work on that tomorrow. We'll pay the Goldberg lad a visit. See if we can't ruffle his feathers a little and see what drops out.'

'Thank you. And I'll continue the work here, trying to give these poor unfortunates back their names.'

The room was growing dark, and Cuthbert realised he had kept Hogg and Anderson longer than he had intended. When they left, he studied the investigation board that was now taking shape on the wall. At last, a picture of what was going on was beginning to emerge, but there was still so much to do.

*

After another fretful night's sleep, Cuthbert was back at the mortuary the next day. He and Ogilvie were seated at the desks in the small office at the side of the dissection room that they had been allocated for the investigation. Both were writing up their findings from the series of examinations they had performed earlier that morning.

Rather than trying to establish cause of death, which commonly occupied the pathologists in their work, in these cases there was little doubt how these men, women and children had died. What was seriously in question though, was who they were. Both men knew that the biggest and most difficult task they faced was identifying these victims.

However, that morning Cuthbert had made one observation that he knew did not easily fit. Without glancing up, he asked Ogilvie, 'How good is your ballistics laboratory at the university?'

'I'm embarrassed to say, sir, that we don't have one.'

Cuthbert who was writing, stopped in mid-sentence. Ogilvie could see that Cuthbert was unsure if he had heard correctly, and he repeated the admission: 'You see, sir, Dr Henderson is not a great advocate of forensic ballistics, and in fairness we do see very few cases of gunshots in this city. It's really all about knives on the streets here.'

Cuthbert was still incredulous that a department of such renown should have such a gap in its armoury. Given the nature of the report he was writing and what he knew would have to be done, he stood up from the desk and asked Ogilvie to join him at the slab nearest the window, where the white sheet was obviously covering something much smaller than a body. He asked the junior man to talk him through his examination, as much to test him as to reassure himself of his own findings.

'Dr Ogilvie, I wonder if you could give me the benefit of your opinion here?'

Ogilvie was pleased to be asked, and he removed the sheet and studied the dismembered head closely and carefully without touching it before taking it in both hands. It had been lying on the slab on one side and now Ogilvie examined it from the front. He also tilted the head back to study the ragged mess that had been the neck and looked closely at the state of the features, checking for damage. Finally, he turned the head around and probed the back with his fingers for any wounds.

'Sir, this is the head of an adult male that has been crudely separated from its body, most likely by violent explosive force. The head is intact apart from some deep scratches and abrasions that appear to have been caused by post mortem trauma. The most notable finding, however, is the gunshot wound.'

Cuthbert nodded but maintained a studied silence to encourage the junior pathologist, as he had often done when grilling Simon Morgenthal at St Thomas's.

'We have a discrete entry wound above the right eye, but no obvious exit wound. Thus, we would classify this as a penetrating rather than a perforating wound.'

Cuthbert neither agreed nor disagreed with Ogilvie's initial appraisal, but the young man was confident he understood what he was looking at and needed no encouragement to continue.

'The wound ballistics – that is to say, how the bullet affects the tissues it interacts with – depend on a number of factors. These are the size and composition of the bullet, the angle at which it enters the body, the location and track of the impact through the tissues, but most importantly the speed at which it is travelling when it hits. In summary, the higher the velocity, the greater the energy the bullet brings with it and the more damage it will do.'

'Why do you think there is no exit wound?'

There was a time when Ogilvie's nerves might have got the better of him when facing a blank-faced examiner like Cuthbert, unsure if what he was saying was remotely right or wrong, but not now. This was a field of forensic medicine that he had studied recently and extensively. He continued almost as the teacher rather than the pupil.

'The fact that the bullet passed through the skull but did not exit is indeed interesting and suggests a number of important things. First, we are probably dealing with a low-velocity rather than a high-velocity projectile – most likely delivered by a hand gun rather than a rifle. Second, because bullets lose speed as they pass through the air before hitting their targets, this would not be what we would expect with a shot delivered by a gun pressed against the head, as in a suicide or at very close range. Note also that there are no powder burns around the entry wound which would support this. Third, and this, I suggest, may be a deciding factor, the shape of the entry wound is not perfectly circular, suggesting some lateral movement or yaw as the bullet flew through the air. That would seriously reduce its velocity, such that when it broke through the skull it would have enough energy to do a great deal of damage but not enough to escape through the back of the cranium.

'Once you remove the brain from the skull and follow the track you will know a lot more. There may even be evidence of ricocheting within the skull cavity, which would further deplete the bullet's energy and, I'm afraid, result in even more catastrophic tissue damage.'

Cuthbert could not help but be impressed by Ogilvie's assessment. 'Professor Glaister has taught you well, Dr Ogilvie.'

'Oh, I'm sure you must realise by now that Glaister teaches us nothing. If he's not away speaking at some medical symposium or other, he's sitting on examination boards up and down the country. And when he is here, he's never in the department. He spends all his time playing politics with the senate, I think. And I doubt he even knows the other juniors and I are in his department.'

'Dr Henderson, then? Is he to thank for your training?'

'I think you know the answer there too. No, we have to teach ourselves, and that's why we were so excited when we heard you were visiting. Your reputation precedes you, sir, and the thought that you might be coming to take over the lead of the department was just . . . well, we all thought it would have been a breath of fresh air.'

Cuthbert was treading carefully for he did not want to be drawn into a game of criticising his colleagues, although he was sure Ogilvie was telling the truth. He decided to change the subject and make further use of Ogilvie's expertise.

'Perhaps I could entrust you to open the skull and complete the post mortem examination. Would you be comfortable with that?'

'Certainly, sir, and if the bullet hasn't fragmented, I will take care to recover it intact.'

'That bullet may be crucial, so, yes, blunt dissection first and then retrieve it with your fingers, not your forceps. The only marks I want to see on that bullet are those the gun made. Am I clear?'

'Absolutely, sir.'

*

Back at his desk Cuthbert completed his notes on the finding and then started to jot down his thoughts about the consequences of this discovery. He concluded that this man was already dead when the explosion ripped him apart.

Given the fact that his head was blown from his body meant that he must have been close to the bomb, perhaps even on it, but it didn't kill him: this did. Cuthbert circled the drawing he had made of the single gunshot wound to the head.

It was imperative that this head be identified, and perhaps the only way to do that was to find the rest of the body. His clothes, his wallet, maybe even any identifying marks might be crucial. To that end, he consulted the chart of the site that now hung on the mortuary wall. This specified the location where each numbered find had been retrieved.

He started by taking a note of those remains that had been flung from the detonation point in approximately the same direction. He reasoned that smaller pieces might have been thrown further than larger ones, and he selected several he thought might be possible components of the body belonging to the head.

Many of the smaller body parts were laid out in numerical order on a large bench in the laboratory area adjacent to the main dissection room. Cuthbert was quickly able to match two pieces of leg due to the fragments of dark blue serge still attached to them. There was also an incomplete upper male torso that might be a possible match, but all the clothes had been ripped from it. Almost adjacent to that on the bench was a mass of flesh that comprised the stump of a neck, a right shoulder and upper arm and part of the chest. Again, it was clearly an adult male and there were no clothes. However, amid the cuts and scratches to the skin, Cuthbert could detect lettering and symbols that looked to be crude, amateur tattoos on the upper arm and neck.

He took the partial torso and arm to the slab in the dissection room where he had better light and the facility to wash the skin. After cleaning away the surface dirt, he could make out a heart and the word 'Mary' on the shoulder and on the neck some lines that ran into the ragged wound of the decapitation.

It wasn't much to go on, but Cuthbert thought it was a start. If there were any matching tattoos on the portion of the neck still attached to the head, he may have found a significant part of the body.

Ogilvie still had the head and was busy trying to retrieve the bullet, but Cuthbert consulted the notes he had made after he had examined it both at the scene and later in the mortuary. Sure enough, he had recorded the presence of some dark lines in the shape of a cross on the neck which at the time he thought may have been post mortem staining or trauma. When Ogilvie was finished, he would revisit the examination and confirm whether there was a match.

In the meantime, he got out Hogg's file and went through the details of the missing persons. Finally, he came to one that looked to be a possibility. Male aged 20, 5 foot 11 inches in height, with a tattoo of a sword on the right side of his neck and one of a heart with the word 'Mary' on his right shoulder. When Hogg phoned shortly after to report in, Cuthbert took the opportunity to bring him up to date.

'Sergeant, I think we have an identification for one of the victims. He is Robert or Rab McDiarmid from Bridgeton. His injuries are unusual, and it would help immensely if we knew a lot more about this young man. Might you and Constable Anderson take a look?'

Hogg knew that W.P.C Anderson had been the one to track down McDiarmid's family when they were compiling the identification file, and he thought they might get more out of them now about the boy's story if he sent the constable back on her own. He said this to Cuthbert, who expressed some concern over her safety, working alone in that part of the city. Hogg, however, reassured him that she could take care of herself, although he would be on hand.

*

The officers parked outside the Olympia Cinema at Bridgeton Cross. Hogg planned to stay put in the car, but he would be able to watch the constable as she walked past the Umbrella towards the top end of Main Street where Mrs McDiarmid lived.

'Wave if you need the cavalry, lassie.'

'I'm sure anything that might happen to me will have already happened by the time you make it across the cobbles, sir.'

She walked smartly over to the Umbrella. This was designed as a shelter but served as much as a meeting place. It had stood for over fifty years and was like a large cast-iron bandstand surmounted by a fifty-foot high, four-sided clock tower. Today being dry, the benches under the canopy were occupied by a few old men digesting their newspapers.

Outside the close entrance at number 12 a group of women had gathered. When one of them saw W.P.C. Anderson approaching, she alerted the others and they fell silent. The sight of a policewoman rarely brought anything but bad news.

'Is this about Rab?'

The policewoman had been headed off by a middle-aged woman in a wrap-around apron under her coat.

'Bessie's beside herself over there. If it's bad news, you'd better tell her quick and get it done with. Is it the worst, hen? Is it?'

The policewoman hesitated, not knowing who she was speaking to, but it was enough for the woman to read her expression, and she called over to the others, 'It's the worst, Bessie. Rab's deid.' Anderson tried to locate the boy's mother in the throng to mend the damage, but Mrs McDiarmid was already bent double and clasping her hand to her mouth to staunch the wail of grief she was trying to hold in.

'Mrs McDiarmid, I'm sorry to bring such bad news.'

The aproned woman was still trying to act as police spokesperson and shouted in Bessie McDiarmid's ear, 'The lassie says she's sorry he's deid.'

Anderson moved in closer to make herself heard and took the grieving mother's hand. She in turn looked up and sobbed, 'I always said he would come to no good running wi' that mob. How did he die? Was it a knife? Was it quick, hen?'

The same shawl that had once swaddled her son to her when she scrubbed the close stairs was now threadbare; she used it to wipe the tears she shed for him. Bessie was held up by her daughter who was more angry than sad. She had no time for grief and would not share her mother's tears.

Anderson needed to know more about Rab McDiarmid but could already sense the distrust of his sister. A police uniform in this area did nothing to reassure the locals. All they saw was a sign of brutal authority. She proceeded gently. 'Mrs McDiarmid, I'm very sorry for your loss. He was so young. We're just trying to find out what happened to him. Do you know why he was on the Green that night?'

'She doesn't know anything about it. So can you no just leave us in peace?'

Lizzie was trying to turn her mother away from the policewoman, but the older woman turned back only to say again that it was the mob he ran with that were to blame for everything. She was hushed again by Lizzie, who led her away, back into the close.

Anderson had written nothing in her notebook and looked about in frustration. The small crowd that had gathered to see what was going on was dispersing, and she doubted anyone else would speak with her.

She was putting the notebook back in her pocket when she noticed a young woman leaning against the wall looking at her. She had dyed blonde hair, and her coat and shoes were cheap but had been fashionable when they were bought. She took a long drag on her cigarette and eyed the policewoman from head to toe. 'Do you no want to know, then?'

'Miss?'

'Mary Callan. He lived up this close. We were tight for a while. But he always wanted to be a big man. He ran with the Brigton Boys. You knew that, aye?'

The policewoman shook her head, but she was already taking notes.

'You don't know much, hen. He was gettin' high up. Right thick with that Alec Jamieson.' She snorted and flicked her cigarette butt away. 'Wee boys playin' at bein' big men. That's all it comes down to. But even wee boys can get themselves killed. Wasn't a knife, was it? You'd have said, if it was. I knew it would be sooner or later. None of them last that long.'

Anderson didn't want to stop her speaking, but she was keen not to be drawn on the nature of McDiarmid's death, so she probed a little further. 'Do you know why he was on the Green, Mary?'

'Well, they were all there, weren't they? The Brigton Boys are the bodyguard. Bloody rubbish! They get a few bob and are told to dress up and act like hard men. It's all show until it isn't, and the blades get flicked. They're saying it was a bomb. Well, I don't know much, but that wasn't Rab.'

'Who's saying it was a bomb?'

The young woman pushed herself away from the wall, checked the seams in her stockings and tightened her coat belt. She shook her head at the policewoman and walked away. Without turning, she called back, 'Who'd you think, sweetheart?'

*

All the time Anderson was trying to piece together Rab McDiarmid's story on a street corner in Bridgeton, Ogilvie was carefully dissecting his brain in the mortuary. After almost an hour of slow work, Ogilvie asked to see Cuthbert and presented him with an enamel dish containing a bloodstained nugget of metal about the size of a tooth. Cuthbert raised his eyebrows and said, 'Intact?' Ogilvie nodded.

After washing the bullet under running water so as not to touch it, Cuthbert could see that its head had been deformed and flattened as it passed through the victim's skull. This sort of deformation was to be expected, and it was often extensive enough to obliterate any tell-tale markings that might be used later for identification, but in this case, as Cuthbert studied the bullet under the examination lamp, he could see that it was largely intact.

'"A silent witness". Are you familiar with Goddard's work, Dr Ogilvie?'

The junior pathologist knew the name in connection with the science of forensic ballistics, but he could hardly claim any real familiarity. However, as it turned out the question was rhetorical, merely an opener for Cuthbert to share his reading.

'Calvin Goddard has done more than anyone else to take the field forward, and that's what he would call this insignificant-looking lump of metal. He even goes so far as to say that old-fashioned expert witnesses, like us, are obsolete and all because of this little piece of metal that he calls "a silent witness". He prefers this because he claims a bullet has the two qualities so desirable, but never attainable, in the human witness – the inability to tell anything but the truth and a freedom from all personal prejudice.'

Cuthbert smiled and knew at once what needed to be done next.

Chapter 8

Bridgeton: 1 May 1926

The speaker was standing on one of the benches under the Umbrella at Bridgeton Cross, and the crowd was huddled tightly around him, keeping out of the lashing rain. Alec Jamieson was a raw-boned man in his late twenties, dressed in a three-piece suit that had seen better days. He was small, just over five foot tall, but with the voice of a much larger figure. He had taken off his flat cap and was waving it, folded in his hand, as an orator's prop.

'Aye! Those Fenian bastards came here and they took your jobs. They came here and they took your houses. Your women. They're breeding like rats, and soon you'll be outnumbered in your own country. The scum from Ireland with all their papist ways are taking o'er, and we can't let that happen. I won't let that happen. Are you with me? Are you goin' to let that happen?'

His supporters led the rhythmic response of 'No! No! No!' and urged everyone to join in. Soon the small crowd was punching the air and pulsating with the chant.

Shouting over the throng, Jamieson called for them to help him clean the streets, and as he spoke, his gang were already passing around their bunnets. Refusals to contribute to the cause were met with a glower held just long enough to convince the reluctant donor that his face might be remembered one night on a quiet street.

The speech was designed to inflame, but it was also designed to swell the coffers of the gang. Of course, it was pennies compared to the sums they would extort from shops and pubs, but Jamieson knew these small sums were even more important.

The amounts themselves were immaterial. What mattered was that the people of Bridgeton felt they were contributing to their community when they threw a penny or twopence into one of his lieutenant's caps. It was commonly believed that what they gave was redistributed to help those in need in the area. However, this was one of those myths that people choose to accept to allow them to justify their bigotry.

Alec Jamieson was certainly not any kind of Robin Hood figure, no matter how much he might have tried to portray himself as such. He was in fact the leader of one of the largest organised crime outfits in the city.

The 'Brigton Boys' were, to the outside observer, a group of disaffected young men who had found a common purpose in their sectarianism. They were bonded by a common loathing of Roman Catholics and a burning desire to reclaim their East End streets for the Protestant majority. However, this was only one view, seen through the lens that distorted everyone's view of them.

Jamieson had gathered about him men who found it easy to be loyal. He promised them much and offered them an opportunity to fill their empty, unemployed days with purpose. Many of his men were taken in by the stories he perpetuated about helping the community in which they lived. And Jamieson was careful enough to offer the occasional very public handout or take up some petty injustice for a scorned wife or a mistreated worker, to make it all credible. However, some young men were simply in his ranks because of their need to lash out at the world, violence being the only means of communication they had at their disposal.

Jamieson gave them plenty of opportunity to vent their anger and provided them with the weapons to make sure the fights would be remembered. He also drilled them and made them march through the streets to show their number and their discipline. This was not a gang: it was an army, and Jamieson styled himself as their general.

He took the adulation of the small crowd under the Umbrella and slipped away through the rain that was even heavier now. He pulled his cap down and ran towards his tenement in Franklin Street.

His men in the crowd had gathered up the takings and knew they were to meet him later to hand it all over. They would get their usual cut, their expenses to keep them smartly dressed and the extra they needed to save themselves from having to find a job. There was some work around, although much of it was dirty and some of it was dangerous, but a man could make a living as long as he was willing to graft hard.

The path the Brigton Boys had chosen was an altogether easier one in that respect. They only got their hands dirty with other people's blood and spent much of their time loafing around the streets of Bridgeton waiting on the call.

*

That weekend, the weather was turning milder after a cold spring and there was a freshness now in the air. More people were on the streets than usual, taking advantage of the first dry days for weeks. Children were playing without coats, prams were being pushed along to the Green, washing was drying on lines in the back courts, and there was a real sense that the summer might not be that far away.

The first that many of the people of Bridgeton knew of the strike was when they woke up on the Monday morning to see soldiers with their rifles at Bridgeton Cross. That first day, the streets were unusually quiet with no trams and little other traffic. There were no papers printed and those with radios listened intently to the news bulletins from the B.B.C. Prime Minister Stanley Baldwin was heard calling for the people of Britain to trust him.

'I am a man of peace,' he said solemnly. 'I am longing and looking and praying for peace. But I will not surrender the safety and the security of the British constitution. Cannot you trust me to ensure a square deal and to ensure even justice between man and man?'

The listeners, huddled round the radio sets in the tenements of Bridgeton that morning, were not sure what their answer was. They were told on the bulletins that it was the miners who had gone on strike over a dispute about their pay and their hours with the mine owners. 'Not a penny off the pay, not a minute on the day,' was their defiant cry as they walked out of their jobs across the country. But that was just the beginning, and other unions had pledged their support, beginning an avalanche of sympathy strikes throughout the country.

Now, transport workers, dockers, tram drivers, builders, printers and many other workers whose toil kept the wheels of the country rolling had laid down their tools in support of the miners. This, the listeners were told, was not a strike but the beginning of a revolution and some two million workers had answered the call to action.

Looking out on Bridgeton that day, people saw no revolution. They only saw empty streets, as though it was a

Sunday, but with the same poverty and dirt and hopelessness as always.

By the second day, there were small groups of men blocking the entrances to various workplaces. These men stood sentry on the picket lines in front of their workplaces, defiant but unarmed. They had already heard of blacklegs, fearful for their jobs, trying to sneak back into work, and of others who were volunteering to act as scab labour to dilute the efforts of the strikers and break their resolve. But the pickets were having none of it.

Many of the business owners of Bridgeton had spent the previous day discussing how to deal with the alarming situation. Most of them were connected with each other through their common religion and politics. They were uniformly Protestant and Conservative and many were active Freemasons and members of the Orange Order.

They employed Catholics because they needed a lot of unskilled labour, but they were not about to be dictated to by them. Perhaps it was only natural that they should turn to Alec Jamieson and his men for a solution.

The Brigton Boys were mobilised to take over the driving of delivery lorries and trams. They even took to directing the traffic around the busier streets of Bridgeton. Jamieson made them highly visible so that everyone could see that they were on the side of the ordinary people and would not allow the communists, or the Catholics, or whoever it was that could be conveniently blamed for all this, to win.

The people in their turn accepted the line they were being fed. In those few days, the reputation of the Brigton Boys rose in proportion to their apparent benevolence. What was not visible was the money that had changed hands. In backrooms, Jamieson had taken more in the last day than he had in the last year, and he was not about to disappoint his clients.

The atmosphere on the streets over the following two days shifted from one of bemusement to one of defiance, which would erupt into violence. And Jamieson's boys were always there to help. The police had been given orders to break up the picket lines by any means and to allow those who wished to return to work to do so peacefully. The strikers had other ideas.

Clashes took place with strikers jumping the officers, fists flying and boots kicking, but in return they received severe beatings about the head from heavy police truncheons. The Brigton Boys would watch out for these instances and rush to help not the strikers but the police. An unholy alliance was formed between old enemies, and the police, often outnumbered, turned a blind eye when the razors and the knives came out.

On the fourth day of the strike, on Fielding Street outside Barclay's Engineering Works, there was a picket line of about twenty men. Amongst them was Wullie McDiarmid. He was hardly committed to the strike but knew that to do anything other than join in would have made his life very difficult.

That morning, the men had managed to turn a few misguided workers away who were trying to enter, and they were now trying to brew tea on the brazier they had burning in the street.

'Wullie, where's that big son o' yours?'

'He's no here, that's for sure. And he should be.'

Rabbie was now 15 and had been employed at the engineering sheds since he left school nearly two years before. While most of his schoolmates working around the area were still little more than children, Rabbie had grown and matured quickly. He now stood six inches above his father, had the strength of a grown man and had been shaving for a year.

His relationship with his father had never thawed and with every passing year Rabbie had taken greater care of his mother and sister. Now, his father never dared to raise his hands to them, but he was still as verbally abusive. Instead of hitting out, he waged a slow psychological war against his family. Rabbie could now protect them from his father's blows, but he was still powerless to fight against something as intangible as poisonous words.

At work, the two rarely spoke, but the men knew he was Wullie's son and most understood why the boy would give such a father a wide berth. Now, on the picket line, they thought they could use Rabbie's heft in case things got rough.

They were about to quiz Wullie further, when Rabbie appeared running down the street. He stopped at the line, ignoring his father and speaking directly to Mr Summers, the foreman.

'The police are up around the corner, and they look as if they might be comin' this way. The Brigton crew are right behind them as well.'

'That's all we fuckin' need. Listen, lads, I don't want anyone gettin' hurt, right? Stand your ground. This is a legal protest and we have a right to be here. Just don't provoke them. And let me do the talkin'.'

Frank Summers had always been good to Rabbie even before he started work under him in the engineering sheds. His son had been Rabbie's best pal all through school until he died that day three years ago, collecting birds' eggs. Rabbie had not been with him, and he had always thought that if only he had, maybe Jimmy might still be here. Maybe he wouldn't have tried to reach that last nest under the bridge, lost his footing and fallen into the freezing waters of the Clyde.

It took them a week to find his body, and God alone knows what his father had to go through when he was called to identify him at the mortuary. Since then, Mr Summers had always had a kind word for Rabbie, and, without any bitterness but with understandable regret, he had watched the boy grow up.

In the next moment, there was a police whistle and the men on the picket saw a line of officers come running towards them with their batons raised. There was going to be little chance for negotiation, and the men braced themselves for the attack.

Instinctively, Rabbie kicked over the brazier, and the burning red-hot coals spilled across the road in front of them, forming a barrier. The police sergeant began to shout, but his words were drowned out by the roar of the Brigton Boys behind him who pushed through, jumped the coals and started slicing the air.

Wullie McDiarmid stepped back and grabbed his son by the arm. Whether he was trying to protect him from the fight or pull him across his body to shield himself was not clear, but Rabbie pushed him away. Panicked, his father lashed out and slapped the boy hard across the face.

Rabbie had been hit many times by the man, but not in recent years, and in the sting of the blow, he was transported instantly back to his childhood. The same old fear and hatred rose up in his throat, and he froze, staring down at his father, who was now cowering before him regretting his action. But Rabbie had no time to respond before his father was jumped by two of the Brigton Boys.

He watched as the man was dragged to the ground and kicked in the ribs. With every blow, he let out the kind of yelp Rabbie had heard from his mother. Once they had him curled in a ball, they stopped to take out their razors from their waistcoat pockets. The smaller of the two bent down and forced his father's eyes open so he could see the glint of the blade.

'Listen up, auld yin, you'll no be hitting the boy any more. Is that crystal? But, here, you look as if you might need a wee minding, so have this for free.'

In a deft movement he ripped the blade across Wullie's

face from eye to mouth and squealed with laughter as he did so. The blood spurted everywhere, and Wullie rolled on the ground in shock as much as in pain. He clamped his hand to his wet face and began choking and spluttering as he realised he was bleeding.

Rabbie turned away to see the picket line scattering. Some were being pursued by the officers, others by the Brigton Boys who had yet to wet their blades.

He turned back to his father who was still whimpering on the ground, but he couldn't look at him any more. He knew the man was finally finished – not dead, but finished in any meaningful way – and a sudden peace descended upon Rabbie. This must be what freedom felt like, he thought.

Rabbie didn't realise that the man who had slashed his father was still standing nearby so that he could watch the effects of his handiwork. When they caught each other's eye, Rabbie tensed, but the man just wiped the blade, folded it and put it back in his waistcoat.

'All part o' the service, big man. We've no met, but we should. I could do with somebody the size o' you. We've got a lot more battles to fight and there's a lot more faithers like him that need a seein' to. Come and see me. The name's Alec Jamieson. Maybe you've heard o' me.'

Jamieson tapped his cap with his forefinger to salute the boy, turned and sauntered back up Fielding Street. For a moment, Rabbie watched him go. Then he stepped over his father and ran after the leader of the Brigton Boys.

*

What came to be called the 'General Strike' collapsed only nine days after it began, largely through the efforts to undermine it by countless strike breakers. In Bridgeton, Alec Jamieson claimed a very public victory for the people and privately collected a bonus from the group of employers who had contracted him.

By the end of the week, he also had Rabbie McDiarmid at his side, now kitted out in a new suit, good leather shoes and the trademark flat cap of the Brigton Boys.

'Stick close, son, and try to catch on quick because I've no got time to say anything twice.'

Jamieson saw to Rabbie's induction himself as he did with all his new recruits. He outlined the nature and scale of the problem they faced and presented irrefutable proof that just about every ill faced by the people of Bridgeton was due to the undesirables in their midst.

'We need to get rid o' the Catholics, son. If they had one throat, I'd slit it myself. But there's too many. So we need to work clever and make them want to leave. We need to make them realise there's no place for them here amongst clean, decent folk. And how do we do that? With a wee bit o' persuasion here and there, that's how. Course, we need money to keep the show on the road. And everybody needs to chip in if we're going to make a difference. I'm going to need you to use they big arms o' yours to bend a few to our way o' thinkin'.'

Rabbie nodded and said little when he was in Jamieson's presence. He was still overawed by the man and was ready to believe everything he said.

'Let's start with the Shawfield Bar. George Niven, the landlord, hasn't really been keeping up to date with his contributions to the cause. So we need to go and remind him. Watch and see how it's done.'

The pub was on the corner of Main Street and Trafalgar Street. This early in the day it was closed, but after a sharp double rap on the door from Jamieson, the door was unlocked. It was Niven himself who opened up, and he was far from pleased to see who his caller was.

He immediately started making excuses about the slowness of trade in recent weeks, and the downturn in profits, but Jamieson invited himself in and brought Rabbie along. The pub stank of stale cigarette smoke and spilt beer. The darkness in the bar was only broken by the shafts of daylight that fell like huge fallen rafters from the windows to the spit-and-sawdust-covered floor.

'For Christ sake, Geordie, do you never clean the place?'

'As I was sayin', Mr Jamieson, things are no great at the minute. Maybe you could give me a wee bit o' leeway wi' the payments.'

'No problem, Geordie. No problem at all. I'll just put the whole operation on hold so that you can get yourself sorted out. The thing is, there's mouths to feed. Widows with weans, women with men in the jail, and the auld folks that can't do for themselves any more. There's the fines to cover for the good men in my charge that have fallen foul o' the courts, and then there's my men, like this new yin here, burstin' with energy, so they are. If I just leave them with nothin' to do, God only knows what they'll get up to. I mean one o' them might come in here and start droppin' things.'

Jamieson picked up an empty beer glass from the counter and tossed it to Rabbie, who caught it and then, quickly catching on, let it slip to the floor.

'Butter fingers. And then there's your nice chairs. I mean, if a fight should start in here, some o' them might get broken. They don't look that strong. What d'you think, Rabbie?'

The boy picked up one of the bentwood chairs and smashed it hard against the wall. The wood splintered and the chair broke in two. Rabbie threw the pieces to the floor and shrugged.

'See what I mean, Geordie. Things are never as strong as they look. Oh, and there's your nice windows. It would be an awfy shame if anything happened to them.'

'All right, all right! I can give you last week's right now and the rest at the end of this week.' The landlord went to his till drawer and took out four ten-shilling notes. He handed them to Jamieson, who counted them and shook his head.

'The thing is, Geordie, when I have to collect in person like this, there's always a wee surcharge, so get your hand back in that drawer and give me another quid. That way, I'll no have to send Rabbie here to pay a wee visit to that wife o' yours. She's a good-lookin' bird, so she is, but she wouldn't be half as nice with a fuckin' great scar, now, would she?'

Alec left the bar with the three pounds in his pocket and walked up Main Street to the Cross with Rabbie in tow.

'And that's what you'll be doin'. Now, tell me how auld you are, son?'

'Sixteen next month, Mr Jamieson.'

'Christ, you're a big boy for that. Wonder if you've even stopped growing yet. Tell me, what about you and the lassies? Gettin' much, son?'

Rabbie blushed in response.

'Well, we'll have to sort that out pronto. Away home the now and meet me at the Cross at eight.'

*

As spring was turning into summer, the days were lengthening. By eight o'clock that night it was far from dark and there was still a bustle on the streets. The queues outside the Olympia were waiting for the second showing of the latest Jimmy Cagney film, and there was piano music spilling out from the Anchor Bar.

Rabbie arrived early because he had learned that Jamieson expected punctuality. The leader was often late himself, but no one else was allowed that slack. When Jamieson approached, there was a young blonde woman on his arm, and when they were close, Rabbie could see she was wearing bright red lipstick and had painted eyebrows.

'Well, young yin, this is Mary. She's a very special friend o' mine and she's agreed to do me a wee favour. Is that no right, hen?'

Mary Callan was 17 and had been with Jamieson on and off for the last two years. Lately, it had been more off than on, but he wasn't the kind of man you said no to. She looked at Rabbie without smiling and then at Jamieson. She tugged at his arm and said, almost pleading, 'Alec.' He took her arm off his and pushed her towards Rabbie.

'Here you go. Mary'll show you a good time.'

The girl took Rabbie's arm and led him across the street. 'C'mon, you. Quick.'

There was a gas lantern in the close, high up at the corner near the foot of the stairs. It cast a feeble, flickering yellow light that barely made it into the recesses. The passageway that went from the entry through to the backcourt and the middens was barely lit at all. It was to the far corner that Mary rushed to find some privacy.

Rabbie's eyes were still adjusting to the gloom, but he could hear her whispers and he followed them.

He found her leaning against the wall, already hitching up her skirt and pulling her underwear to one side. He could barely see her, but this close he could smell her hair and the perfume on her skin. He leaned in to kiss her the way he'd seen them do it at the pictures, but she turned her head away. 'C'mon, quick, before he comes.'

Rabbie could sense her fear and was infected by her anxiety. She pulled him closer and reached for his trousers, fumbling with the buttons of his flies. She did the work, guiding him towards her, and in no more than seconds he was panting against her neck, unable to tell her what he was feeling.

She straightened up and tried to push him back so he would take his own weight, but he was still feeling weak at the knees. She thumped his shoulder with her small fist, and he straightened and pulled out.

She took a handkerchief from her bag, folded it and used it as a pad between her legs, before adjusting her clothes. Rabbie was still breathless, and looking at her in the dimmest of light, he thought she was the most beautiful thing he had ever seen.

'Next time, son, try and hold onto it a wee bit. The lassies like it when they can feel you're making an effort.' Mary looked past Rabbie to see Alec standing in the darkest shadows of the passageway, where he had been all along. She had been watched before but thought that this time she had been quick enough to elude him.

'Aye, is that no right, hen? So Rabbie's a man now. Listen, Rabbie's a wean's name. From now on, you're just Rab. And there'll be plenty more like her if you just do what I tell you. C'mon, I've got some work for you.'

Rab looked at Mary, who was hanging her head low. He wanted to thank her, to say that it was more than nothing, that it was the best thing that had ever happened to him. But he said none of these things and rushed out after Alec, leaving her in the back close to deal with her shame alone.

*

In the following weeks, Rab would see Mary around the streets. She was always dressed well, her face always made up. He never saw her pushing prams full of laundry to the steamie, mopping the close or getting messages from the shops. She never had children strapped across her in tight shawls or pulling at her hemline crying to be lifted.

He saw her walk by and be ignored by the women in the

streets. He saw some muttering as she passed, and once an old woman even spat at her feet as she approached.

The path Mary Callan had taken was not one that found any measure of approval from the Bridgeton women. They had no time to dress up and paint their eyes and lips, but they told themselves that they still had their self-respect.

Rab knew she had been Alec Jamieson's girlfriend and that it had given her considerable standing in the community. But that lasted only as long as she was seen on his arm around the Cross. While she was his girlfriend, she could afford to look down her nose at all those exhausted women who spent their days scrubbing and trying to eke out a broken pay packet until the end of the week. That kind of life was never going to be for her.

She was only 15 when she started with Alec, and she believed him when he told her she was the one. Now, only two years later, he had moved on to other girls who hung on his arm as she had done. His string of girlfriends would look at 'sad wee Mary Callan' with the same pitying looks she had used when it had been her turn.

Now, Jamieson used her as and when he saw fit. There were lots of young men who were interested in her because of her past – the pretty blonde who had been good enough for Alec Jamieson. She kept most of them at bay and took the money Jamieson gave her now and again.

Rab called to her across the street when he saw her looking in the Italian café window. She turned and saw him running over. He was tall and good-looking – where had she seen him? It took her a moment, but when she remembered, she turned on her heel to walk back up the street.

Rab ran after her, his big strides making short work of the distance between them.

'Mary, did you no hear me shoutin'?'

'Get away from me. I mean it. Get away!'

'Mary, I just wanted to talk. C'mon, hen, I'm no goin' to hurt you.'

'Hurt me? You're damn right you'll no. I don't care who you are, I'll stick you as quick as look at you, if you lay a finger on me.'

Rab was alarmed by the wild look in her eyes. Every moment of that night in the close was still so vivid, and he so wanted to talk to her and to tell her what it had meant. Now, he could see nothing but cold hatred in those dark eyes of hers.

'I just wanted to say I'm sorry. I'm sorry I just went away after, you know. I wanted to stay with you. To say what I felt about you. I didn't want you to think I was just usin' you. It wasn't like that.'

'Oh, aye. Then what was it like? I was your wee treat courtesy of Alec Jamieson. He must like you. He doesn't make me go with just anybody, y'know. And don't give me any story about how I was the best you'd ever had. I was the only one you'd ever had. But nobody asked me what I wanted. You never do, the damn lot o' you.'

Rab didn't know how to speak to the girl, and he was getting nowhere trying to make her understand. She was breathing hard as she spoke, and he knew she wanted to walk away. However, he had come this far and decided to try one last thing.

'Listen, can I buy you a coffee?'

'What?'

'A coffee. You were looking in the café window and I thought maybe you'd like a coffee.'

'Do you even like coffee?'

'I don't know. I've never tried it.'

She didn't laugh, nor did she smile, but she did stop frowning just long enough to give him hope.

'I get to introduce you to all the delights, don't I? C'mon, then. And don't touch me!'

They walked back up the street and went into the Italian café. They sat at a table in the corner furthest from the door. Mary ordered for them both and soon they were sipping small cups of frothy coffee.

'That's no bad. No bad at all. D'you like it, Mary?'

She looked him over. He was younger than anyone else she had been with and there was something in his eyes that might have been goodness, but she was far from sure. He certainly didn't talk like the others or act like them for that matter.

'What's your game, son? Are you just trying to get me back up a close, 'cause that's no going to happen.'

'I just wanted to see you again. You're just that lovely. A real doll, Mary. And you smell better than anybody I've ever met.'

This time she laughed and rolled her eyes. 'Aye, that's how to get a lassie, son. Tell them they smell better than all the rest of Brigton. It's no much o' a compliment when you think about what they smell like around here, is it?' She shook her head and sipped the coffee.

'Listen, can I see you again? Maybe we could go for a walk. Or I could take you to the pictures.'

'So you can kiss me again, eh?'

'I never kissed you, Mary. You wouldn't let me.'

She turned her face away, remembering the night. She was becoming confused by her thoughts. 'Naw, that's right enough. I suppose there's no harm in a walk. But just a walk, mind.'

Rab's face brightened, and they made a date. He paid for the coffees with a shilling from his waistcoat pocket and told the waiter to keep the change.

'Is that supposed to impress me?'

'Naw, I'm just happy, that's all. It's no every day the loveliest lassie in Brigton says she'll go out with you.'

'Away you go, you big sook!'

She turned to go, and Rab watched her walk back up the street in her high heels. She knew he was watching and made sure she didn't turn back to look, but she also made sure she looked as good as she felt.

*

There was a walk on the Green and more talking than Mary had expected. There were also trips to the picture houses in Dennistoun and even in the town centre so that they wouldn't bump into any of the Brigton crew. And Mary let him kiss her and slowly he learned how to make her feel that he was making an effort.

Unusually, she lived alone in her own single end, paid for by Jamieson, and Rab came to spend more and more time there until the neighbours thought he had moved in. They were both playing a dangerous game, but Mary knew that Jamieson was done with her and thought he would no longer care as long as she was available when he needed her for his little favours.

Rab came home to her one evening and took off his jacket. There were spots of blood on his shirt at his shoulder and she rushed over.

'Don't get yourself all riled up. It's no what it looks like. I've only been fighting wi' a needle.'

'What are you sayin', Rab? A needle?'

'It's just a wee somethin'. I did it for you, doll.'

He peeled off his shirt to reveal the tattoo on his right shoulder: a simple heart with her name. She put her hand to her mouth and turned away. She was touched, but she knew the boy would not be hers for much longer, no matter what he wrote on his skin. She knew he would be led away by Jamieson and the gang, that he would end up like so many of them, either in jail or in the morgue.

*

That summer, there was more work for Rab than ever. Jamieson had indeed taken a shine to him and despite his youth he found him to be one of his most reliable lieutenants. He was quick on the uptake and good with his hands, and Jamieson had never seen anyone develop quite such a visceral hatred of all the injustices he filled his head with.

From collecting the dues from the pub landlords, Jamieson promoted him to work the back-court bookies. It meant he was on the streets even more than usual and 'Alec's big yin' became a regular sight.

On one of his regular trips to collect their cut from one of the bookmakers, Rab saw her. The teenage girl was struggling to carry the bag of groceries, but when he approached her and offered to help, she turned away.

'I don't need your help, Rabbie McDiarmid. None of us do.'

'Lizzie, let me help you. It's too heavy.'

She was only 14 but could already convey the same rebuke in her eyes that she got from their mother. She took the bag in both arms and quickened her pace. He ran alongside her, and every time he tried to take the bag she twisted away.

'Lizzie, don't be daft.'

'Daft, is it? Aye, that's me all right. I'm the one that stays at home and has to scrub the close stairs and make his dinner. My maw's no up to it but see if you care.'

'I give you money.'

'Aye, that's no all you give us. Heartache, that's what you give your maw.'

'I'm tryin' to make somethin' o' myself, Lizzie.'

'That's what you call all this.' She stopped and flicked the collar of his suit and the peak of his cap and then pulled open his jacket and pointed at the blade in his pocket. 'Aye, that's makin' somethin' o' yourself, right enough. You're makin' yourself just like him. If you could make yourself six inches shorter, you probably would, just so you could be even more like that Alec Jamieson.'

Rab looked around to see who might be listening. His sister was loud when she wanted to be, and right now she didn't care who heard her.

'And I'll tell you who else you're like, Rabbie. You're just like your auld man. He likes to hurt people, and it turns out you're just the same. Like faither, like bloody son.'

Rab grabbed her, and she dropped the bag. She didn't scream this time because the suddenness of his strength took her breath away. He held her by the upper arms and shook her as he spoke. 'No, I'm no like him. I'll never be like him. Don't say that. It's no true.'

She could see the anger welling up in him just as she had seen it so often in the past with her father. They had the same temper, but Rabbie could do much more damage, not just because he was stronger, but also because he was fearless. She knew her father was a bully, and like all bullies he was a coward. Rabbie, though, was frightened of nobody, except perhaps himself.

*

Apart from dropping money off with his mother every week, Rab gradually saw less and less of his family. His sister continued to shun him on the street and his father would hide when he saw him coming, in much the same way that Rab himself had done as a young boy when he saw his father. Only his mother would still embrace him and hold her big son close.

'Tell me you're lookin' after yourself, son. You need to be careful who you're runnin' about with.'

'You don't need to worry about me, Maw. I can take care o' myself.'

'Aye, that's what they all say afore they get jumped. You watch yourself, and don't get into any bother. And I don't want you carrying a knife. Are you listening to me, Rabbie? No knives!'

'Right you are, Maw. No worries on that score. No knives, I swear.'

Rab McDiarmid held his mother and kissed her on the cheek before parting and told her he would see her again the following week. Between then and now, however, he knew fine he would be called upon, more than once, to use the knife he swore he did not carry.

The very next night, Jamieson was lighting a cigarette up the close and Rab was waiting for him to take the first long drag before he spoke.

'It's like this, Rab. Chick's skimming the take. And I can't have that kind o' thing. Bad for morale, if I let that go. Know what I mean?'

'Sure, Mr Jamieson. D'you want me to sort it out?'

'See that's what I like about you, Rab. You've got initiative. You see a thing that needs done and you go and do it without bein' asked. That's rare, so it is. Let me know when it's sorted.'

Rab nodded and left, feeling for the knife in his pocket as he went. Chick Donaldson had gone to the same school as Rab, and although he was three years his senior, he'd known him before they met again in the ranks of the Brigton Boys. Chick was Jamieson's debt collector for the bars along London Road and Landressy Street.

Rab couldn't understand why anyone would cheat Mr Jamieson and undermine the cause they were all fighting for. Surely he must know that by stealing the money that was collected, he was really stealing it from those in Bridgeton who were in greatest need. Jamieson had indeed done one of his finest jobs on young Rab McDiarmid, and the boy was only too pleased to be able to teach the thief a lesson.

The lesson itself was quickly delivered as Donaldson was walking out of his close on James Street. Rab followed him until he turned onto Mackeith Street, and there in the shadow between the streetlights he jumped him.

Rab had the advantage in both weight and strength, and, coupled with surprise, Donaldson stood no chance. The cut was savage yet precise and severed his right ear clean off. Rab held his big hand over Donaldson's mouth to stop his screams and wiped the blade on the man's jacket before whispering in the other ear, 'Mr Jamieson sends his regards, but your services are no longer required.'

Rab bent to pick up the severed ear, wrapped it in a handkerchief and put it in his pocket before walking back up to the Cross, whistling as he went. Jamieson took receipt of the prize with a squeal of delight and rubbed Rab's cheeks with both hands.

'That deserves something special. Here, I want you to have this.' From the inside pocket of his jacket he took out a slim black case and handed it to Rab. 'On you go, open it.'

Inside was a cut-throat razor with a fine tortoiseshell handle. Rab took it out and unfolded it. The hinge was smooth and expertly engineered, and the blade mirror finished and honed and stropped to the sharpest of edges.

He turned it in the light, and it flashed just as it had when he had seen Alec slash his father's face. He looked at Jamieson and nodded his appreciation, unable to find the right words to thank him.

'No bother. I just wish you health to use it, son. Now, c'mon, there's more work to be done.'

Chapter 9

Glasgow: 15 February 1931

Cuthbert telephoned his department at St Thomas's and was quickly put through to Simon Morgenthal. Since their last call five days before, the young pathologist had heard nothing further from his boss and was delighted now to hear his voice and his request.

'I need your help, Simon.'

'Anything, sir.'

'I'm arranging for a bullet and casing to be sent to you, and I would like you to do what you can in identifying it. I know what you're going to say – why can't they do that up in Scotland? – but I'm very disappointed to say that Glasgow has yet to discover the benefits of forensic ballistics. Can you do this for me?'

'Of course, sir. But I thought it was a bombing. Is this another case?'

'One and the same, Simon. It just keeps getting stranger. I won't prejudice your analysis by giving you any other details at this stage, but I'll call again. You should receive the bullet by tomorrow afternoon. Could you have it analysed by the following day?'

'It'll be a priority, sir. And if there's anything else you need, please don't hesitate to ask.'

'There is one thing – I need you to keep the department running for a little longer without me.'

*

When Cuthbert hung up, he was confident that he could count on Morgenthal's competence and loyalty. The latter was almost more important to Cuthbert, for the former could be taught, but loyalty, he knew, was always earned.

He looked at the growing number of files on his desk. As each victim was tentatively and then positively identified, the team of pathologists would complete a report of their findings and append it to the original identification sheets provided by Hogg and his team. From that original file of some twenty-four pages, there had grown over eighteen files, one for each of those identified so far.

One name that was not yet amongst those was Alistair Henderson. Cuthbert had made a start on his case shortly before the human remains had been transferred from the bombsite to the mortuary, but his attentions had been diverted to performing the post mortem examinations on the largely intact corpses. Now those were completed, he returned to Henderson.

He looked again at the photograph of the would-be politician pinned to the board behind his desk and tried to find some sort of communion with the man that might guide his next steps. He went back to the description of his clothing and to the roster of body parts and clothing fragments prepared by Currie and Mathieson, and came again to the same conclusion: that his suit might be the best and perhaps only way of identifying him.

This time he did not have to rely solely on the written

descriptions; he could directly examine the remains with any shreds of clothing still attached. The laboratory area was still being used to house those body parts that had not yet been identified. Many of the larger pieces, and therefore the ones easier to assign, had been removed, leaving an assortment of smaller body parts.

He found the foot and ankle with the attached fragment of light-coloured cloth and studied the material closely. It was indeed a pale grey flannel and was consistent with the description of Henderson's suit that night. He took the foot into the dissection room and placed it at the end of one of the now empty slabs.

He scoured the remaining records and studied the remains, looking closely for any other evidence of pale grey material that might match the piece around the foot. He identified seven other pieces and laid them out carefully on the slab to see if any consistent picture would emerge.

One was a section of leg that did seem to match the foot and ankle in terms of skin colour, while another was a portion of the left upper arm and shoulder. Again, the body proportions were right, and they could all have belonged to the same corpse. What he could not find was an intact head; however, there were some very charred remains that merited a closer inspection. At first glance, it was impossible to identify which parts of the body they were, but in a good light and after some removal of the blackened surface layer, he could see that this was the left side of a face. Part of the left ear was gone, but there on the lobe was an unmistakable mole.

Cuthbert consulted the sheet from Hogg's file again and noted that one of Henderson's few distinguishing marks was just that. He laid the charred mass at the top of the slab and stood back. Might this half of a man that he had managed to reconstruct be the best that he could do? Henderson had been practically on top of the bomb when it went off and even to recover this much of his body was surprising. For the next part, he knew he needed help. The mortuary technician whom he had managed to estrange that first evening was still keeping his distance; Cuthbert decided to seek him out.

At a small desk in what might otherwise have been a broom cupboard, Cuthbert found him, sifting through a pile of paperwork. When Cuthbert knocked softly on the open door, the man jumped.

'I'm very sorry I startled you. I was wondering if we might have a little chat, and I promise to be a lot more civil this time.'

Cuthbert waited to be invited into the tiny office, although in truth he was unsure whether he would fit.

'There's not much space in here, doctor. Shall we go to your office?'

'No, no, I don't want to inconvenience you. I can stand. I really wanted to apologise for my tone to you and your colleague. It was quite inappropriate, and I feel thoroughly ashamed of myself. I could tell you I was tired, anxious about the terrible task we had to undertake, thrown by the unfamiliar surroundings, but none of that would in any way excuse me. I hope you might allow me to start again.'

The technician had never in his twenty years working at the city mortuary received an apology from a police surgeon. Cuthbert's tone struck him as genuine, and he responded warmly. 'Think nothing of it, sir. It's a terrible business, and you must be up to your eyes in it. Are you finding everything you need?'

'The place is very well-appointed, and I suspect that's entirely down to you ... do you know, I don't know your name.'

'Young, sir, Sandy Young.'

'Mr Young...'

'You can call me Sandy, sir. No need to stand on ceremony with me.'

'Well, Sandy, I was hoping I might ask for your advice.'

'My advice?' Sandy Young was starting to think this was going to be a whole day of firsts.

'The fact of the matter is, I have a problem. Might I discuss it with you in the dissection room? I need to show you something.'

The technician was now being led by Cuthbert along the corridor of his own department to be shown the partial remains of Alistair Henderson.

'We've had some sights in here, I can tell you, but this is a real mess. Do you know who he was?'

'That's just it. I think this is all that remains of Alistair Henderson, the candidate who was speaking at the rally. He was the brother—'

'—of Dr Henderson. Aye, I heard. And this is all there is?'

'I believe so.'

'Well, we can't give him back like that. If you leave it to me, I'll see what I can do to make him more presentable.'

'I was hoping you might say that. I know we can never prepare him for any viewing by the family but just knowing they have a body rather than a bag of bits might help them at what must be one of the worst times of their life.'

As Cuthbert was speaking, Sandy Young was already appraising exactly what he had to work with, so the pathologist left him to his task.

*

When Morgenthal took receipt of the package the next morning from the police courier, he opened it immediately. As expected, he found a sealed bag labelled in Cuthbert's handwriting with the details of the bullet and the shell casing. In the package was a letter.

City Mortuary
Saltmarket
Glasgow

15th Feb. '31

Dear Simon

I trust the enclosed has arrived safely into your hands and that you are able to perform the necessary analyses to make some useful identification.

The work here proceeds slowly, and the scale of the task is at times daunting. I think you have yet to see this level of violence in a single setting, and I can only be thankful that you have been spared the kind of wartime experience that I have had, where such sights were, regrettably, all too common. We deal with terrible things, but to walk in the aftermath of men, women and children being ripped apart in an instant is quite beyond anything we are trained to deal with.

The case is a political one, and already there are signs that we may be dealing with a Jewish reprisal killing. Mankind has always chosen to make our differences a matter for hatred and violence. It seems even in this modern age we still have medieval minds.

Forgive my rambling. The courier is at my side awaiting the dispatch.

In haste.

Cuthbert

As it turned out, the examination was more straightforward than Morgenthal expected, and after some consultation with the textbooks, the identification was simple.

As he wrote up his findings, he reflected on what Cuthbert had written in the letter about differences. He knew that society regarded him as different. Although he had been born in London, as his father had been before him, he would always be seen as a Jew first and an Englishman second.

He worked in a profession that for the most part tolerated Jews, but even he had encountered blatant prejudice. Once at a job interview for a position he sought before he started work with Cuthbert, he had been informed with a smile that although he was suitable, he could not be considered seriously for the position. 'No Jew, you see, can ever be a gentleman,' he was told.

His schooling had been punctuated with casual anti-Semitism almost on a daily basis, and his way of dealing with it had always been to meet it with a smile, to laugh it off and never to show that it stung him to the core.

His family were wealthy and that allowed them some protection. They were accepted, if grudgingly, into London society, but Simon had heard his father's associates disparaging others as 'dirty Jews' while drinking his finest brandy before saying to his father, 'But of course we don't mean you, Morgenthal.'

Their exceptionalism was a sham, and he knew just how much it hurt his father. All it did was allow these fair-weather friends to enjoy the patronage of a rich Jew at the same time as firmly holding on to their racist beliefs.

Once, as a teenager, he had confronted his father about it. How could he sit at the same table as these men? His father, having endured more prejudice than Simon could yet imagine, was matter-of-fact about it all and told his son that Jews always had to accept that they were unwelcome.

'It is our destiny as a people, my son. We have no home, and we are always the guests wherever we live. One day you will realise that sometimes just to live you have to swallow your pride. Our life here is a good one. I have made you a gentleman with a fine education, no matter what they might say, but you will never change the way they think. Don't try, my son. Just live.'

At the time, Morgenthal was horrified by his father's weakness and acquiescence, but with the passing years he had grown ever closer to his way of thinking. Simply living without rocking the boat that bears you seemed the most pragmatic solution to it all.

*

At the city mortuary, W.P.C. Anderson was adding some new information to the case board behind Cuthbert's desk while she updated her colleagues.

'The victim of the gunshot wound has now been positively identified as Robert McDiarmid, known as Rab. He was twenty years old from Bridgeton, and we now know he was an active member of the Brigton Boys and a close associate of the gang leader, Alec Jamieson. We also know that the Brigton Boys were serving as Alistair Henderson's bodyguard that night and according to witnesses made themselves conspicuous.'

Hogg tried not to look at the post mortem photograph of McDiarmid's remains that she had pinned to the board and asked, 'Do we think he was killed at the scene?'

Cuthbert sighed and agreed that that was a good question. 'In normal circumstances, if you can call any murder normal, the body would provide us with good physical evidence of whether it had been moved and we would also be able to estimate the time of death. That's not the case here. What little we have of this young man has managed to tell us how he died, but not when or where. Did anyone report hearing a shot fired?'

'No, nothing like that, I'm afraid, but by all accounts there was quite a lot of noise in the crowd, especially leading up to the speaker's arrival. It's not impossible that the shot could have been lost in the commotion or even mistaken for something else. A car backfiring or suchlike.'

'So,' Cuthbert continued, 'without further evidence we cannot establish the circumstances of his death. What about motives? Who might want this lad dead?'

Hogg took up that question. 'He was in a razor gang, sir. He had no shortage of people who wanted him dead. They're extortionists when they're not play-acting at being bodyguards. Some people they will just push too far. And then there's rival gang members. He had probably taken quite a few scalps on the streets of Bridgeton. Constable Anderson says he was close to Alec Jamieson. He wouldn't have been that if he'd not shown his loyalty, and that would mean cutting, maybe killing, to prove himself.'

'And we shouldn't forget his own gang,' Anderson added. 'They're not exactly a band of brothers. They're all vying for position, so it wouldn't be too hard to imagine one of them taking it upon himself to get rid of an obstacle in the way of their own progress.'

Cuthbert stood up to pace the room while he was thinking. 'What about others though? I mean, he was part of the bodyguard for a fascist politician. Surely that might put him in the firing line from one of the Jewish groups. What about the Jewish Socialist League?'

Hogg was still puzzled by Cuthbert's fixation on finding a Jewish connection to the violence. It was time to air his concerns, but Anderson got there first. She joined in and said again that she thought it would be out of character given everything they knew about the League.

'It just doesn't fit, sir. And, if I may say so, apart from the fact that they were present at the scene on the night of the bombing, we don't have anything that links them. Or do you have other information?'

Cuthbert realised he had to come clean. He sat down and told them both of the anonymous phone call he received.

'He said he was from the Ministry and he made it clear who the perpetrator of the bombing was, or at least who my report should identify as the perpetrator. The leader of the Jewish Socialist League was mentioned specifically. Clearly, my report will say nothing of the sort unless it turns out to be true. That's why I've been so insistent on following up that line of inquiry. I need to establish if he is being set up. I need to find evidence to exclude him as a suspect. I apologise that I did not tell you sooner, but I didn't want to bias your investigation with what might be nothing more than a crank call.'

'Or what might have been a high-level tip-off. You should have told us, Dr Cuthbert. We are on the same side after all.'

Hogg was clearly angry, and Cuthbert realised he had undone some of the trust that they had built.

'So, doctor, do you think we should bring this David Goldberg in? I think we need to be guided by you here. After all, we don't know what else you haven't told us.'

Hogg's tone was brusque, and Anderson remained silent, aware of the tension that was developing between the two men.

'I apologise to you both. I was wrong not to mention it, and I assure you I am keeping nothing else back. I think it would be good to talk to this man – if for no other reason than to give him a chance to clear himself of the accusation.'

Hogg could see that Cuthbert was genuinely contrite. In fact, had he himself received an anonymous call from Whitehall ordering him to be fraudulent, he wasn't sure who he'd tell either.

'We'll bring him into the station and see if we can't get him talking. One thing though, sir, did your mystery caller also tell you to fit this man up for the shooting?'

'No, that's the interesting thing. He didn't mention a shooting. It made me wonder later if he knew anything about it.'

*

Davie Goldberg was collected from the Workers' Society reading room in the Gorbals, where his mother told the uniformed constable he could be found. He came willingly to the station for he knew nothing could be gained by resisting, and he was assured that he was not under arrest, at least not yet.

Goldberg was already seated in the interview room when Hogg entered. A tall, slim man with sullen eyes, he sat, long legs stretched out, swinging rhythmically on the bentwood seat that seemed too small for him.

When he saw the sergeant, he said nothing, nor did he adjust his relaxed pose. All he offered by way of acknowledgement was a frown.

Hogg was used to young men who thought they were too big, too important or too clever to be in his interview room. Goldberg was just the latest in a long line of lads that he could break in two if he chose.

'Where are you from, son?'

'Glesca. Did you think I was going to say the promised land, or deepest Russia, or somewhere else you think we Jews should be from? We're always supposed to be from somewhere else, aren't we? Never here, we never belong here, do we?'

'So you are Jewish?'

'Would you like me to get my cock out so you can check?'

Hogg snorted and turned over a page in the file in front of him. 'Look, son, I don't care what you are, but this is a line of inquiry I have to follow. I'm not saying we think it was

Jews who were responsible for what happened on the Green the other night, but–'

'Aye, you do. That's exactly what you and the rest of them think. And that's why I'm here. Can you not see what's happening? They're already pointing the finger. They're saying it was us, the Jews. Aye, it's always us when anything bad happens.

'D'you know they even smashed the windows of the Jewish bakery in the Gorbals the other night. Isi makes fucking bagels, for God's sake! He's got nothing to do with this. None of us have. But try telling that to them with their bricks in their fists and their paint brushes dripping with hate. "Jews Go Home!" they scrawled across his door.

'Aye, great. And where exactly would that be, eh? Isi was born round the corner from me, and I was born just up from Gorbals Cross. So it's not going to be a very long journey, is it?'

Hogg could see the rage and utter frustration in the young man's eyes and changed tack. 'Tell me about the organisation you run in Govanhill, son, your Socialist League.'

'It's the Jewish Socialist League, and I don't run it. We're a collective. We don't believe in all that hierarchical shite.'

'But every organisation needs leadership. Are you their leader, son?'

Goldberg stopped swinging in the chair and leaned forward, pushing his face towards Hogg. The sergeant didn't flinch, having been menaced in the same way by much harder men than this one. 'If you think I'm the leader, then maybe I am. You seem to know all about it. Don't know why you even need to talk to me.'

'I'm talking to you, son, to give you a chance to explain.'

Goldberg sat back again and looked a little less angry and a little more puzzled. 'Explain what?'

'We have witnesses that place you and your League at the scene of the bombing last Monday night. So explain: what were you doing there?'

'Well, we weren't planting bombs, if that's what you're asking.'

Hogg didn't react; he started writing slowly and deliberately in his notebook. A few moments later, Goldberg was becoming disconcerted by the sergeant who had now put down his pen and was simply staring at him, waiting for a better answer. Almost a full minute passed, and the silence, which Hogg was using as his own form of menace, was causing the young man to fidget.

'What do you want me to say?'

Again, Hogg did not react; he simply waited for Goldberg to speak.

'Look, we were just there to make our protest. As far as we're concerned, fascists shouldn't have a platform like that. All they do is spout lies and hate. They prey on people's fears and tell them everything that's wrong with their lives is the fault of somebody else. Somebody different with a foreign-sounding name. Somebody like me and every other Jew in the Gorbals. They say they want to deport Jews. More likely they'd line us up and shoot us if they had half the chance. But can you imagine what that's like? Being hated like that, being told you're not wanted. I shouldn't have to take that. None of us should.'

Hogg was taking notes again, and quietly he said, 'And how strongly do you feel about that? Enough maybe to put a stop to one of the men that's saying it?'

Goldberg was an angry young man, but he wasn't stupid, and he could see where this was leading. He stood up suddenly and slapped the table in front of him.

'No. No. No. You are not going to pin this on me. We went to that protest to shout the bastard down, not to kill him. Ask any of your witnesses. We were over by the trees; we were up them. We had flags and our banners. We were shouting and banging bits of metal. We were making a right racket – and it worked. He had to stop and start again. Looked right pissed off, so he did. And then . . .'

Goldberg stopped shouting and sat down, trying to recall exactly what had happened next. All he knew was that he had been in the trees along with several of the League. Becca had fallen down, and he saw Sally and Josh rushing to see if she was all right. He had turned back to see Henderson and then he, himself, was on the ground, his ears were ringing, and he had banged his side on one of the tree roots. He had struggled to his feet and had looked for Becca and Sally. They were sitting on the ground nearby under the tree from which Becca had fallen. Her frock was covered in blood, and Sally was holding her. He remembered no flash, no loud bang, no sudden rush. All he could recall was an emptiness in the air about him and a buzzing inside his head.

'. . . and then it must have happened. I never saw it, and I don't know if I even heard it. You must think I'm daft, but that's the honest truth.'

Hogg, who had been close to more explosions than he cared to recall, did not think the young man was anything other than truthful. He half-remembered some of the huge shells at the front that destroyed whole trenches and half his company, and however hard he tried he still could not hear them, he still could not see them.

'Did you see anything suspicious? Anything out of the ordinary?'

'It was a fascist rally. There was nothing ordinary about any of it. But if you're asking did I see anybody with a bomb? Then, no. What does a bomb even look like?'

'You have to see that you and your group have both motive and opportunity to commit this crime. You were there and you hated the man. I need you to convince me otherwise. That's why I'm talking to you rather than arresting you for murder, son. Do you get that?'

Goldberg was sitting still in the chair now, his long legs folded under him, and he was leaning forward not to intimidate Hogg but to engage with him. He realised he was in a very dangerous position.

'I can't prove to you that I didn't want to see Henderson dead, but the honest truth is that I didn't. I wanted to see him silenced, to shut him up, to make him stop saying all his lies, but we don't try to kill people. That's what they do. Not us. We were there, I can hardly deny that, but we never went near the platform. The bomb must have been planted there, but it wasn't us.'

'And what about means? What do you know about bombs?'

'Nothing! I just told you! Why would any of us know anything like that?'

'So none of your crowd was ever in the war? None of them ever learned about explosives, ordnance – is that what you're saying?'

Goldberg looked rattled by the question and thought hard about the League members. Most were men and women in their early twenties like himself. None of them had been old enough to go to the front, but there were a few slightly older members who had served.

'It occurs to me, Davie, that in your ranks, you probably did have the expertise to do something like this, if you really wanted to. So that's "means" we can add to the "motive" and the "opportunity". It's starting to pile up against you, so I think I need you to start taking this seriously because unless you can give me some better answers, son, you'll not be going home the night.'

Now Goldberg grasped the situation he was in. He sat with his head in his hands ready to answer anything.

Hogg slid a pad of paper across the table and placed a pencil on it. 'I need you to make a statement. First, I want the names of all the League members who were on the Green that night. And I want to know when they came and exactly what they did from the time they arrived. Then, I want to know the names and addresses of any of your members who served in the war or in the army after it. That'll do for starters. Start writing, son. We've not got all day.'

There was a firm knock on the interview-room door, and W.P.C. Anderson came in. She looked at Goldberg, who was now busy writing his statement, and passed a note to the sergeant. She waited while he unfolded the slip of paper and read it. He looked up at her and said, 'Are you sure?' She nodded and left. 'Stop writing, son.'

Goldberg looked up, confused, only to see a marked change in Hogg's expression. Gone was the face of a slightly irritated uncle to be replaced with that of a hardened policeman who thought his time was being wasted.

'While we've been having this wee talk, the men have been taking a look through your room. You're a dark horse, son. Under your bed — some might even say hidden under your bed — there was a wee surprise for us. Tell me, where did you get the gun?'

Goldberg blanched. He knew this was worse than anything so far. He stumbled for the words to explain. 'It's not what it looks like. It was just to put the frighteners on them. I would never use it.'

'Did you take the pistol to the rally that night? And don't lie to me, son.'

'No, I mean, aye. I had it in my bag, but I never took it out. I never used it. And anyway, it was a bombing, not a shooting.'

Again, Hogg stared at the young man in silence. He didn't want to believe that he and his group had anything to do with all this, but, by God, he thought, this one wasn't making it easy.

He knew he couldn't let him go, not until the gun had been examined and they had spoken to some of the others in the League to cross-check his story. If the gun was a match for the bullet that killed McDiarmid, the boy would likely hang for it, never mind any involvement he might have had in the bombing. He was only 23 with a life still to be lived. Hogg shook his head at the waste of it all and got up to go.

'We're keeping you, son. There'll be more questions after we get a few other bits and pieces sorted out. In the meantime, you'll need to settle yourself down. The constable will take you to the cells. Don't give us any more bother than you already have.'

Goldberg reached out to the sergeant as if to grasp the freedom that was being wrenched from him and then sat back and stared dully at the table. The uniformed constable took him firmly by the upper arm and lifted him up from the chair to march him downstairs.

Outside the interview room, Hogg was quizzing Anderson about the gun. It had yet to be identified and was now in the evidence store.

'Dr Cuthbert has sent the bullet to be checked by his team in London. We should know more soon. Do you think it's him, sergeant?'

'Christ knows. It would certainly suit Cuthbert's anonymous caller. But the thing that's niggling at me is that if it is him, if Davie Goldberg is guilty, why all the mystery? Why not let us just do the investigation and find it out on our own?'

'Maybe they felt we needed a nudge in the right direction, sir.'

'No, I don't buy that. I still think they're fitting this boy up for it. But why does he go and get himself a bloody gun? The young fool.'

Hogg marched off and phoned Cuthbert at the mortuary to bring him up to date with developments.

'Thank you, sergeant. Not what I was wanting to hear, but thank you nonetheless. I presume D.C.I. Black knows you've brought Goldberg in for questioning. I expect he's had plenty to say about it all.'

'He certainly knows, sir, but he seemed far from interested. It's difficult to know what exactly would grab that man's attention other than the prospect of another promotion dangled in front of his face. And the thing is, he's too stupid to see that solving a case like this would go a long way to shutting up all his critics who say he's just a useless pile of . . . I beg your pardon, sir.'

'Shite, sergeant. "Shite" is the word you're looking for. I have heard it before, and it does seem an appropriate description. All right, I'll be getting the report on the bullet shortly. That might help in sorting out just how significant the boy's gun is. Let's hope for his sake it's not a match.'

Chapter 10

Gorbals: 8 January 1929

The chill of the damp morning air was broken by the blast of heat from the bakery. Inside the shop on Oxford Street at Gorbals Cross, the lights had been on since long before dawn, and the musical babble of Yiddish tumbled through the doorway onto the pavement, along with the fresh smell of bread. Davie stopped to breathe in the mouth-watering warmth.

Isi Feinstein was arguing loudly with his father inside as he did every morning. He wanted to modernise, to improve, and all his father wanted was a little peace. White-aproned, they waved their arms and stabbed floured fingers at each other to make their point, all the time crafting the black bread and bagels that would feed the Jewish families in the nearby tenements. And as it was Friday, there was also challah, the traditional egg bread for the Sabbath, but only those who lived in the room and kitchens on Rutherglen Road would likely have enough money left to buy that.

Old Moshe shuffled across the road towards the bakery through the slush, his hacking tubercular cough announcing his approach.

'*Gutn morgn, shalom aleichem.*'

'Good morning, Moshe. May peace come to you too. How are you today?'

'Feh! So Yiddish is not good enough for you any more. So *chosuv*, you are now. It was good enough for your *tatte*, may peace be upon him. It was good enough for your *zeyde*, though you never knew him. He was a *shlimazl* and definitely still owes me money, may peace be upon him too. But you young people with your modern world – you want to change everything. Everything! Now, make way for an old man. I need words with Mr Feinstein senior.'

'Davie, why are you waiting down there? Get yourself up here, man.' The voice came from above the bakery, and as soon as he looked up, the window was already being slammed shut.

He called back, 'I didn't know you were already in. I was waiting for you to open up.' But his words were lost in the sleet that was just starting to fall, and he pushed open the street door and climbed the stairwell to the first-floor landing.

The door of the Workers' Society, whose offices occupied the two rented rooms above Feinstein's bakery, was as battered as the bare floorboards of the landing. The door had once been painted red, but all that was left now was a memory of revolution.

Rumour had it that the society only rented the rooms to take advantage of the heat from the ovens downstairs. Certainly, every expense had been spared in providing comfort for the readers of the books and pamphlets in the cramped library, and the only heating in the office was a small, inefficient paraffin stove. But there was always tea.

A large brass samovar had already been fired up by Doron Frossman, who had opened up that morning. He preferred 'Ronnie' to the point that he would refuse to answer to anything else, and only his mother would get away with using his proper name.

'Is there any milk?'

'Not unless you brought some. D'you think we're made of money? Anyway, milk would spoil that lovely brassy taste you only get in your tea here.'

The two men were both 21 and had known each other ever since they had met in short trousers on the first day of school sixteen years earlier. They had become instant friends out of necessity because at the time they were the only two Jewish boys in the class. They found some solace in each other from the taunts and name-calling.

Only a few years later, the boys were no longer the oddities they had once been when other Jewish families arrived from Eastern Europe. Their children had the misfortune not only of being Jews but of also having thick German or Russian accents, that is when they could speak English at all. Davie and Ronnie by contrast were two Glasgow boys from the outset and even joined in with the others poking fun at the newcomers.

Now, looking back, they were ashamed of themselves and realised they had more in common with those gaunt, frightened boys from Berlin, Warsaw and the shtetls of Russia than with the loud Protestants and Catholics they had been born amongst.

The two friends might be born-and-bred Glaswegians, but they now realised they would always be outsiders. The heritage their parents had brought with them, along with their Yiddish from the East, bound them more strongly to the newcomers than any ties of nationality.

It was the arrival of one boy when they were 13 that changed their outlook for good. Salomon Finkelstein had moved to Glasgow with his parents and his sister Marta. They had travelled across Europe from the slums of Berlin, a city the boys had only ever heard of in connection with the war.

Salomon was their age and ended up in their class, where the teacher seated him beside the other Jews at the back. The boy quickly learned to keep his mouth shut when he found his accent stirred the others to violence.

One day in the playground, Salomon was on the ground with Geordie Kenneth straddling him and punching him hard. The young German had done nothing to deserve the beating other than simply being there.

As he tried to defend himself against Geordie's swings, he made not a sound. Ronnie watched as Salomon's nose started to bleed and silent tears welled up.

'Come on, Davie. We can't have this.'

In a single movement, the two young boys heaved Geordie off his victim and threw him to one side. They stood over Salomon, who was still on the ground, curled up to protect himself from the two boys he thought were about to take over his beating.

Ronnie growled at Geordie, who knew better than to stand up to the boy who was a head taller than him and physically much stronger. Davie was not far behind his friend in size, and between them they presented a formidable defence that made everyone else lose interest in the little German boy.

The crowd, who had been watching the fight and egging Geordie on, dissipated, and games of chase and marbles and a makeshift kickabout with a half-brick gave them all new purpose.

Ronnie bent over Salomon, who winced in fear but still made not a sound.

'Don't be daft. We're not going to hit you. Get up. You're with us now. No danger.'

'*Adank.*'

His voice was as thin as his legs, and the boys had rarely heard him speak. But this they both understood, for it was the language of their dinner table, their scoldings and their nursery rhymes, and it was Davie who replied by way of reflex.

'*Ir zent zikher*. You're safe with us. So, come on, don't worry. But, listen, Salomon's an awful mouthful. Can we call you Sal?'

By now the boy's nose had stopped bleeding and his tears had dried, and although he was still shaking, he nodded. '*Yo, itst meyn nomen iz Sal.*'

And so it was from then on.

*

In the offices of the Workers' Society, Ronnie tossed a book to Davie who fumbled to catch it and missed.

'For Christ's sake, you need to learn to catch like a man.'

'And you need to learn to swear like a Jew. What is it anyway that needed to be sent by air mail?'

'I told you. It's that book by that German bloke. Boring as fuck, but you should take a look – wait till you read it, he just loves us.'

'*Mein Kampf* . . . It's in German.'

'It's nearly Yiddish. Or you can get the man of the moment to help you – our wee Sal. Well, speak of the Devil.'

A slim young man with dark glossy hair and pale blue eyes was standing in the doorway, brushing the sleet from his sleeves and removing his cap.

'Well, shut the fucking door. We don't want to heat the landing, do we?'

'Always the charmer, Ronnie. Hiya, Davie. You well?'

'Never better, Sal. I hear you've got some news. It's all around the streets.'

'No secrets in the Gorbals, that's for sure. Aye, me and Becca are going to tie the knot.'

'Well, it's the only way the wee man's going to get his leg over,' said Ronnie.

Sal's German accent was long gone, but he was still the smallest of the three, and Davie at least was still protective of him. He shook his head in sympathy and just scowled at Ronnie, who was tidying the bookshelves ready for the morning readers.

Since his father had died, Davie had been spending more and more time in the offices. It was a change of scene, and he needed to get out from under his mother's feet and away from his little sisters. When he had been in work, he'd only been a regular on Wednesday nights and on Sundays, but for the last three weeks he had spent every morning above the bakery.

The Workers' Society was part meeting place, part library, part reading room – a socialist hub. It had become an informal sanctuary and gathering place for the Gorbals' immigrants, chief amongst them the Jews. It was funded by the trade unions and by small subscriptions from those who could afford it when they were in work. Ronnie was the only paid employee of the society, and he was the only real communist amongst them. Davie and Sal just came to keep warm and find some company.

'Any work this week, Sal?'

'No, Davie, but they're taking on casuals at the foundry on Monday, so you never know. Horrible, dirty work, but I need any money I can get, what with the wedding. What's that you're reading?'

Davie had forgotten he was still holding the book Ronnie had tossed, and he held it up so Sal could read the cover.

'Well, that'll be a right load of shite. Those bastards were why we left to come here. They hate everybody but themselves. And you know what they think of us, don't you? It's not like here where they just treat you like dirt. There, they beat up old women and piss on Jewish graves. They laugh while they're torching our shops and kicking us to death in the streets.'

'Well, they're in Germany and we're here,' said Davie.

'Wake yourself up, man,' said Sal. 'They'll not be staying in Germany.'

'The wee man's right. We've always had to run away or be killed. Look at Russia before the revolution. And it's not just about being a Jew, it's as much about poverty and oppression. The only chance is for the workers to unite. There's undeniable strength in numbers. It won't matter if you're a Jew, Catholic, Protestant or nothing at all, we'll all be workers standing together.'

Ronnie had stopped fixing the shelves and had joined the other two beside the samovar. He was only sure about one thing in his life: his politics. He had watched his own father go on strike back in 1926, and he remembered the hunger and his mother's weeping at the table. He had seen how when the strike was broken, his father had never worked again, blacklisted as a troublemaker. And two years later he had watched him die in the box bed in agony because they had no money for the doctors.

His socialism was deeply personal, unlike his religion which he had quietly discarded when his grieving mother was no longer looking.

'So how's the communism coming along, Ronnie? Planning a wee trip to Russia any time soon?'

'You can mock, Davie Goldberg, but communism is the modern way forward. It's the only practical solution – politically, philosophically, economically. You watch and see where we all end up.'

Davie and Sal enjoyed it when they could tease Ronnie onto his soap box. Davie decided to push him a little further. 'Listen Ronnie, the communists and the Jews are fighting the same enemies, right? There's a lot of common ground. We're at war with the right-wing factions, the fascists, the tsarists, the oppressors of the people everywhere. So why are the rabbis so against what we do here?'

Ronnie instantly took the bait. He turned to face them and

put down the books he had been carrying because for this he needed his arms.

'That's easy. Politically, the right wing has always linked the spread of left-wing views to the Jews. And the elders know that. That's why they're so down on us for being openly left-wing. They don't want us raising our heads above the parapet, being socialists – and especially communists – and embracing everything that means. "Why make it hard?" they say. "Why give them another rod to beat you with?" As far as I'm concerned, they're just cowards. They think if we pretend not to be Jews at all, the bastards will just overlook us.'

Davie and Sal were biting their lips trying to suppress their laughter. It was always the same when Ronnie took flight. He had a particular expression he adopted when he thought he was addressing the masses, and when he started throwing his arms in the air to emphasise his points, that's usually when the other two spluttered into their tea and lost control.

Ronnie was used to their ridicule but could do little about it. The three had grown from boys into men together. Things as simple as politics and passion weren't going to come between them now. However, he did like to remind them both how startlingly ignorant they were.

'When was the last time either of you two read a book? A real book, like the ones on the shelf over there? You live in a bigger world than the Gorbals, my friends, and the doorway to that world is through those books. You need to read some early Keir Hardie. Here, *From Serfdom to Socialism*. It's a seminal work.'

Ronnie could hear them sniggering at his use of the word 'seminal' but he ploughed on. 'And there's the *Fabian Essays on Socialism*. George Bernard Shaw. Essential. And then you've got the big guns, Marx and Engels.'

'Light reading, then, Ronnie.'

'You think this is all a joke. But one day you're going to wake up and find you're older and no wiser. This is the time to educate yourselves – while you're young.'

The pair felt suitably chastised but not enough to want to pick up the copy of *Das Kapital* that Ronnie had thrown at them as his parting shot. Sal rose to make fresh tea and wondered if they had really upset Ronnie this time. He thought it best to get him talking again.

'The thing is, Ronnie, the communists and the fascists are as bad as each other. You might take the communists for your allies now, but it just looks like that. Just because we share a common enemy with them doesn't make us all pals. But the thing that gets me in a knot is trying to figure out what I am. I'm a Jew, right, but I live in Glasgow so I'm Scottish, but I must still be a wee bit German. See what I mean?'

Davie chimed in, seeing what Sal was doing and knowing that Ronnie liked nothing better than to argue about the politics of Judaism.

'That's a good point, Sal. What d'you think, Ronnie? Are we Jews or are we British?'

Their friend was trying his best to sulk over at the book stack, but it wasn't coming naturally. Instead, he turned and joined in. 'Read Rifkind – he's got the right idea. He says we're given this false choice: either we adapt or we leave. We have to give up our Jewish culture and assimilate blandly and anonymously into society, or we have to fuck off out of it. Why can't we be loyal British citizens and at the same time be Jews, real Jews, bound together by a common culture, language and literature, never mind religion? And he says international socialism is how we're going to achieve it. Everywhere that they hate Jews, it's because of what we're forced to become. We're the moneylenders, the sweaters, the wee businessmen living off others like bloody parasites. He says we need an occupational transformation; we need to get back to our roots on the land: we need agriculture, not usury.'

'In the Gorbals? Aye, right! That's just another bloody utopia that'll never happen.'

Davie shook his head and returned to his tea, but Sal was undaunted and tried again to keep Ronnie engaged. 'So we should be voting for the Jew in the election, then. Bloch is standing again, isn't he?'

Ronnie shook his head and Davie looked puzzled.

'No? So you wouldn't vote for a Jew despite all your ravings?'

'Maurice Bloch might be a Jew but he's also a Unionist. Until there's a bona fide communist on the ballot paper, I'm obliged to support the only socialist, whatever party he stands for. Buchanan and his Labour Party will be getting my vote.'

This time it was Sal who shook his head and said, 'I can't keep up with you sometimes.'

'But the fascists will never get in here, will they? Surely everybody can see what they're about.'

'You think everybody's like us, Davie? They're not. We talk politics here, we read, we learn, but Glasgow? It's hardly a place of political sophistication. These fascists are hoodlums masquerading as politicians, and they offer nothing to the people other than somebody to blame. They stand on their soap boxes and shout about the divides between *them* and *us*; they preach a hatred of *them* while they pretend to be *us*. And people are easily swayed. They always have been. Look at them. They're done in, worn out from work and poverty. They live in slums along with the rats and watch their children choke to death on the diphtheria. Wouldn't you want someone to blame for it all? It's an easy lie to buy, and these fucking fascists are selling it cheap.'

It wasn't that Davie was uninterested in all the discussions, it was just that sometimes he wanted to talk about matters much closer to home and about things that were less intense and troubling. The atmosphere created in the Workers' Society by Ronnie was always serious and one of impending crisis that could only be averted by a call to arms and action.

Sometimes Davie just wanted to talk about lassies and the dancehalls and leave the revolutions to somebody else. When there was a lull between lectures, Davie asked Sal again about his fiancée.

'You and Becca, eh. I hope you don't mind me saying, but she's a lovely-looking lassie. You're a lucky man, Sal. So is it a bit of a rush job, the wedding, I mean? D'you have to?'

'Fuck's sake, Davie. That's a terrible thing to say. She's not like that.'

'Sorry, sorry. I just thought maybe you'd been a wee bit careless up the close, y'know.'

'Becca and me, we've never done it.'

'You're kidding me.'

'Why would I kid? I told you, she's not like that.'

'Like what? Normal, you mean.'

'Look, Davie, just 'cause you've got sex on the brain, doesn't mean everybody else does too.'

'You're twenty-one, Sal. If you've not got sex on the brain, there's something wrong with you.'

'Aye, well. She'll not let me.'

'Fuck's sake! Anyway, I'm going to the Pally the night. Can I interest you in the jigging? Maybe get a wee lumber as well? You're still a free man, and it looks as if you could use the experience.'

'Thanks all the same, but I better not. I'm going round to Becca's house the night. Her maw's making some dinner.'

Davie could barely conceal his pity for the young man. 'No bother, maybe next week.'

*

The Dennistoun Palais was a large modern white building off Duke Street, and the streets around it were already full of young men and women gathering for a good time. The Denny Pally, as it was commonly known, was a place to forget yourself for a few hours, to enjoy the live dance band, and where a young man like Davie could hold some lovely girls close to him in a foxtrot or a quickstep.

It was a dry venue, serving only orange juice and milk by way of refreshments, but quarter-bottles of gin and whisky would be smuggled in, tucked in handbags and back pockets just to make sure the night went well.

Davie had not been working for nearly a month and his funds were low. He could afford his own entrance fee, but he could take no one with him tonight or any night until he found another job. He had been earning eighteen shillings a week, and any savings were almost gone.

Tonight, he told himself, would be the last outing for a while. He had dressed smartly and had oiled his thick jet-black hair. He was over six feet tall and his height caught the eye of many of the girls. The fact that he could also dance meant that he rarely had trouble finding someone to walk home at the end of the night.

The hall inside was like a different world from the cramped, dingy spaces of the Gorbals. Stepping through the doors, everyone was transported to the other side of the screen at the cinema.

Suddenly, they were in a grand space with a polished wooden floor and a high ceiling painted with golden stars. And the band, dressed in evening wear, were playing the latest songs. There would even be singers – glamorous young starlets hoping to make a name for themselves on the dance-hall circuit on their way to radio fame. And the girls were all beautiful. Every one of them had spent hours fixing their hair and their make-up just so. And, although money was scarce, they all wore their simple, often homemade frocks as if they were haute couture. However, with their youthful bodies and good looks, they could have worn anything and still looked wonderful.

Davie scanned the room and saw some familiar faces from the Gorbals. Old school friends, workmates and a few of the girls who lived on Crown Street. They nodded and smiled and chatted when they bumped into each other. The evening was easy and convivial, and it was just the escape he needed.

The first hint he had that something was amiss was when he saw the man whom he knew to be the manager walking smartly across the dance floor towards the entrance from a door behind the stage. He was dressed, as always, in a white evening jacket and black bow tie. Davie knew that whatever had drawn him onto the floor that night must have been of some concern.

From inside the hall, it was difficult to know what was happening outside or to hear anything because of the band, but curiosity got the better of him and he wandered across to the entrance. There he saw the commotion that was developing, as a group of young men, perhaps as many as six, were trying to enter. The manager was blocking their way and tempers looked as if they were about to flare.

'They'll be tryin' to bring in drink, I suppose,' said a voice in Davie's ear. He turned and saw it was Minnie White, a girl he had spent his school days avoiding for she always seemed to be wanting to hang on to his arm and walk with him, even before he had developed his own interest in such things.

'D'you think that's all it is? I mean, half the folk in here have got bottles with them. They look a rougher crowd to me.'

'Naw, it's no the drink. It's the Brigton Boys.'

Davie turned to his left to see Dougie, one of the apprentices at the shipyard where Davie had worked. 'How d'you know?' asked Davie.

'Look at them. Three-piece suits, bunnets and that look in their eyes as if they own the place.'

As they spoke, the manager yielded either to persuasion or coercion and allowed them in. First through the door was a tall, heavy-set man who removed his cap and took a scrap of paper from his pocket. He stood in the foyer and ran his eyes down the names on his list and then started to scan the crowd. When he identified his first target, he smiled and went straight across to him.

The man was with a girlfriend, and he moved her to his side and slightly behind him to get her out of harm's way. The man with the list bent down to whisper in his ear and then patted him lightly on the cheek. The requested sum was counted out in small change and handed over. His name was duly ticked off the list. Davie watched this happen again and again, and each time the target's pockets emptied into the outstretched palm of the collector.

'What's going on, Dougie?'

'Subscription night. I think it's time to go. This is going to turn ugly.'

'What d'you mean?'

'The Brigton Boys are collecting. They're working their way through their list, and sooner or later they're going to find one who's skint and the worse for drink. And that's when it all kicks off. Trust me, you don't want to be anywhere near them when that happens.'

Davie knew of the gangs in Glasgow, everyone did, but he could honestly say he had never seen any of them in action. There were stories about what they got up to and the fights they had, but although he had seen plenty of petty crime and had encountered many thugs in the Gorbals, he had never come across anything that could be described as a razor gang.

Now, he watched them even more intently, trying to see what they did, to hear what they said. What kind of fear could they instill that would make men hand over their hard-earned cash just like that?

Davie turned again to ask Dougie a question, but he was gone. So was Minnie, and as he looked about, he could see that the crowd was much thinner than it had been only minutes before. As the tall man turned away from his latest target he looked again at his list and then raised his eyes and looked directly at Davie.

Rab McDiarmid did not recognise the tall, dark-haired man but he could see him taking a special interest. And he decided to have some fun. He walked towards Davie and, as he did so, purposefully drew back his jacket to show the razor in his waistcoat pocket.

'See something you like, big man?'

Davie froze, unsure what was being asked. He could feel those around him draw back and away, leaving him isolated.

'Naw, just here to enjoy the dancing like everybody else. Don't want any bother.'

'That's good, big man, 'cause neither do we. Just here to do a wee job. So what's your name?'

'I'm from the Gorbals.'

'That's no what I asked you.'

'Davie. Davie Goldberg.'

'Is that a fact? We don't like your kind here, dancin' with our lassies, touchin' them up. I don't like Catholics, but I like Jews even less. Catholics are dirty bastards, but the Jews give me the boak. I don't want to see you here again. Is that clear?'

Davie was seething, but he knew he had no way of fighting back. There were six of them, all armed with knives and razors, and, more importantly, they were unafraid to use them. There was nothing to do but yield. He nodded.

'On your way then before I change my mind about stickin' you here and now.'

One of the girls who had been standing close by Davie gasped as she heard the threat. Defiantly, she stepped forward. 'You've no right to speak to anybody like that. You're just a big bully, so you are.'

Rab smiled at her and then turned to her boyfriend, who was trying to silence her. 'Good idea, son. You need to shut the wee bitch up, before I do for her as well.'

Calmly, Rab turned to continue working his way through the list. Davie stood for a moment, fists clenched in frustration, and then he left.

In the street outside, he slunk into the shadows across the road from the entrance. He wasn't sure what he intended to do, but he knew he couldn't simply walk away from this and still respect himself.

It was only about twenty minutes later that Dougie's prediction became a reality. Bodies erupted from the dance-hall entrance onto the street with a man reeling, arms flailing, followed by three of the gang. Leading them was the tall one, and this time his razor was out and open.

'Nothin'. That's what I'm giving you, nothin'. 'Cause that's all I've got. You're a bunch o' fuckin' bastards, the lot o' you. You should be ashamed o' yourselves with what you've done to this place.'

As far as Rab was concerned, the time for discussion was over: an example had to be made of the man. Subscription nights only worked if everyone knew that this was how they could end.

Rab was too quick for the drunk man's wild punch. He caught him first on the arm, slicing through the cloth of his jacket and drawing first blood. The man fell, clutching his arm in pain, and the other two starting laying into him with their boots. Their kicks were brutal, and they went for his head even though he tried to protect himself with both arms.

Davie watched the attack, unable to move. He saw the men's grinning faces, their enjoyment of the violence, and he suddenly thought he was going to vomit.

The man on the ground stopped screaming and then stopped responding to their beating altogether. As he lost consciousness, his attackers lost interest for they were clearly feeding on their victim's pain. Only the tall one was still engaged, bending down towards the man, but Davie could not see what was said or done. The next moment, there were police whistles and running feet, and when Davie looked back, the Brigton Boys were gone and all that remained of their work was a crumpled figure in the middle of the road.

Davie rushed to him. He steeled himself and bent to see if he was still alive. There was the faintest groan from his lips and Davie shouted for others to get help. It was only then that he saw it: on the man's cheek was carved a bloodstained letter 'R'.

*

On the walk home, down through the Green towards the Gorbals, Davie could not get the sight of the man out of his mind. He knew that, given slightly different circumstances, he would have been the one lying bloodied and beaten on the street.

When Sal talked about Berlin and what the streets had been like for the Jews, about the hatred and the mindless aggression, for Davie it had all been just a story sanitised by distance and time. That was something that happened there and then, but not here and now.

Tonight, he had witnessed up close just what people who

hated you could do, and he knew that none of them were safe while there were men like that around. He knew he couldn't help everybody, but he could stand up for his own people, and in that instant, that's what he resolved to do. This wasn't about Ronnie's brand of politics. This was about something much more important: survival.

*

The next week, not far from the Gorbals, in Govanhill, the Jewish Socialist League was holding its regular Wednesday night meeting. Davie arrived at the door of the hall and waited nervously before entering.

He had got the name from one of the pamphlets at the Workers' Society and was already having second thoughts about spending an evening in a room full of Jews. Just as he was about to pull on the door, it burst open, pushed from the other side, and a girl, no more than 16, came rushing out.

'Don't let them start without me, will you?'

He opened his mouth to speak, but she was gone. The door was still swinging on its hinges, and he could see inside for the first time. There was a small group of young men and women all about his age and they were arranging the chairs in a circle. The air was filled with warmth and friendship, and he was drawn in. He stepped through the door and into the hall, only to be pushed forward by the girl rushing back in and bumping into him.

'I've got it now. Sorry.'

She turned to Davie and said, 'I'm Ruth. What d'they call you?' He told her and she shouted to the others, 'Everybody, this is Davie and I think he's a shy one. So that probably means all the lassies'll have to watch him.'

There was laughter, and one of the young men rushed over to welcome Davie. He introduced himself as Josh and apologised for his wee sister.

That evening Davie found exactly what he was looking for in the group. They talked not of the kind of high-minded political theory so beloved of Ronnie, but of the practical problems faced each day by Jews in the city. They shared their experiences, they laughed at the ridiculous and they found hope in each other.

By the end of the night, Davie confirmed his membership and pledged his loyalty even though no such pledge was required.

'So, Davie, will we see you again next week?'

Ruth was eyeing him up, deciding whether he would be worth the effort of flirting with.

'Aye, you will. I've things to do and I want to do them with people like this. There's that much energy in this room, that much spirit, it all feels right.'

'Spirit? I've never really thought there was enough spirits in here. Maybe you could bring a wee half-bottle next time you come. Would liven things up.'

'You don't need livening up, hen.'

'Is that right? I don't think you know what I need.'

From the back of the hall where everyone else was stacking chairs, there was a sharp call from Josh, who was reaching the end of his fraternal tether.

'Would you leave the poor man alone, Ruth? And stop frightening them all away.'

Davie called back to Josh, 'It's fine, honestly. I'll be back next week. You can count on it.'

Ruth watched the tall, dark-haired stranger walk away and sighed. Yes, she thought, he would do.

Chapter 11

Glasgow: 17 February 1931

There was a brisk rap on the office door and Cuthbert looked up from his desk.

'Sorry to disturb you, sir, but there is a Dr Henderson from the university to see you.'

He saw the mortuary technician's head peeking round the door. He had gone out of his way to bring him into the fold of the investigation, but Sandy Young was still a little wary of the 'big, important pathologist from London'. Cuthbert had, however, called upon his expertise in trying to prepare the fragmented body of the target of the bombing, Alistair Henderson.

In Cuthbert's book, what Young had managed to do was nothing short of miraculous, and he had told him so. With only about half the body it was never going to be possible to have an open coffin at the funeral, but by obtaining a set of funeral clothes for Henderson from his family and placing the body parts carefully alongside padding and even some straw he was able to give the impression of an intact man of five foot ten inches in height.

The head was the most problematic, but the technician had neatly packed the fragment with cotton wool till it was the right size and shape and then carefully bandaged it, leaving the intact parts of the ear and the cheek visible.

In spite of their rocky start, the technician's face was drawn now not because he was frightened of Cuthbert so much as he was of the visitor, with whom he had had many fractious conversations over the years. Dr Henderson was the police surgeon who in other circumstances would have been leading this forensic investigation, and it was his desk that Cuthbert now occupied at the city mortuary.

'Please show him in at once, Sandy,' said Cuthbert, rising and straightening his waistcoat in readiness for whatever was to come. However, if he expected the same arrogance and disinterest Herbert Henderson had shown him when he visited the department of forensic medicine just over a week ago, he was to be disappointed.

The man who came into the office was a shrunken version of the one he had met before. His complexion was grey, he looked worn-out, and he stretched out his hand to Cuthbert as much to seek support as to offer a greeting.

'Please take a seat, Dr Henderson. Can I get you something to drink? Tea perhaps?'

'No, no, please don't go to any trouble. I didn't come here today to cause you any more inconvenience than I already have. I realise I was less than welcoming when you visited us, and for that I humbly apologise. Professor Glaister is not at all keen on our dean's plans for the department, and let us just say I have my standing orders. No, I simply needed to come to thank you. Not just for myself, you understand, but for the family and especially for Millicent.'

Cuthbert was unsure if he was expected to understand, but he could see that Henderson was struggling to keep his emotions in check, and he thought it best to let the man speak without interruption.

'Millie is so grateful. We all are. For what you've done. I expect I am one of the few people who understands exactly how difficult what you've had to do is, and I want to thank you for the time and care you have devoted to the task. My brother didn't deserve what happened to him – to die like that. But you gave him back to us. You put him back together for us so at least we could bury him with some dignity.'

Cuthbert now understood but chose to say nothing. This was not a task for which he could take all the credit, nor one for which he wanted praise. Neither was it a time to revisit old prejudices.

'Alistair had strong views, and I didn't agree with everything he said, but after what happened, after those filthy cowards did this, perhaps he was right all along. You have quite a reputation, Cuthbert, and I trust you'll live up to it and give my brother some justice. You need to find the damn Jew who did this.'

Cuthbert watched the man in front of him almost contort with the rage and hatred that was eating him from the inside out. Again, Cuthbert chose to say nothing and merely helped Henderson to his feet. He called for Sandy Young and quietly asked him to show their visitor out.

*

That afternoon, Cuthbert telephoned Morgenthal to check on his progress with the bullet.

'It's a rimless, straight-cased shell, sir, with a coated steel jacket and lead core. Based on the calibre and weight of the bullet and the letters "D.W.M." on the head stamp of the brass cartridge, I am certain it's a 9mm Parabellum. It was probably manufactured during the war, although dating ammunition from that era is imprecise.'

'Parabellum?'

'I believe it's from the Latin motto of the manufacturer in Berlin, *Si vis pacem, para bellum.*'

Morgenthal could hear Cuthbert sigh at the end of the phone and sensed he was slowly shaking his head as he always did when confronted by foolishness.

'Yes – if you wish for peace, prepare for war. For millennia, they've been using that one as an excuse – the arms manufacturers and all those warmongering politicians who've never had to pick up a sword, a bayonet or a gun.'

'There's more, Dr Cuthbert. I have also completed the preliminary analysis of the striations on the bullet and the firing pin mark on the cartridge. Fortunately, there are some very clear identifications that will be unique to a specific firearm. There's a very good chance of identifying the weapon from comparisons with any other fired rounds. If any candidate weapon is recovered, we could test-fire it and do a direct comparison of both bullet and cartridge. Or, of course, the local C.I.D. in Glasgow may already have photographs of recovered bullets in their archives. As for the gun that fired the bullet, that could be any one of a number of different 9mm pistols, but I would say the most likely, given that the bullet is of German manufacture, is the Luger P08. They're really quite common in this country as so many were brought home from the war.'

'We have a gun that could be the weapon and it will need to be examined.'

'It should be a straightforward identification process as to the make and model of the weapon. And then of course the bullet could be compared with test-fired rounds from the candidate gun to confirm if it's the one used on the victim.'

Cuthbert sighed deeply, and this time Morgenthal wasn't sure if he had been the cause. He thought it best to say nothing else and wait to let his mentor speak.

On the contrary, however, Cuthbert was more than impressed by his assistant's almost encyclopaedic knowledge of handguns and ammunition. What troubled him was the dearth of expertise on ballistics there in Glasgow. Morgenthal was growing increasingly tense as the silence continued, but he was surprised by how it was broken.

'The problem with all this, Simon, is that no one here knows as much about this as you, and I certainly don't trust anyone else to do the job. I know you are busy at St Thomas's, but I think I need you here. I realise it's a terrible imposition, but could you get the overnight train and be in Glasgow tomorrow morning ready to start work?'

This time it was Morgenthal who fell silent, only to be nudged by Cuthbert saying, 'Well, laddie?'

'Of course, sir. And . . . thank you.'

*

Later, Morgenthal received another call, this time while he was in the department preparing a case with the necessary reference books and equipment he thought he may need in Glasgow. He recognised Madame Smith's distinctive accent but was surprised to hear her voice.

'Dr Morgenthal, please forgive me for disturbing you at the hospital, but I had hoped you may be able to do me a small service.'

'Anything at all, madame. Is everything all right with you, with Dr Cuthbert? I spoke with him not an hour ago and I'm travelling to Glasgow tonight to be with him.'

'That is why I am calling, sir. Dr Cuthbert also telephoned me to let me know that his stay would be further extended, and although he would never ask, I am sure he needs fresh linen and other items. I was hoping that if I were to pack a small case you may be able to take it to him. Of course, I can bring it to you at the hospital.'

'I would be more than happy to, madame. But there's no need to come here. I'll pick it up this evening on my way to the station. Shall we say eight o'clock?'

*

Morgenthal had only visited Cuthbert's terraced townhouse in Gordon Square twice before. The first time, he and Sarah had been invited to dinner shortly after they were married. The second time, he came alone. In his less than finest hour, he had spent the night there after Cuthbert had discovered him sleeping rough in the department when his wife had thrown him out.

He thought it was one of the most tasteful homes he had ever visited. Sarah, on the other hand, said she had found it somewhat spartan, even rather dull, but to Morgenthal's eyes it was almost oriental in its minimalist décor.

And he remembered there were books and exquisite works of contemporary art everywhere. For someone who so openly professed his love and admiration for the classics, Cuthbert seemingly found it easy to accommodate the modern into his life.

Morgenthal rang the bell and was greeted warmly by Madame Smith.

'This is really very kind of you, sir. I know Dr Cuthbert will appreciate it.'

'Nonsense. It's the very least I could do to help.'

'You will take a seat? May I offer you some refreshment?'

Morgenthal was already lost in looking around the white walls of Cuthbert's home and at the series of framed pen and ink drawings that lined the entrance hallway.

They were abstract images of dancing punctuation marks, black ink on bright white paper framed in black lacquered wood. They hung on the wall above a similarly black lacquered console table that was obviously Japanese. The carpet was a subtle grey, and the only colour in the room was provided by the crystal bowl of luxuriant and heavily scented pink and lilac roses on the table.

Madame Smith was used to visitors being somewhat taken aback by the style of her employer's home. She too had been surprised when she first walked into this hallway some years ago, but she had grown to love the uncluttered beauty and simplicity of Cuthbert's taste – not least because it was easy to dust.

'I see you are admiring the Kandinsky drawings. He is a Russian artist, you know, and every time you look at them you see something new and unexpected. I think that is perhaps why Dr Cuthbert finds them so interesting. He is always searching for something just out of reach, don't you find? Now, may I offer you that refreshment?'

Morgenthal was still early for the Euston train and gratefully accepted the offer of tea, which Madame Smith served in the study, another of Cuthbert's white rooms. He had never been in this part of the house and realised it was probably Cuthbert's inner sanctum. As such, he suddenly felt ill at ease. Should he be here at all?

Madame Smith laid the tea tray on the small table by the window and proceeded to pour. On either side of the fireplace and on the long wall opposite the window, there were plain bookshelves in white wood from floor to ceiling. Every book in the large collection was carefully arranged, and Morgenthal was quite certain that his mentor would know exactly where each and every one should be.

Looking around the room, he noted that there were no framed photographs, family portraits or any evidence of his past. A single, large oil painting dominated the room and hung unframed above the marble fireplace. It was a bold composition of primary-coloured squares and simple straight black lines.

Morgenthal stared at it quizzically, not altogether sure he regarded it as art. Madame Smith enjoyed observing her visitor's reaction to the painting. Indeed, that was the reason she had served the tea in Dr Cuthbert's study.

'It is by a Dutch painter by the name of Mondrian and very new. It's so striking, don't you think?'

'I'm not sure I've ever seen anything like it.'

'At least not hanging above someone's fireplace. Am I right? We have to forgive him his little foibles. They are, after all, so few and far between. Milk or lemon, Dr Morgenthal?'

The conversation turned from Cuthbert's taste in art and design to the case in Glasgow, and Madame Smith expressed her concern that her employer was working too hard.

'I encouraged him to go because I thought it would provide an opportunity for some rest and relaxation. I see now that I could not have been more wrong. I was so glad to hear that you are to join him. He finds you such a help and I know you feel as I do.'

'Madame?'

'We both care a great deal for him, do we not?'

Morgenthal could see that she spoke with a depth of feeling that he shared but would find difficult to confess. He merely nodded nervously, and she saw she was right.

'Let me get the case for you. It is very small, and I hope it will not inconvenience you unduly.'

'I am only too happy to help, madame. Do you have any message you wish me to convey?'

She thought for a moment with her head bowed almost as if she were praying and said, 'No, there is nothing. It is simply my job to ensure he is comfortable. But' – she stretched out to touch his arm lightly – 'thank you for asking me.'

*

It was Simon Morgenthal's first time in Scotland. He had been looking forward to the trip north both because of the thrill of the overnight train journey and because Cuthbert had asked for his help.

He walked along the platform of Glasgow Central Station, followed by the porter with his luggage trolley. Hogg spotted him from the concourse. Cuthbert had described him, but the smartly dressed young Englishman was unmistakable.

People were spilling from the train, wearied by the journey, but not this one. He was beaming like an excited child as he took in the great glass station roof, the bustle on the concourse and the morning trains sliding into their platforms from the suburbs. As he approached, Hogg saw the measure of him and wondered just what they must be feeding folk in London to make them all so tall.

'Dr Morgenthal? Detective Sergeant Hogg, sir. Dr Cuthbert told me to expect you.'

'I say, it's jolly good of you to meet me! What a magnificent station you have here in Glasgow. I didn't expect anything quite so grand. I expect the rest of the city is just as marvellous. I really can't wait to see it.'

'Indeed, sir. I see you're travelling light.'

'Oh, they're not all mine, sergeant. One is for Dr Cuthbert, and one has all my equipment. I'm not that much of a liability, I promise you.'

Hogg nodded, thinking it best to keep a civil silence. 'This way, doctor. I'll take you to the mortuary.'

'Righty-ho. Lead on, Macduff.'

Hogg winced.

On the drive across the city to the East End, Morgenthal drank in the sights, his gaze everywhere but mostly up. He gave Hogg, who was seated with him in the back of the police car, a running commentary on his observations and by the end of the fifteen-minute drive, the sergeant was more than eager to help him out of the car.

'I'm sure I'll be seeing you again, sergeant, but let me just say what a pleasure it's been to meet you.

'Yes,' said a weary Hogg. 'I'm sure our paths will be crossing over the next day or so. For now, I'll just leave you to it, sir.'

*

When they met, Morgenthal was surprised by the strength of Cuthbert's handshake. Apart from their first meeting and a few other occasions over the years, there had been no call for such a warm greeting.

Cuthbert looked delighted to see his assistant and was still gripping his hand tightly as he spoke. 'Thank you for coming all this way, Simon. I'm sure Sarah will be very cross with me for taking you away from her and your laddie. How is my little namesake doing?'

'Jack's thriving, sir. Five months old already, thank you for asking. And Sarah more than understands the job. To tell you the truth, sir, I think she might even be a little pleased to see the back of me for a few days. I think she enjoys having the house to herself every now and then. Heaven knows, I'll probably go home to find the place redecorated. She's always threatening that.'

Morgenthal was as talkative as ever, and although there had been times when Cuthbert found his cheerful chatter to be an annoyance, today he welcomed the familiar lilt of his voice.

'Let me show you around, Simon, and, of course, introduce you to Dr Ogilvie over here, who has been an enormous help on this case.'

Ogilvie looked up from his bench and smiled at the visitor after assessing him. He could see the warmth Cuthbert had extended to him and realised that it was only to be expected;

after all, they were colleagues. However, he was a little piqued to be introduced into the conversation almost as an afterthought, considering he had been in the room all along. He stood when summoned and gave a small nod of acknowledgement.

'Dr Morgenthal, I have heard so much about you. Dr Cuthbert here is always singing your praises. It's good to finally put a face to the reputation.'

To be polite, Simon would have liked to return the compliment, but in truth he had heard nothing at all of the young pathologist from Cuthbert, so he simply smiled and held out his hand.

'You two should have a chat later – I'm sure you'll get on famously. You're both at exactly the same stage of your training, and I'm sure you'll have a lot of notes to compare. But first, Simon, do come into my office. Dr Ogilvie, perhaps you would be kind enough to put Dr Morgenthal's bags safely out of the way.'

Ogilvie looked from Cuthbert's smiling face to the three leather suitcases and nodded somewhat half-heartedly.

Simon, however, was suddenly uncomfortable and intervened. 'Oh, thank you, but I wouldn't hear of it. Besides, this one here is actually yours, Dr Cuthbert, from Madame Smith no less. And this one is the equipment I brought to help with the ballistics analyses. As for the other one, I can take care of that.'

Ogilvie nodded again without smiling and got back to his work.

In the office, Cuthbert had already forgotten about Ogilvie, if indeed he had registered his annoyance at all, and he asked Simon to fill him in on everything that had happened at St Thomas's in his absence.

'It seems you have things under control.'

'Oh, I don't deserve any credit, sir. The staff are excellent. Everyone knows exactly what's expected of them, and I'm pleased to say the workload has been relatively light of late. I've just had to provide the occasional guiding hand. Nothing much at all.'

'You do yourself a disservice, Simon. It takes more than that to keep a department going, and I think I should know. But enough of London. I take it you have brought back the bullet and its casing?'

Morgenthal took the evidence bags from his briefcase as well as a brown envelope from which he drew the photographs he had taken. 'These are the enlargements of the markings on the bullet. You can see the striations quite clearly.'

'Excellent. You'll need these to compare with the Glasgow C.I.D. files. Since we spoke on the phone, I've been able to ascertain that headquarters does indeed have ballistic files. Quite what state we will find them in, I don't know, but that's what I'd like you to get started with. Search the files and find any matches that you can.'

Morgenthal was keen to get going, but Cuthbert insisted he first go to his hotel, check in and freshen up after his journey.

'I'll arrange for Sergeant Hogg to take you to the police headquarters after that and introduce you to the people you'll need to work with there. I'll catch up with you later and you can let me know how bad it looks.'

'Oh, I almost forgot, sir. I have a letter for you from Chief Inspector Mowbray. It was delivered by hand to the department with instructions to forward it on to your address in Glasgow, but as I was coming, I thought it would be quicker to bring it myself.'

The letter was handwritten and not on official notepaper. Cuthbert knew it must be the information he had asked Mowbray to unearth regarding D.C.I. Black.

'Thank you, Simon. That was good of you. Now, get yourself to the hotel and I'll see you later at the archive.'

As soon as he had gone, Cuthbert sat at his desk and slit open the envelope.

London
16th Feb. '31

Jack,

I have done some rooting around on the quiet and it does looks like your D.C.I. is a piece of work.

Very much off the record, he's had a meteoric rise through the ranks with no real achievements to back it all up. He seems to have been in Glasgow his whole career, which given the size of the place is not that surprising.

What is surprising is that he worked in uniform as a constable before transferring to C.I.D., making sergeant the following year. He seems to have worked vice in the city, which is always an alarm bell for me, given my experience of vice officers and all the troughs they manage to dip their snouts in. But he's never worked homicide until now.

Given the high-profile nature of this, his first case, I expect somebody will have to do some explaining as to why a more experienced senior officer was not in charge. At least that would be the case here in the Yard. Maybe they do things differently up in haggis-land.

I did speak to one inspector here who transferred down from Glasgow, and he'd worked with Morrison Black. He was quite tight-lipped about him, and I got the impression there was no love lost there, but he wasn't willing to say anything against him.

Those are the facts, and here are the rumours for what they're worth. He's certainly in the lodge, perhaps pretty high up in it, which might have helped him up the ladder. Also, there's talk of who he knows and more importantly what

> he knows about those in charge in Glasgow. You know, the skeletons in the closet. But there's always gossip like that. It's what some of them say here about me, and I don't have any secret files on the commissioner, let me assure you.
>
> Therefore, nothing that concrete, but I do think you need to be careful, my friend. He definitely has the ear of the top brass and probably their trust.
>
> Regards,
> Jim

Cuthbert was surprised by nothing in the letter. It tied in with what Sergeant Hogg had been saying all along and certainly fitted with what little he himself knew about the man.

*

When Hogg called Morgenthal's room from the Central Hotel reception to inform him he was waiting for him downstairs, he was greeted with another burst of cheer.

'Well, I said we'd be seeing each other again soon. Who'd have thought it would be the very same day! Thank you for coming to collect me. I could have got a taxi, you know. I'm sure you must be frightfully busy and all that. But it's very kind and much appreciated. Shall I come down now?'

'Yes, that's the idea, sir.' Hogg scratched his head and pulled on his hat and wondered if he could sit in the front with the driver this time.

At the police headquarters on Turnbull Street, Morgenthal signed in as an official visitor at reception. The uniformed constable on the desk looked him over and turned to Hogg for some form of confirmation that he should be letting this Englishman into the station at all.

'Dr Morgenthal will be working in the archive rooms. He'll need access to ballistics records and for that I think we're going to need to speak with Bob Armitage. Can you get him on the phone, son?'

Armitage was a humourless, bald little man who took a dislike to Simon Morgenthal the moment he met him. Possibly on account of his height and jollity. Certainly, the young doctor did nothing but exude the same guileless charm he always did, but his perfect manners were no match for Armitage's prejudice.

'And what kind o' name is Morgenthal?' As he asked the question, he sniffed the air.

'My father's and his father's before him, I should think. I can't claim to have had any say in it. None of us can, can we, Mr Armitage?'

Morgenthal knew exactly what he was being asked and why, but he refused to give the man any kind of satisfaction. 'Might I trouble you to show me the ballistics files? I do have quite a lot of work to do, and the sooner I can get started, the sooner I can be out of your hair.'

It was said with a wide, white-toothed smile, but might just as well have been delivered tied to a poisoned dart.

The cavernous archive rooms were in the basement. Rank after rank of chipped grey metal shelves held buff folders and boxes all numbered by hand.

'How far will you need to go back?'

'I don't know, Mr Armitage, but I think the gun that fired the bullet in question was probably not made before 1914, so shall we start with the last decade? If that draws a blank, I'll keep searching.'

Armitage was yet to smile and yet to look his visitor in the eye. He shuffled off, limping slightly, and Morgenthal noticed for the first time that his left shoe was built up to accommodate a shortened leg. He rushed after him to the shelves where the diminutive man was attempting to lift down a large box.

'Can I help you with these? They must be heavy.'

'Please yourself. It's those three there. Leave them as you found them and do not remove anything from this room without my permission.'

'Of course. You've been most helpful.'

But the words were lost on the man who was already limping back to his office at the back of the archive room.

'Yes, you really are one of life's little treasures, Mr Armitage.'

The boxes were indeed heavy as they contained files of photographic evidence. Morgenthal took the first box to the table under the main light in the room and pulled over a chair. Inside were photographs, similar to the one he had brought from London, showing the patterns of the markings on bullets recovered from various gun crimes.

With each photograph were details of the associated crime and the circumstances of its retrieval. In the box, there were well over a hundred such files, and there were two more boxes to go. The process of comparing his photograph with each of these was going to take some time. But he knew the best way to get something done was to start.

Rather than spend a lot of time comparing each photograph, he decided on a strategy of quickly going through the whole box to eliminate all bullets that were obviously not a match. This might be because they were the wrong calibre or because they had grossly different markings.

With the field considerably narrowed, he could then spend much longer on the remaining files. After two more hours, magnifying glass in hand and with the benefit of a tool to measure the distance and angle between certain grooves in the photographs, he had narrowed it down to some five contenders.

These all had very similar markings, but any differences

between them would be revealed in the fine detail. For that Morgenthal would need better light than was available in the archive room.

Armitage had not come back to check on him, and Morgenthal was quite sure he would be no help even if he did. Instead, he repeated the process with the contents of the other two boxes and found a total of twelve possible matches.

He was in the process of stretching to relieve the cramp in his shoulder muscles when Cuthbert arrived.

'Well, Simon, have I caught you engaging in some callisthenics?'

'Not at all, sir. It's just a very uncomfortable place to work. Not that I'm complaining. I'm happy to do the job.'

'It's all right, Simon, I can see it's a rat hole of a place. I mean, how can you see anything with that light?'

'I've made progress, sir, but you're right: we need to examine this shortlist of possible matches elsewhere.'

Cuthbert marched to Armitage's office, knocked and entered only to be met with the scowling face of the man hunched over his desk.

'My colleague requires a space with better light. Can you provide this?'

'Your colleague? You mean the big Ikey Mo?'

'I beg your pardon?'

'The big Jew boy? I hope he's no stinkin' the place out. They always smell, that crowd.'

'How dare you! Dr Morgenthal is a qualified pathologist, and he is a guest in your station assisting in an important murder investigation. You will afford him the same courtesy and respect you would me if you wish to remain on this force. Am I clear?'

Armitage snorted by way of reply.

'Am I clear, you vile little man?'

Morgenthal, who had been listening to the exchange, rushed over and put his hand on Cuthbert's arm.

'Please, sir, leave it. It means nothing.'

Cuthbert turned, still enraged, and saw Morgenthal smiling. He was doing everything he could to show his mentor that he was fine and that no offence had been taken, however much it was intended.

'But, Simon . . .'

'No, leave it be, sir. Mr Armitage will require your signature so that we might remove these files for further examination. Perhaps, Mr Armitage, you could furnish Dr Cuthbert with the necessary form, and we will both be on our way.'

Mechanically and in silence, Cuthbert added his signature to the release paper as Morgenthal collected his jacket and the twelve files. Outside, in the fresh air, Cuthbert gripped Morgenthal's shoulder. 'Simon, I'm so sorry.'

'Please, Dr Cuthbert, it's nothing new. And at this stage it's more important that we get on with this case than start crying over some name-calling, don't you think?'

There had always been a childishness about Simon Morgenthal that Cuthbert had found simultaneously attractive and infuriating. He now saw for the first time just how mature the young man was. He could not easily staunch his own outrage, but for the sake of his young assistant he would try.

'Shall we go back to the mortuary? It's a short walk down the Saltmarket, and the dissection lamps should give you a better look at those photographs.'

'My thoughts exactly, sir.'

Little was said during their walk down the cobbled thoroughfare that led to the river. However, when they reached the low red-brick building that was the city mortuary, Cuthbert paused before they entered.

'I know you don't wish to talk about what happened there,

but I must. I need you to know that although there is much ignorance and bigotry in the world, it is not everywhere, and it certainly isn't here between you and me.'

Morgenthal was touched that Cuthbert felt the need to say such a thing and assured him that he had never been in any way discriminated against let alone abused at St Thomas's. Nevertheless, he could see how much the incident had upset Cuthbert and he added how appreciative he was that he had stood up for him.

'It means a great deal to me, sir. Now, I must get to work, or that charming little man will be sending the police around to collect his precious files.'

*

It took Morgenthal the rest of the day to do the necessary detailed comparative work. However, he knew it was worth it when he identified not one but two positive matches with the bullet that had killed Robert McDiarmid.

He had been invited to stay and join the daily case update in Cuthbert's office and knew he would be called on to report his findings then. In the meantime, he completed the written report that Cuthbert would insist upon.

When Hogg and Anderson arrived, the sergeant saw that Morgenthal was sitting eagerly awaiting them in Cuthbert's office. Hogg introduced W.P.C. Anderson, and the young man took her hand warmly. He told her how magnificent he thought Central Station was, and he was just about to enumerate the other architectural wonders he had observed in the city when Cuthbert arrived.

Anderson whispered in Hogg's ear, 'He seems like a lovely young man.'

The sergeant, who found the silly Englishman almost unbearable, looked at her quizzically. Were they talking about the same person?

'Simon, I see you've met everyone. Good, perhaps you can update us on the ballistics findings.'

Morgenthal stood in front of the board and described in detail the analysis of the bullet and casing that he had performed in London. He showed the photographs he had taken of the bullet's markings and then pinned them to the board beside the photograph of McDiarmid's remains.

Anderson, who was fascinated as much by the story as by the man telling it, interrupted to ask, 'Do we know what kind of gun fired such a bullet?'

'Indeed. The calibre and casing markings all point to it being a Luger 9mm P08. It's a standard German officer issue, many of which were brought back from the front as trophies at the end of the war. It carries an eight-round magazine loaded into the pistol butt. It is recoil-operated and, if kept clean, reliable and very accurate. It's really quite a remarkable piece of engineering.'

'And it kills people.'

Morgenthal was silenced by Hogg's remark. The sergeant had no love for guns and had no time for anyone who did. Cuthbert sympathised with Hogg's point of view, but he needed Morgenthal to finish so he urged him on with a small circular gesture of his hand.

'Yes, and there's ... there's more. I've been through the C.I.D.'s ballistics archives here, and the bullet is a very good match for two other bullets used in gun crimes here in the city over the last five years.

'The first was in 1926: an armed robbery in the city centre where several shots were fired. One of these bullets was recovered from the leg of a woman passer-by caught in the crossfire and the striations on that bullet match those on ours. The gun was not recovered during the investigation, which is why we find it being used again some two years later at what was believed to be a gangland execution. The victim was a William Baxter...'

'I worked the Baxter case. Are you saying that was the same gun that killed Rab McDiarmid?'

'Yes, sergeant, according to the bullet markings, one and the same.'

Cuthbert noticed Hogg looking uncomfortable. 'What is it, sergeant?'

'It could be nothing, sir, but the thing is, we got the wee hoodlum that did for Baxter, and as far as I remember it, we also got the gun.'

'So...'

'So... if Dr Morgenthal here is right, the gun in question should be safely under lock and key in the police evidence store and not being used to kill someone on Glasgow Green.'

Morgenthal consulted the files he had brought from the archive. When a gun had been matched to the bullet there was a separate yellow sheet attached to the photograph complete with a detailed description of the firearm and its location marker in the archive.

The photograph of the bullet that had been used to kill Baxter two years previously was attached to the usual forms, describing the details of the case, but there was no yellow sheet.

'There's no record of the gun in the files, sergeant.'

'Not now there isn't.'

Chapter 12

Glasgow: 18 March 1931

Cuthbert asked the question as delicately as he could, but he knew that whatever he said was likely to cause offence.

'Is it possible, sergeant, that you may have misremembered the details of the Baxter inquiry?'

Hogg took umbrage at the very suggestion, but in truth he was even starting to doubt himself. There had been so many cases in the last few years, but relatively few had involved firearms. He had not been the officer who recovered the gun and, indeed, had never even seen it. So was it possible his memory was playing tricks on him? Yes, it was. But then again, he felt so sure of it.

He tried to recall who else had worked the case but drew a blank. He knew he could consult the records, but he decided to do that on his own time in case it might be construed as a sign of his submission. Instead, he ignored Cuthbert's question and refocused the group's attention.

'Perhaps we should turn our thoughts to the pistol found in Goldberg's room. It would be useful if Dr Morgenthal could examine that and either rule it in or out as the murder weapon.'

Morgenthal nodded enthusiastically, but when Hogg

suggested that the young man go and collect it from Bob Armitage in the police archive, Cuthbert intervened.

'Dr Morgenthal is going to be very busy tomorrow morning with me. Might I propose that the gun be delivered here to the mortuary by W.P.C. Anderson?'

All was agreed, and Morgenthal found Cuthbert's protectiveness touching, if unnecessary.

*

When the gun arrived the following morning, Morgenthal's first look at it confirmed that it was a German Luger 9mm P08. It was in quite a state, however, and he wondered if it could have been safely fired so recently.

He unclipped the magazine from the hand grip and found it to be empty. Looking down the barrel there were accumulations of grease and dirt, and the toggle was stiff and almost jammed when he attempted to pull it back.

W.P.C. Anderson had asked to remain and watch the examination. As she observed Morgenthal deftly and expertly handling the gun, she was impressed with his knowledge. He talked her through everything he was doing at length and was pleased to have such a captive audience. Usually, he was the one being taught, but it felt rather good now to be the teacher.

'So what you're saying, sir, is that you think this could not have been fired within the last seven days.'

'Precisely, constable. I mean, look at the dirt in the mechanism alone. That's built up over quite some time. I would say no one has cleaned this particular gun for months, probably years. It is unmistakably the right make and model for our murder weapon, but this gun didn't kill anyone, at least not recently.'

Anderson took the information back with her to headquarters, where she told Sergeant Hogg. He was pleased that

Goldberg had told him the truth about not firing the gun, but he still intended to give the young man a hard time for having it in his possession in the first place. He arranged for him to be brought up from the cells and placed again in the interview room. This time he asked Anderson to join him, so she could hear his explanation firsthand.

'We meet again, son. I hope your little stay with us has made you think about the trouble you're in.'

Goldberg was hunched in the chair. No one had ill-treated him, but another night in the cells had certainly focused his mind. Any bravado he had three days before was now long gone.

'Where did you get the gun?'

'It was my father's. He brought it back from the war, and it was always in the house. Up high, so we couldn't play with it. He died a while back and, well, I took it. I thought . . . I don't really know what I thought . . . maybe that it might be useful, that it might look good on the protests. You know, put the fear of God into some of them. I never had any bullets, and I don't think I'd even know how to use it. Honestly. I'm sorry. I should've told you about it.'

Hogg took some quick notes as Goldberg spoke and then fell silent. The young man was used to the sergeant's silences now, and he was in no hurry to talk just to fill the space. He looked across the table at Anderson, who was clearly finding him nothing like the young firebrand she had expected. He half smiled at the young woman the way any young man might, albeit in different circumstances.

'Let's put the gun aside and go back to the bombing. I'll be quite frank with you, son. I don't think you had anything to do with it. But you're going to have to help me convince my boss of that fact. So let's get to work.'

Anderson could see the tears of relief welling up in Goldberg's eyes only to be blinked back hard. Hogg reviewed every detail of his partially written statement from the day before and asked him now to complete it.

Objectively, Hogg knew that without any physical evidence it would be almost impossible to charge Goldberg with setting the bomb. Equally, he knew that given the young man was present at the rally, it would be very difficult for him to prove that he hadn't.

There was undoubtedly motive, but perhaps it was not nearly as strong as Hogg had made out in the last session. After all, the lad had a gun, and if he'd wanted Henderson dead, he could have shot him, and that would have been much less messy. Why indeed would Goldberg want to put his own people in danger by using explosives?

None of the Jewish Socialist League had been killed, but that had been more to do with luck than anything else. The case was weak against the boy, and Hogg knew he would be releasing him, but not before he had garnered every detail that he could about what happened that night.

Later, outside the interview room, Hogg asked Anderson her opinion.

'He wasn't lying in there, sir. I was watching him very closely. He didn't do it, and I don't think he would know who did. I thought he would have been a tougher nut though.'

'There's not many that stay that tough in there, constable. I've seen some right hard men greeting like weans over the years. C'mon, we've got to get all this written up. The D.C.I. will need a copy and Dr Cuthbert. Trouble is, is we've got too many bosses. Plays havoc with my paperwork, so it does.'

Anderson smiled and took the notebook from her sergeant. 'Why don't you just leave it with me, sir?'

*

The next morning, Hogg met Cuthbert at the gates of Glasgow Green. Since the night of the bombing, the park had been cordoned off and patrolled twenty-four hours a day by uniformed officers. Now that the forensic investigation had shifted to the mortuary, it was time to sign off the site for reopening and clearing.

Cuthbert walked with Sergeant Hogg to the site he had first seen over a week ago. That time the smell of the explosive had been fresh in the air and the sharp tang of charred flesh had elicited painful memories in both men. What had been covered in grey ash then was now a softer grey, with the sleet that had been falling for days. Cuthbert looked around the empty site and shook his head.

While he was surveying the bomb crater for the last time, over at the perimeter rope a young girl tugged on the trouser leg of the constable who was standing guard. He looked down, but it was her older sister who spoke.

'We need to see the big man. Wee Greta here found it.'

The small girl looked affronted and folded her arms with a scowl. 'I told you, Jessie, my name's Margaret.'

'Aye right, hen.' Jessie looked up at the policeman. 'Well, are you going to get him?'

'Everybody's very busy here, so away with the pair of you.'

Margaret pulled at her sister's sleeve, 'Tell him what I found. Go on.'

'Greta found a gun. So there.'

The constable looked sternly at the 12-year-old. She had the same bright blue eyes as her little sister, but she was even more haughty.

'Give it to me, and I'll see he gets it.'

'Away and raffle yourself. D'you think our mammy knitted us. We'll give it to the man with the shiny shoes or nobody.'

The constable grew tired of negotiating with the two

children and made to seize the brown paper bag Margaret was clutching. Both of them screamed and kept on screaming, forcing him to take a step back.

Cuthbert heard the commotion and looked over. He recognised the girl who had commented on his boots and strode over to the perimeter rope, grasping the constable's arm just as he was about to slap the older girl.

'Constable, what's the meaning of this?'

The young officer mumbled some incoherent reply, and Cuthbert looked to the girls for some explanation.

The smaller of the two elbowed her older sister. 'Tell him, Jessie.'

Cuthbert remembered the little girl's eyes and was once again charmed by her serious expression. 'Ah, it's Margaret, is it not?'

'See,' she said to her sister, who was in no mood for any more games and just sighed.

'Greta found a gun. Under the trees, down by the water. It was in the slush but it's quite clean. The wean said you would want it, so here it is.'

'A gun? Are you sure?'

'D'you no think we know what a gun looks like, mister.' And turning to her little sister, 'I thought you said he had shiny shoes. His boots are aw muddy. And he doesn't believe us anyway.'

'You should take a look, mister. Here.' Margaret handed him the paper bag, and Cuthbert looked inside. It was unmistakably a German Luger.

'Margaret, can you show me exactly where you found this? It's very important.'

'Aye. But will you gie us a penny, if I do?'

'I'll give you a sixpence each if you show me. That's how important it is.'

The girls' eyes widened, already imagining spending their reward on candy balls and liquorice sticks at Glickmann's sweet shop, and they nodded. Margaret took Cuthbert's hand and led him across the grass to the riverbank.

*

After Morgenthal examined the gun, he confirmed that it was a Luger 9mm P08 and could well be the murder weapon. He offered to rig up a test-firing so that a comparison could be made with the shell recovered from McDiarmid.

'Can you do that here, Simon?'

'Certainly, sir. I just need some sandbags and a few metal brackets and clamps. Alternatively, I could use the water tank method. The Americans are using that with very good results. It shouldn't be too difficult to set up in the university. I might have to improvise if they don't have a comparator microscope, but one way or another, I'll get an answer for you, sir.'

'Apart from the barrel markings is there any other way to identify the pistol?'

'Yes. Lugers all have manufacturer marks as well as acceptance marks showing who used them – you know, army, navy, police and so on. They also have unique serial numbers on the main component parts, if they've not been scratched off that is. Are you thinking it might be a known weapon?'

'If it were Scotland Yard, I would be more hopeful, but I have to say I am still surprised by the lack of ballistics expertise here in Glasgow. But C.I.D. must surely have such records. Can I leave that with you to follow up?'

Morgenthal nodded. Like Ogilvie, he took a keen interest in ballistics, and it was an area of forensics he had been studying. To be given charge of this part of the investigation made all the unpleasantness when he arrived worth it.

Morgenthal took the gun to the university to examine it

the following morning. After brushing off some leaf mould sticking to the oil in the mechanism, he checked for any residual fingerprints on the barrel, but found nothing usable.

He proceeded to polish and oil the gun with care, revealing its high-quality blue steel finish. He checked for the presence of serial numbers and found clear matching stamps showing '15026' on the bottom of the barrel, the front of the frame and the left side of the receiver.

As expected, he also found an abbreviated serial number consisting of the last two digits on the smaller component parts of the pistol, including the breechblock and the trigger.

Although not a unique identifier, he also spotted a small, ornate stamp on the toggle at the top of the pistol consisting of the three intertwined letters 'D', 'W' and 'M'. He knew this was the manufacturer's mark for *Deutsche Waffen und Munitionsfabriken*, a Berlin company that produced around half of all the Luger pistols used by the German army during the war. It was also the same abbreviation he had found on the brass cartridge recovered at the scene.

He held the pistol in his hand, feeling its weight and the comfort of the grip, then turned it to allow the light to catch the polished grooves. He held it at arm's length to look down the barrel, using the sight to find his imaginary target.

Morgenthal knew it had been used to kill, and probably more than once, but despite what Sergeant Hogg had said, he could not help admiring the beauty of the craftsmanship. The more he read about firearms, the more fascinated he became with their design. He knew Cuthbert had only a perfunctory interest in ballistics, and, understandably, like most of his generation, had no love of guns at all, so Morgenthal could see an opportunity where he might be able to complement his mentor's knowledge and perhaps even excel.

Now that the pistol was clean and safe to use, Morgenthal

built his temporary firing range from sandbags in one of the small laboratories at the university department. The magazine housed in the pistol grip still contained six bullets, and it was a straightforward procedure to fire two of them into the sandbag wall he had constructed.

As he pulled the trigger, he felt the sharp jolt of the gun in his hand. The spent brass casing ejected from the mechanism flew back and hit him on the chest. For his second shot, he held the gun at full arm's length, and this time the casing was ejected safely onto the floor beside him.

He recovered the two brasses and carefully bagged them. He then spent the next half-hour excavating the bullets from the sandbags. Just as Ogilvie had exercised great care when retrieving the bullet from McDiarmid's brain in case he altered the markings caused by the firing, Morgenthal now avoided the use of any sharp tools that might do the same with the test firings.

If he hoped to find a conclusive match between the bullet that killed McDiarmid and one of these, he could not afford to damage them. He also could not repeat the tests for he knew that the tell-tale striations caused by firing could change very subtly with every three to five bullets fired from any gun.

Now that he had the test-fired bullets, he had to do the comparison, which required a microscopic analysis of the shells. Much to his delight, Mathieson surprised Morgenthal by showing him the recently acquired comparator microscope that was still sitting unused in the corner of his own lab.

Morgenthal collected the bullet that had killed McDiarmid and mounted it on one of the microscope stages. He then mounted the first of the test firings on the other, adjusted the position of the bullets so as to align their orientations and viewed both stages simultaneously through the optical bridge that linked the two microscopes.

What he saw through the eyepieces was a split image, with one bullet on the left and the other immediately beside it on the right at the same magnification. While looking down the microscope he made small adjustments to the position of the bullets to bring their respective markings into alignment.

As he studied the two bullets, it was immediately obvious that there was a match. He completed the analysis by attaching the camera and photographing the comparison. He also compared the brass casings from the test-firing with the one recovered from the scene. Again, there was no mistaking the similarity of the marks made by the gun's firing pin on the heads.

He locked away the gun securely before preparing his written report for Cuthbert.

*

The following morning, Morgenthal collected the developed photographs and made his way with the evidence bags and the gun to the city mortuary. When he arrived, he made straight for the pinboard and added details of the new evidence.

Cuthbert came in from the laboratory area where he had been working on the last of the body parts recovered from the scene. It was all but impossible now to assign the remaining nondescript fragments to any one body and the pathologist was feeling disappointed that he had failed some of the victims. When he saw Morgenthal, his spirits lifted. 'Good news?'

'Indeed, sir.'

'Wait there, I want to call in Dr Ogilvie. I know he shares your interest in ballistics.'

The young pathologist joined Cuthbert and Morgenthal and tried to look as if he was pleased to be there.

'It was Dr Ogilvie who recovered the bullet from the head, of course,' said Cuthbert. 'Without his dexterity you might not have had anything to work with.'

'Only too happy to be of some small service, sir.'

Ogilvie, however, looked far from happy. Morgenthal had wondered what he had done to incur such peevishness, but now he realised that it was just a case of old-fashioned jealousy. He resolved to say something later to try to sort it out. Now, however, he had evidence to present.

'I used the Goddard technique, sir, and I'm pleased to say we have a match.'

'Ah, Goddard, remember I told you about him, Dr Ogilvie. You've heard of Calvin Goddard, Simon?'

'Of course, sir. No one has made a greater contribution to forensic ballistics. He was the co-inventor of the comparator microscope, you know, and when it comes to the identification of bullets, he reminds us that "no two objects, either of God's or man's fabrication—"'

'"—are ever identical in detail." Yes, a truly remarkable man indeed.'

Morgenthal showed the comparative photographs he had pinned to the board and talked the pair through the detailed matching of the markings on the bullets.

'So I conclude that the Luger recovered on Glasgow Green is definitely the one used to fire the bullet that killed McDiarmid. I have my full report here for you, sir.'

'Excellent work. We finally seem to be getting somewhere.'

'And where's that?' Ogilvie, who had been listening in silence, now spoke up. 'I mean, yes, you've matched a gun to a bullet, but since it was a ditched weapon, you have no way of linking it to any suspect. Anyone could have tossed it away that night. I don't doubt your expertise, but I really can't see that it takes you any closer to understanding what happened.'

Cuthbert thought Ogilvie's tone petty and unnecessary. The man should have been interested to see the outcome of Simon's work, but now he could see that he was annoyed.

The young man's behaviour struck him as unprofessional, but before he had a chance to rebuke Ogilvie, Morgenthal piped up.

'You know, Dr Cuthbert, Dr Ogilvie makes a very good point, one I think it is worth addressing. Perhaps we might go over the findings together and see if we can extract any more information. In fact, Dr Ogilvie and I could put our heads together now and let you return to your work.'

A distracted Cuthbert left them to it and went back to the thankless task of scrutinising the remaining body parts.

'Did you just save my bacon, Morgenthal?'

'Nothing of the sort. I just think we might have got off on the wrong foot. Thought it might be good to clear the air a little without the grown-ups in the room.'

Ogilvie smiled and shook his head. 'I envy you, you know. Working with him, that is. He's remarkable, isn't he? So interested in it all and so knowledgeable about everything. It's all rather different here. There's no support or mentorship. We do what we can, but there's only so far you can get on your own.'

'Well, if you don't mind my saying, you seem to have got pretty far. I'm well aware of your knowledge of this field, and I know Dr Cuthbert was very impressed with your evaluation of the gunshot wound and the retrieval of the bullet. And as for your fieldwork–'

'Oh, stop! He's never said anything about my fieldwork. You know, I was really hoping he would take the job.'

'Job?'

'You didn't know? That's why he's in Glasgow. Glaister's chair of forensic medicine. The dean's been headhunting him, and if it wasn't for old Glaister hanging around the department like the ghost of Christmas past, we might have stolen Cuthbert from you. But don't worry, it's not going to happen. You'll have him back in London, but make sure you look after him because I don't imagine this will be the last university that comes calling.'

Ogilvie patted Morgenthal on the shoulder, told him he was sorry for his childishness over the last couple of days and went back to his work.

Sitting alone now at Cuthbert's desk, Morgenthal realised just how much he did not want to lose Cuthbert, and he understood precisely why Ogilvie had reacted the way he had.

He had known nothing about the job in Glasgow, and he began to wonder how Cuthbert might have told him if he had accepted it. He also began to wonder if Madame Smith knew, and quickly he realised that of course she did.

*

In the duty room at police headquarters, Hogg was doing his own wondering. He had reached a brick wall in the case and could find no traction to get himself going again.

As he looked through the files in front of him there were no obvious leads and no suspects for the bombing or the shooting now that he had put the idea of Davie Goldberg to bed. He went back to the Mary Callan interview statement written up by W.P.C. Anderson.

Rab McDiarmid was in the Brigton Boys, and they were there that night, so how does one of them get himself shot in the head? There were too many unanswered questions, but he thought one place he might start asking them was with the gang leader himself.

He called his constable and arranged for Alec Jamieson to be brought in. 'He's been here that many times, I'm sure his boots could find their way in all by themselves, but maybe you can go and give him a helping hand.'

*

The next afternoon, Alec Jamieson was picking his teeth when Hogg and Anderson entered the room. He was smartly dressed, his grey bunnet lying on the table beside him.

He looked up and winked at the constable. 'Well, they're sure gettin' better-lookin' since the last time I was in this place. How's it goin', doll?'

'Mr Jamieson, this is W.P.C. Anderson, I'm Detective Sergeant Hogg and we would like to ask you about the night of ninth February.'

'Why, what happened then?' He giggled like a cheeky little child. 'Shouldn't laugh about it, should I? Terrible affair, so it was.'

'Where were you that night, Jamieson?'

'Is it no Mr Jamieson now? I was at home mindin' my own business.'

'In Bridgeton?'

'The very same, and a lovely part o' the world it is.'

'Your gang members were present in force at the political rally on Glasgow Green. Why weren't you with them?'

'I don't know what you mean. Gang? I'm no in any gang. You must have me mixed up with some other handsome fella.'

'You run the Brigton Boys, son, so don't come the smart arse with us. Your lads were actin' as Henderson's bodyguard. So where were you?'

'Och, now that I think about it, I did hear somethin' about the Green that night. Now what was it? Oh, aye, *boom!*'

He giggled again, and Hogg repeated his question, unaffected by the man's antics.

'I wisnae there. I told you already: I was at home.'

'You lost men that night, Jamieson. Three of them killed

and five still in the infirmary. Are you not keen to find out who did it?'

'Folk died, right enough. Hell of a thing. But sometimes that's the way it is in a war.'

'Is that what you think this is, a war?'

'Aye. The streets are no safe, and we need to take them back. Take back control. Clean up the filth.'

'But it was the man saying all that who got killed.'

'Like I say, that's the way it is in a war.'

Hogg doubted Alec Jamieson had any political conviction beyond caring for number one, and he wondered where all this was coming from. He had interviewed him on two previous occasions and both times he'd had solid alibis placing him miles from the scenes of the crimes in question. However, both times Hogg knew that he was as guilty as anyone he had ever met.

The man was a vicious, indiscriminate thug who slashed his way through the East End of Glasgow. He was an extortionist, a racketeer and a pimp. It was only of late that he had formed any connection with the world of politics.

Recently, there had been a picture of him published in the press, walking side by side with Oswald Mosley on Glasgow Green of all places, and it was clear to all which end of the political spectrum he was inhabiting. The right-wing's anti-Semitism aligned perfectly with the extremist views of the likes of the Protestant League, also supported by the Brigton Boys.

Jews as well as Catholics were their targets now and regularly received the full brunt of their razor-sharp forms of justice. But none of this added up when it came to the bombing. The Brigton Boys were there to defend Henderson, not to see him killed. Jamieson had failed publicly and spectacularly in doing the job. Why, then, was he making light of it? Hogg knew that reputation to these men was, after all, everything.

'Do you have a gun?'

'Naw, we don't use guns. Guns are for cowards; real men use knives. With a knife you have to get up close to your man, and you have to look him in the eyes when you're sticking him . . . so they tell me. What would I know about it?'

Without warning, the door of the interview room opened, and a figure tailored expensively in black swept in. The man was silver-haired, in his sixties, and his eyewear placed him in a different era.

He put a document on the table and straightened it so that it lay directly in front of Sergeant Hogg.

'Carlton of Carlton, Hicks and Blake. My client, Mr William Jamieson, is being questioned without my knowledge, and I demand that you desist immediately. Failure to do so will result in a suit against you and your commanding officers for harassment and failure to follow due process. I'm waiting.'

He stood beside Alec Jamieson, who looked up at the man from his seated position and then smiled at Hogg. 'Looks the part, doesn't he?'

Hogg had never encountered this particular brief, but he knew the type well. He had not once looked at his client, let alone spoken with him, and Hogg doubted they had ever met. Besides, he was too expensive for Jamieson's pocket, so who was paying for him?

'Well, sergeant, I'm waiting . . .'

'Sir, Mr Jamieson has come here today voluntarily and has agreed to answer our questions relating to a very serious matter. He is not under arrest, and he is free to leave at any time. I would, however, appreciate his continued co-operation in this case.'

'Are you pressing charges against my client? No? Then I think that concludes our business here, gentlemen. We'll find our own way out.'

Alec Jamieson departed just as cockily as he had arrived. With a smirk he put on his bunnet and gave a sarcastic salute to the sergeant.

'So long, auld yin. If I don't see you through the week, maybe I'll see you through the window.'

Still laughing at his joke, he was encouraged out of the room by his lawyer.

Hogg sat back in his chair and looked across at the empty seat. Anderson, who had been beside Hogg throughout the interview, asked, 'What are you thinking, sir?'

'About Jamieson? Oh, he's involved. That wee toerag is a career criminal, and he doesn't give a damn if we know he's guilty. I'm surprised he didn't just come out and confess it right there and then. He would've enjoyed it, along with the fact that we could do bugger all about it. What I don't know though is, why? It's not their style – a bomb, I mean. And he was right, they don't use guns. So where does it all leave us?'

'Perhaps we need to get all our heads together around Dr Cuthbert's case board at the mortuary, sir.'

Hogg snorted. 'You know, I never thought I'd say this, but maybe you're right. Let's go and see what the brains of Scotland Yard can come up with.'

*

In the mortuary office, the two pathologists and the two police officers huddled around Cuthbert's desk in front of the board.

'So let's start from the beginning. What do we have, sergeant?'

With the aid of the photographs on the board, the map of the site and the various pieces of string that had been pinned between different items to emphasise their connection, Hogg proceeded to outline the case as it stood.

'We have a bombing on Glasgow Green and associated

mass murder of twenty-four men, women and children, at the centre of which we believe is a targeted political assassination of a known right-wing anti-Semite – Alistair Henderson, a prospective Member of Parliament for the New Party. In addition, we have the shooting and killing of Rab McDiarmid, member of the Brigton Boys, a lawless gang of thugs known for their anti-Catholic and more recently anti-Semitic targeting. This shooting we believe to have taken place on the Green at approximately the same time as the bombing. We have witnesses who confirm that McDiarmid was alive earlier that day and then present at the rally. The recovery of the gun that fired the fatal shot also supports the idea that he was killed there.'

Cuthbert got to his feet to study the board, looking from the post mortem picture of Rab McDiarmid to the smiling, very much pre mortem photograph of Alistair Henderson.

'Sergeant, I suppose the obvious question is: do we think they are connected – the bombing and the shooting?'

Hogg took his seat again and shrugged. 'Well, you already know my thoughts on coincidence, Dr Cuthbert, so these are not independent crimes. In my view, they are very much one and the same, and I would lay odds that the same man carried out both.'

'All right, I think I would agree with you there, sergeant. So who is that man? What have we got?'

Hogg handed his notebook to Anderson and gestured for her to get up. She hesitated for a moment and then realised he was deadly serious. 'Our initial suspect, sir, Davie Goldberg, leader of the Southside Jewish Socialist League, has been questioned. He owns a Luger, which we now know could not be the murder weapon and therefore makes it very unlikely he would be McDiarmid's killer. He and his group have motive and opportunity to do the bombing, but we have not found any evidence that they had the means. We have questioned a number of the League members, and none has access to that kind of expertise, let alone the materials.'

Cuthbert nodded as he studied Goldberg's mugshot. 'Please go on, constable.'

'Alec Jamieson, the leader of the Brigton Boys, has also been questioned although the interview was terminated by his lawyer—'

Hogg interrupted, 'An expensive brief from a big city law firm, which would be way out of his league. Somebody is looking after our Alec, which makes me think he's got something worth hiding. He's an arrogant little thug and all the more so now because he knows he's got a guardian angel. That one knows nothing's going to stick to him.'

Cuthbert, who was still at the board, scrutinised the mugshot of Alec Jamieson that had been brought from the police files. He was snub-nosed, with bad skin and a sardonic smile.

Hogg continued where Anderson had left off. 'We can't place him at the scene, but he has no one to support his alibi that he was at home at the time of the rally. Although he's been in and out of here many times over the years, he's never been involved in anything with guns or bombs. He's a razor man, and God knows he does enough damage with that. There's also the issue that his own men were killed and injured in the bombing. You have to wonder if he would really do that . . .'

Cuthbert looked at the eyes in the picture and was reasonably sure that he would. He turned to Hogg. 'And there's no way to connect the gun to Jamieson?'

'If I may . . .?' Morgenthal went to the pinboard and began to answer Cuthbert's question. 'The normal tests we might do, like looking for powder residue on a suspect's hands, are useless here because of the time gap. It's been nearly two weeks since the fatal shot was fired, and any evidence will be long gone. And as for fingerprints' – he pointed at the photograph of the Luger pistol on the board – 'it's notoriously difficult to recover prints from the textured grip of a pistol like that or even from the oiled steel of the barrel. Remember too that the gun was found by two small girls – we're more likely to recover their prints than the killer's.'

'What about . . .?' W.P.C. Anderson started to speak and then checked herself. 'Mmm, no. It's stupid.'

'No idea is too stupid to say out loud when we are dealing with a murder investigation. Go ahead, constable, what was it you wanted to say?'

She shifted in her seat as the eyes of the room turned to her, but she had nowhere to hide. 'It's the fingerprints, sir. I know Dr Morgenthal said that none could be recovered from the gun, but I was wondering if that was the only place they might be found.'

Morgenthal looked at Cuthbert, both initially puzzled but both arriving at the same conclusion a second later.

'The bullets,' they said in unison.

'Excellent, constable. Might that be possible, Simon?'

'I haven't touched them since the gun was given to me. I did check the magazine to see if it needed to be cleaned, but it was spotless and contained six bullets. The full complement is eight, so it's likely only a single shot was fired. I fired two more test shots for comparison, so the other four bullets should still be in place. If the killer was the one who loaded the gun, his fingerprints will be on those brass casings. I can get onto it right away.'

Cuthbert asked Morgenthal to proceed and smiled warmly at W.P.C. Anderson as she and Hogg left to return to headquarters.

*

Morgenthal took the gun into the laboratory and unclipped the magazine from the pistol grip to examine it under the strong bench light. There were indeed still four bullets stacked one above the other. As he tilted the magazine and the brass surfaces of the bullet casings caught the light, he thought he could see faint markings.

With a magnifying glass he studied these, and his eyes widened as he realised that they were very possibly finger marks. To recover these, he needed to free the bullets from the gun, but he realised that this evidence could be readily lost. The non-porous nature of the metallic surface made it especially important that care was taken when handling the unused bullets. Otherwise, the marks might be smeared and rendered useless.

In order to release the bullets from the gun, Morgenthal decided to completely dismantle the magazine by releasing the small holding screws. He lifted the top section clear allowing him to hold back the spring mechanism and extract each of the remaining four bullets with forceps and a steady hand.

He laid them carefully on a wad of tissue paper on the bench and assigned each an identification number. Next, again using his forceps, he orientated the bullets so that the faint markings were uppermost. With a soft brush, he dusted each with a fine black powder.

When he blew the excess away he was pleased to see that there were likely to be clear, usable partial marks on three of the bullet casings. He planned to lift these with gelatinous strips, but in case of any damage or distortion in that process, he had them photographed first. The curved nature of the bullet surface made both approaches difficult, but soon he had photographic records as well as stable acquisitions and could move to the next step.

He called police headquarters this time instead of trying to get past their reception in person and asked to speak to the fingerprint technician. He turned out to be a very helpful young man, most unlike Armitage the archivist, who was keen to assist the pathologist.

'All our reference fingerprint cards are held in the Central Criminal Records Office in Glasgow. If you can provide me with the photographs and the marks you've lifted from the bullets, I can work out the Henry Classifications for you and conduct the preliminary search of what's on file.'

'That would be a great help. We will need to take a wide swipe at this, but there are two specific named records I would like to look at in detail first. Could you pull those for me, as well?'

Morgenthal gave the technician the names of Alexander Jamieson and David Goldberg and thanked him for his help. He then proceeded to reassemble the gun's magazine on the bench. He had enjoyed taking it apart and was now getting even more pleasure from putting it back together.

Everything was collected within the hour by a uniformed officer and taken to headquarters, and it was only a few hours after that when the technician called back.

'Excellent news, sir. I have a match with the very first mark to print comparison I tried. That's never happened before. I thought I'd be at this for days.'

Morgenthal took note of the findings in his notebook and after asking some further questions thanked the technician and hung up. He went straight to find Cuthbert who was working at his desk.

'Sir, we have an answer. I have excluded Goldberg – they are definitely not his fingerprints on the bullets. However, there is a positive match for Jamieson. We can conclude that he handled the bullets that were in the magazine of the murder weapon and that he likely loaded the gun.'

Cuthbert leapt up, clapped his hands and went to the pinboard. He took another look at Jamieson's eyes in the small photograph pinned there.

'So we have a direct link between Jamieson and the murder of Rab McDiarmid, one of his own lieutenants. Get Sergeant Hogg, will you, Simon? I think he and I need to pay a visit to my favourite D.C.I.'

*

Hogg met Cuthbert in the foyer of police headquarters, and both expected to be victims of Black's habitual waiting game, but this time they were asked to go straight up.

D.C.I. Black was looking far from his usual relaxed, somewhat detached self. There was noticeably more paperwork on his desk since their last visit, and as they entered, they caught the end of an irate phone call he was having.

As he swore at whoever he was speaking with, he gestured to them to come in and sit down. Hogg had never been invited to sit before in that room, but he was more than happy to take the weight off his feet, even if it was an oversight on the chief inspector's part.

'Right, where the hell are we in all this? I understand I have a bombing, a mass murder, a political assassination and now a fucking homicide. Is that about the size of it?'

'Indeed, chief inspector. Sergeant Hogg and I have been going over all the forensic findings and we thought it best to bring you up to date in person.'

'Just cut to the chase, will you? I know you all like to talk, but everything's piling up here and I've got Harper breathing down my neck.'

'Then I'll be brief. The bombing was undoubtedly a targeted attack on the parliamentary candidate Alistair Henderson. Twenty-three other men, women and children were also killed.

We have no direct leads as to the identity of the bomber, but Sergeant Hogg and I both feel it's too much of a coincidence for it not to be connected with the homicide. Rab McDiarmid, known associate of gang leader Alec Jamieson, was killed with a single gunshot wound to the head. We think he was murdered on the Green at the time of the rally. Fingerprint evidence on the unused bullets in the recovered weapon implicate Alec Jamieson as the killer. I suggest we must also now consider him as the prime suspect in the bombing.'

Black looked at Cuthbert and then at Hogg. He pushed some files aside and leaned forward across his desk. 'That's quite a conclusion. Hogg, I see you've had Jamieson in already for questioning. Have we got enough to arrest him now?'

'I don't think so, sir, especially with that brief of his who'll be all over us if we don't have a watertight case. We can link him to the bullets in the gun, but that doesn't mean he fired them. And as for the bombing, as Dr Cuthbert here says, that's little more than a joint gut feeling and a dislike of coincidence. We can certainly get him back in to assist with our inquiries, but we're going to need more to arrest him.'

'All right, agreed. This is progress though, and finally it's something I can use to get Harper off my back. Keep at it and see if you can nail that bastard.'

Chapter 13

Glasgow: 9 February 1931

The battered old suitcase was small but heavy, and Jamieson carefully put it down to catch his breath while he checked the crowd. He was standing on the edge of the Green looking over towards the monument. The sun had all but set, but there was a good moon, and the gaslights were already going on along the streets.

People were strolling in groups of two and three across the grass and along the gravel paths still damp from the previous night's rain towards the big open space in front of the obelisk. From this distance he could make out the wooden platform where the candidate would speak later, and carried on the air he could hear the song that everyone was humming that week.

He picked up the case and began to croon along himself: 'Good night, sweetheart, till we meet tomorrow. Good night, sweetheart, sleep will banish sorrow.'

As he drew nearer to the platform, he could see the microphone stand, front and centre, and a flight of steps made of rough-cut pine that allowed access to the stage. He pulled his flat cap a little lower over his eyes as he wove through the crowd, making sure not to bump the case against any legs.

When he reached the front, he heard his name being shouted but chose to ignore it. After all, he wasn't supposed to be there at all.

He strode up to the platform openly and confidently. He knew that being furtive only ever attracted attention, and this way anyone in the crowd would simply take him for one of the rally officials.

He went round the side of the structure beside the steps and pulled back the black material that skirted the platform. Underneath was a large damp space. The air was thick with the smell of the cut pine, and there were cables running down from the microphone and along the side, out to a small van parked behind the platform and to the loudspeaker high on the stand to the right. That van was where the gramophone was being played, and it also provided the power for the public address system.

Jamieson was relieved to put the heavy suitcase down again, and he stood for a moment to orientate himself. He positioned himself directly beneath the microphone above and laid the case down flat on the grass in front of him. He knelt on the wet ground and slid the brass clasps, right and left, and gently lifted the lid of the suitcase with both hands.

The bomb was a thing of beauty, he thought. He had had no hand in making it but had been delighted to be given the task of setting it. There had been very clear instructions, the most important of which had been not to drop it, bump it or treat it roughly.

He knew how to be gentle when he had to, and he had treated it like a newborn all the way from his house in Bridgeton. Now, it was up to it to do the job.

He looked over the components – the black cast-iron pipe, sealed at both ends which he knew was filled with twenty-five pounds of army dynamite, the clock, battery and detonator and the delicate, almost flimsy, wires that linked them all together.

He checked his watch and knew he still had a few minutes before he had to set the timer. As he gently closed the lid of the case, he realised he was not alone under the platform. Jamieson turned to see the figure of Rab McDiarmid, breathing heavily.

'You're a hard man to catch, Alec. Did you no hear me shoutin'?'

'What are you doin' here? Should you no be out there getting ready for the bodyguard?'

'Time enough for that. But what are you doin'? What's in the suitcase?'

Alec Jamieson could have pulled rank on the young man, even threatened him, but he thought better of it. Much easier, he thought, if he could just get him out into the crowd but close to the platform, and then in about ten minutes he wouldn't have to worry that he'd been seen.

'Never mind that. Just getting the platform organised for our speaker. Go on now, get yourself out there. And make me proud.'

'Since when did you get your hands dirty? C'mon, what's in the suitcase?'

Rab made for the case and Jamieson blocked him.

'That's enough now. Away you go.'

'Naw, hang on. What's goin' on here?'

Rab was taller and stronger than Alec Jamieson, and he easily prised him off when he lunged for the case again. Rab kicked it open and saw the clock, the wires and black pipe lying diagonally across the case.

Alec hissed at him. 'Fuck's sake, Rab, watch what you're doin!'

'Is that a bomb? What's happening?'

'It's complicated, son. Look, have I ever lied to you? Naw, and I'm no about to start now. This is an insurance policy, that's all. Just in case things go tits up. We're the bodyguard, remember. The Brigton Boys are here to see that nobody gets hurt, at least nobody that's on our side.'

'And how does a bomb do that? This is no right. That's a big yin. If that goes off, it'll take us with it. And anybody on that platform.'

Jamieson checked his watch and his tone changed. 'Look, I'm done arguing. Get to fuck, Rab!'

'Naw. I'm no goin' anywhere. No until you tell me what's happening here.'

'You just couldn't keep your nose out o' it, could you?'

When Jamieson pulled the trigger, the crack was mistaken in the crowd for a firework. People looked over to the platform from where the noise came but could see nothing.

The bullet hit Rab in the forehead and the force pushed him back against one of the platform's wooden supports. He stood for a moment already dead before slumping like a sack thrown down from the back of a coal man.

Jamieson did not bother to check on him and calmly opened the suitcase again. The pipe was capped at both ends, but three wires protruded: one red, one blue and the other black. He attached the blue one to the detonator and the red one to the clock and battery that had been rigged together and tied to the side of the pipe.

Finally, and very carefully as he had been shown, he wrapped the black wire around a screw that had been inserted into the clock mechanism. He adjusted the hands of the clock and set the timer on the alarm for ten minutes.

He checked his watch one last time and flicked the switch. Gingerly, he closed the case and collected the gun from where he had left it on the ground.

He looked over the heap of awkward limbs where they had fallen and frowned. There was surprisingly little blood, he thought, especially compared to the fatal stabbings he was more used to.

He looked at the gun in his hand and shook his head for he much preferred his knives. He wondered briefly about trying to conceal the body but then realised that he could leave that job to the suitcase and its contents. Before he left, he made sure to go back and take Rab's razor from the dead boy's waistcoat pocket. He'd given it to him, and there was no need for that to go to waste as well.

*

Standing beside one of the trees at the edge of the space, Davie Goldberg was waiting, watching the crowd arriving. There were friends chatting, families with children and courting couples walking hand in hand looking for the best spots to watch the proceedings.

He knew most of the people were just there for a good time and a break from the monotony of their sorry lives, but that didn't stop him hating them. Most of those arriving were oblivious to the political agenda about to unfold. And even if they had known, they would have been indifferent, for what was politics to them?

Old men, with pipes drooping from their lips, stood silent and unmoved by the music, expecting little of the evening. They had seen it all before, but still they came to satisfy some inner need that perhaps this time it might be different.

Women swaddling sleeping children in shawls sought some companionship from other mothers and an escape from the house for an hour. Most were there for the fresh air, some distraction from the confines of their tenement rooms, and most had never heard of Alistair Henderson or his cause.

Davie Goldberg knew that was exactly why the rally was being held. He struck a match and cupped it, protecting it from the wind, to relight the half-smoked cigarette he took from the tobacco tin in his pocket. His face was momentarily illuminated in the shadows and Becca saw him.

'I've been looking everywhere for you, Davie. What's the game?'

'Not a game, Becca. Time these bastards were taught a lesson. Sal with you?'

'He's coming. Says he'll bring them.'

'Aye, he'd better this time.'

After joining the Jewish Socialist League, Goldberg had wasted no time in recruiting others from the Gorbals, including his old school friend, Sal, and his wife, Becca.

Now, he turned and stepped back further into the shadows of the trees and bent to collect the bag he had been carrying. Becca followed and helped him take out the folded flags.

'Quite a crowd, Davie. Should be a good chance to get the word out.'

'We'd need more than wee flags to do that. I mean, look at them. This crowd needs a proper wake-up call.'

Becca watched him toss the flags on the ground as he rummaged in the bag looking for something else.

'Where is the bloody thing?'

His shoulders relaxed as his hands found the gun at the bottom of the bag. He took it out, and as Becca caught sight of the pistol, she jerked back.

'Davie! What are you thinking? That's not the way. That's not what we are.'

'I'm not about to blow somebody's brains out. We just need to get their attention, that's all.'

'I don't like it, Davie.'

Goldberg put the pistol in his pocket, out of sight, and looked about to see if anyone was in earshot. He smiled at Becca and tried again to reassure her.

'There. It's away. Just forget about it. Where the hell's that man of yours?'

Becca was also becoming concerned that her husband had still not arrived. She scanned the path leading up from the suspension bridge over the river. That would be the way he would be coming from the Gorbals.

The light was poor, and with so many people now converging from every direction, it was all but impossible to find a single face in the crowd. Then she spotted the shuffling gait of her husband. He was moving awkwardly carrying what looked to be a very heavy load.

Sal Finkelstein arrived under the trees, where they had arranged to meet, panting for breath. He threw the weighty duffel bag he was carrying from his aching shoulder to the ground and looked for Davie, who was standing scowling behind him.

'Sorry, sorry. I couldn't get away. But I brought them.'

'As if this isn't hard enough, Sal. You always have to take everything to the wire. Get them unpacked and dish them out. It'll be starting soon.'

Davie was tense and angry. He was forced to work with people he thought of as soft and uncommitted, because they were all he had. Trying to get the chapter of the Socialist League all pointing in the same direction was a difficult and thankless task, and it had taken him nearly eighteen months since he took over the leadership from Josh to get them to this point.

He had organised many smaller protests to shout down fascist speakers, but this was by far the biggest operation. For one thing, Becca was right: this crowd was larger than any before.

The New Party was better organised and probably better funded than any of the others, and Goldberg knew that meant it would be the biggest threat. Tonight, they had to make their voices heard over the speaker. They had to show this crowd that they were being sold a pack of lies. But first he had to get his own troops rallied.

'Listen up, everybody. That bastard Henderson is going to be talking in a minute. Spouting his hate. He wants a different world – one that you don't have any place in. If it was up to him, you'd be deported just to keep the streets of Govanhill clean. Or, worse, he'd save the time and money and just have you all put down. He'd drown you in that river, like a bag of kittens. To him, you're a bunch of animals. Worse than that, you're vermin. Are we going to let him talk? Well, are we?'

The seven other members of the Jewish Socialist League shouted their collective 'no', but without the fervour Goldberg wanted. His face was enough to make them shout it louder and longer till he looked satisfied.

'So what are we waiting for? Get the flags up in the trees, lads. Becca, grab one of those hammers from Sal's bag and start making a racket. Bash it against this.' He handed her a sheet of metal from the duffel bag to use as a makeshift cymbal. 'Josh, you take a hammer too and one of those bars. Have we any more banners? They're no use sitting there in the bag. C'mon, get them up!'

There was a scurry of activity in the trees, and those in the crowd nearby strained to read the lettering on the homemade banners as they unfurled from the branches. However, 'J.S.L.' meant nothing to most, and they turned their attention back to the platform and the stirring of the crowd in front of them who had seen the candidate's big black car arrive.

By the time Henderson was getting out, Jamieson was on the other side of the Green, having eased his way anonymously through the crowd. His lieutenants were all around, and he had given them their instructions earlier in the day – to surround the platform in an obvious show of force looking outward to the crowd, razors on display.

He knew they wouldn't all make it home that night, but that was just the way it was: everyone was expendable. And martyrs were always the best recruiting tools.

He stood back, well away from the platform, and watched as the crowd surged forward to get a better view of Henderson climbing the steps up to the stage. He certainly looked the part; he had dressed to be distinctive and easily seen in a light summer suit of pale grey, almost white.

His amber and black rosette could be seen from the back of the crowd, standing out against his jacket like an oversized bumble bee, even if his face could not. Jamieson had never met the man and knew that now he never would. There was nothing personal in what was about to happen: it was just politics.

Henderson raised both his arms, waved to the crowd and received equal measures of adulation and derision in return. All speakers on the Green, whatever their stripe, had to accept the ambivalence of the Glaswegians, but it was a lesson this candidate had still to learn.

He looked uneasy and nervous, having been led to believe by his minders that he could expect an easy ride. Amid the cheers and jeers, Davie Goldberg ordered everyone up into the trees, so that they could be seen and heard by the crowd.

Jamieson was behind the trees at this point and watched a girl hitching up her skirt to climb up onto one of the branches to join the other protesters. He bent to pick up a half-brick lying on the grass, and as soon as they started their racket, he lobbed it with all the force he could at the girl. It missed her, but the shock caused her to lose her balance, and she tumbled from the branch.

The crowd whooped when they saw her fall and two of

the League's young men rushed to her aid. Her nose was bleeding badly, and the front of her dress was spattered with blood. Those who were close enough to see her injuries started shouting that the lassie was hurt.

Jamieson smiled and merged further into the background, edging away from the trees but still keeping the platform in view. He heard a squeal through the loudspeaker and the laughter of the crowd at Henderson's expense.

His boys started moving through the heaving throng to the front as planned, so that Henderson could point out the strength of his well-armed bodyguard to the crowd. As expected, they were dressed in their three-piece suits, making good use of their waistcoat pockets as holsters for their cut-throat razors. The Brigton Boys always put on a good show and that's what Jamieson had ordered.

A uniformed sergeant who had instructed his men to keep a low profile at the event saw the movement and recognised the manoeuvre and swore under his breath. He blew three short, sharp blasts on his whistle and was joined by two of his constables.

'How many men have we got here?'

'Six, sergeant.'

'And a crowd o' nearly five hundred with women and weans! Now that fuckin' gang's here as well. How the hell did this rally get the go-ahead? Fan out and keep an eye on the Brigton Boys. I'm no havin' a blood bath on my watch. Go.'

Jamieson, satisfied that everyone was now in position and his work was done, turned away to leave, reaching the road just as the flash happened.

Earlier, when he had thought about what it would be like, he had imagined screams and wailing, but after the heavy thud of the shockwave hit him from behind and knocked him down, he heard nothing. He was unhurt and got up quickly, the ringing in his ears slowly subsiding. Looking back, there was just a cloud of smoke and dust where the rally had been, and already there were fires, but apart from the crackle of burning pine there was silence.

It was several moments later that the screams came – piercing shrieks of agony as people felt for their missing limbs and found jagged splinters of wood sticking out of their sides. Those furthest from the blast were rising from the ground now, as Jamieson had done, and were starting to crawl, to walk and then to run in every direction.

Some were seeking help; some were seeking safety. Jamieson put his hand in his pocket and felt the heavy metal of the pistol he had forgotten about and instinctively knew that he needed to get rid of it.

As cover, he ran with the crowd, shouting like them for help, even shouting for the police, and quickly found himself near the river. He took the gun and made to throw it out into the middle of the Clyde, but his aim was as clumsy as when he had lobbed the brick, and it hit the stout branch of a tree.

It deflected the gun, which dropped into the gloom below. In all the noise that was now surrounding him, he was unsure whether there had been a splash or not, but either way he had no way of finding the gun in the dark undergrowth.

He made his way east from the Green along London Road. At first, he ran, but then he slowed to a brisk walking pace and eventually a leisurely evening saunter. He wanted to make sure no one would mistake him for anything other than a weary man on his way home from work.

He reached Bridgeton Cross, but he did not want to be seen wearing the shabby, old clothes he had donned to set the bomb. He went up the first close he came to and through to the back court. He crossed over the railings between the courts until he reached his patch on Franklin Street.

When he got to his house, he changed into his good suit and oiled his hair. He smoked a slow cigarette before setting out again on the streets of Bridgeton to allow the news to spread.

By the time he wandered up past the Umbrella, word had reached every door that there had been a bombing on the Green. This time he made himself conspicuous and people came up to him to ask what he knew and what could be done.

They told him some of his lads were there and had likely been hurt. He expressed his concern, offered to help any woman who was widowed and vowed his revenge. It was as much as anyone expected from the leader of the Brigton Boys.

After an hour or more of making himself visible, he again slunk into the shadows and found the phone box. He had the number he was to call and gave it to the operator.

'Is it done?'

'Just as we planned.'

'You mean as I planned, don't you, Alec? Let's not overstretch. Your time will come. I gave you my word on that and intend to honour it. You've made Alistair Henderson a martyr to the cause. They'll probably write songs about him now – you did that for him. In fact, what you did tonight gave him immortality. That's more valuable than any seat in a corrupt parliament controlled by Jews. It's a pity, but there always have to be sacrifices for the sake of politics. It's the price we pay, isn't it? Now, don't use this number again, and if you've written it down anywhere, destroy it. Clear?'

'What's next?'

'Just go about your business, but don't come looking for me. I'll find you if I need you.'

The receiver clicked, and he sighed, fingering the razor in his waistcoat pocket, already dreaming of the next big step up the ladder for Alec Jamieson.

Chapter 14

Glasgow: 23 February 1931

On the walk back down the Saltmarket to the mortuary, after their meeting with D.C.I. Black, Hogg took the opportunity of having Cuthbert to himself to tell him his own news.

'When you asked me if I could have been mistaken about the gun, sir, I don't mind telling you, I was black affronted. But, to tell you the truth, my memory isn't as good as it was, so I did some digging.

'Big Jim Calder was the other sergeant on the case at the time. I had to check the records for the Baxter case, but he was the one whose men found the gun. I spoke to him, and his memory was much clearer than mine. He remembered it was a Luger, and it was recovered among the possessions of John Burns, who went down for the shooting.

'Jim said he saw the gun himself, tagged it for the evidence room and put it in there. But it's gone now, and any record of it has also been removed from the files. And what worries me is that the only people who would have access to it are those inside the force.'

Cuthbert stopped. 'How would an officer be able to access

a gun in the evidence room, sergeant?'

'Evidence is retrieved all the time, for different reasons, so it wouldn't be unusual, but there would be paperwork. You'd have to sign it out.'

'So...'

'So there should be a paper trail. If you don't mind, sir, I'll take a walk back to the station. I think I need to have a word with Bob Armitage and check his books.'

At the mention of Armitage's name, Cuthbert bristled, but he knew now was not the time or the place to say what he thought of the man.

'By all means do so, sergeant. But if I may say, do be careful. If what you say is correct, not everyone in that building can be trusted.'

'I'm well aware of that, sir. I'll see you at the office later.'

Now, freed from the restraints of a walking companion, Cuthbert strode quickly down to the mortuary at his customary pace and was there within five minutes.

*

In the evidence room at headquarters, Hogg watched the slow wheeling gait of Armitage as he clicked his way from the far end of the room.

'Bob, are you all on your own the day?'

'Aye, I am that. The boy's on his day release at the college. Bloody waste o' time if you ask me. His head's full o' lassies with no room for anything else. Anyway, what can I do for you?'

'Just dotting the 'I's and crossing the 'T's on the Wullie Baxter shooting. Somebody asked about the gun, but I think it was signed out. Who would have done that?'

Armitage retrieved a dark blue leather ledger from the shelf beside the counter and placed it on the counter. He flipped through the pages, running a finger down the columns of the yellow pages.

'Oh aye, here it is. Seventeenth November last year. Handgun, Luger P08. Serial number 15026. God, my eyes are terrible. I can't make that out. Here . . .'

He swivelled the ledger round for Hogg to read and pointed at the scrawled signature that was causing him so much bother.

'Grand. Thanks for your help, Bob. That ties things up nicely. I hope you get your assistant back afore long.'

Armitage shrugged. He closed the heavy tome before turning to make the long trek back to his cubbyhole. Hogg considered going straight back to Cuthbert at the mortuary, but instead decided to go upstairs first.

*

When Cuthbert went into the office, Morgenthal was gathering his things together. Now that the ballistics investigation was completed, Cuthbert was keen that his assistant should return to London.

'You've been away from your family for too long, Simon. Take the overnight train to London this evening and surprise Sarah and the baby first thing.'

'But, sir, there are still reports to be filed.'

'No, no, Simon, you've done more than enough here. It's time for others to step forward. As for the final report, that will be my responsibility. The forensic investigation is over. We have given names back to most of those who died, and, thanks to you, we have given the police all the physical evidence they are likely to get regarding the shooting. Thank you for coming to Glasgow; it meant a great deal to me.'

'You know I would do anything for you, sir.'

'Nonsense, laddie. Never promise anyone that. Now get yourself back to that family of yours.'

Morgenthal was almost ready to leave when he looked into the laboratory to find Ogilvie. He was sitting on a stool at the bench in the corner reading.

'That's me off, then. Out of your hair at last.'

Ogilvie looked up from his book and rose at once to say his goodbyes to Morgenthal, who said, 'Look, I was thinking. This might not be your cup of tea, but I wondered if we might keep in touch. I know I'm in London and you're here in Glasgow, but it's just a railway line apart after all and there's always the telephone.

'The thing is, we're going through this together, not just now but for the rest of our lives. In twenty years' time we'll still be working in forensic medicine, and I think we need all the allies we can gather about us. It's not an easy profession, is it?'

Morgenthal started to blush, feeling suddenly self-conscious and a little silly, but Ogilvie looked at him with a renewed warmth.

'I just think it would be good sometimes to have someone to talk to who understands exactly what it's like, maybe to share the worries and the woes. Goodness, what you must think of me. I don't know what I sound like.'

'You sound like a friend, and I can't think of anything I would like better than to keep in touch. I'm planning a trip to London later in the spring – there's a conference at the Royal Society of Medicine – and if you're not too busy, perhaps we could have lunch or even just a coffee if time is pressing.'

'Nonsense! If you're coming to London, you'll be staying with Sarah and me. We have plenty of space and it'll be so much nicer than staying in some ghastly hotel. I could show you round St Thomas's, if you like. Here's my card. It has my home number on it. I shall expect you.'

'Thank you. I don't really deserve this after the way I treated you.'

'Oh, if the boot had been on the other foot, I suspect I might have been a tad jealous too. I'll leave you to your book. What was so absorbing anyway?'

Ogilvie held it up so that Morgenthal could see the title. They both grinned. '*Firearm Identification* by Calvin H. Goddard. I can't help myself. I'm still trying to be teacher's pet. Safe journey, Simon.'

Shortly after Morgenthal's departure, Cuthbert was compiling the last of the paperwork he would need to complete his report. Most important were the identification files that had grown from the original set of pages prepared by Hogg and his team.

Cuthbert studied the collection of files that was now as comprehensive as it would ever be. They were arranged in alphabetical order in three groups – men, women and children. He knew he would have to re-read them all in order to write his report, but before starting he took down the set of children's files and leafed through them.

He scanned their sexes and ages until he found the one he was looking for – a 3-year-old boy. In spite of everything, he could not rid himself of the memory of that innocent lying face down near the bomb crater. Cuthbert was grateful he had not carried out the child's post mortem examination himself. Dr Ogilvie had performed it meticulously. As with the other victims, the details he had collected had been used to cross-match with the missing person's known characteristics to aid their identification.

There was no photograph of the child in the file, for which Cuthbert was grateful. There was just a name.

'George Meikle Wilson. Well, laddie, I promised you we'd find out who you were. At least you can rest in peace now. Sleep well, wee Geordie, while we find out who did this to you.'

Cuthbert closed the file, took a deep breath and set to work.

*

At police headquarters, Hogg knocked on D.C.I. Black's door and waited. The invitation to enter when it came was gruff.

'Twice in one day, sergeant. Have you and the big doctor made another breakthrough?' Hogg's face was serious, and Black put down his pen. 'What is it? I'm busy.'

'It's the gun that was used to kill McDiarmid on the Green, the night of the bombing. We've tracked it down and it's a match for a Luger that we recovered in the Baxter shooting.'

'So?'

'So we recovered it. It was in the evidence room downstairs, or at least it was until somebody signed it out last November.'

'You must have got that wrong, Hogg.

'No, sir. No mistake. It was signed out on the seventeenth of November, and it was signed out by you.'

Black clasped his hands on the desk in front of him and nodded. Hogg could see he was obviously weighing up different versions of the story he was about to spin, trying to decide which one would sound the most plausible.

He sighed and began. 'So it was that gun, was it? The old German one from the war?'

'Do you deny obtaining it from the evidence store, sir?'

'Nope.'

'What did you do with it?'

'I gave it to the person who asked me to get it.'

'Are you saying it wasn't your idea to pull it out of the store?'

'Yes, that is exactly what I'm saying. And this is starting to feel like an interrogation, sergeant, so I should remind you that you're speaking to a senior officer.'

'And maybe this is the point that I remind you, sir, of your right to remain silent, and that this is a murder inquiry that you would do well not to obstruct. Who did you give it to?'

'As I said, the one who asked me to get it. I didn't know that's why he wanted it. He told me a very different story. He said he needed an example for a talk he was delivering on gun crime, and that he'd had a look at the inventory. That Luger would be "just the thing", he said.'

Hogg was starting to lose patience with Black. He had never liked the man, but no police officer wanted to have this kind of conversation with a colleague, let alone a senior one. Hogg wanted straight answers and for it to be over as soon as possible. 'The name, sir.'

'Our friend upstairs, Chief Constable Harper. You don't think I'd be going around doing chores like that for anyone else, do you?'

Hogg was unsure whether he believed Black, but he was inclined to think that if there was a ladder the D.C.I. thought he could climb, he wouldn't ask questions about how it got there. The man was an opportunist and a weasel, but he doubted he was a murderer. And whoever had been responsible for these crimes – the shooting and the bombing – was likely to have much more between their ears than this one.

'If that's the case, sir, what do you suppose we do about it?'

'Well, I'll tell you what we'll not be doing, and that's going upstairs and knocking on the chief constable's door without getting all the facts straight. How do we know he didn't really want the gun to illustrate some lecture he was giving? How do we know he didn't lose the gun, or have it stolen from his room? Maybe he hasn't even noticed it's missing. There are a lot of questions that we need answers to before you go in there firing off wild accusations. Sitting there and doubting me is one thing, Hogg; pulling the same stunt with the chief constable will cost you your stripes and your pension. So why don't you go and get some answers and don't come back until you have.'

Hogg could see that despite Black's bluster he was shaken by the interview. The chief inspector knew he was in very deep trouble and had likely been dropped in it by his boss. He had never been clever enough to ask the right questions, and he was now wondering if he had been taken for a fool for the last time.

Hogg left the building quickly: he knew there was only one place to go.

*

Since the last of the victims had been identified, the mortuary had started to resume its former appearance. Gone were the boxes of recovered remains and the bulging files documenting every detail of the forensic investigation. The only thing that remained of the case was the pinboard above Cuthbert's desk, which still bore the photographs, note cards and strings linking everything together.

When Hogg entered, breathless from the brisk walk down from headquarters, Cuthbert was standing beside the board, wondering if it was time to take it down.

'Ah, sergeant, I wasn't expecting you again so soon. You look as if you need a seat. You don't want to have a coronary in a place like this.'

Hogg didn't even do Cuthbert the courtesy of a smile at his joke and gestured for the pathologist to sit with him. Cuthbert thought the sergeant might be feeling unwell and shifted his tone to one of more serious concern.

'What is it, sergeant?'

Hogg told Cuthbert the story of his discovery and of his meeting with Black as succinctly as he could. Cuthbert listened in complete silence, and it was only after some time that he was fully able to digest what he had just been told – to work through the ramifications of it all.

'Well, sir, what do you make of it?'

Hogg was impatient for Cuthbert's opinion and keen to have someone tell him he had got it all wrong. However, Cuthbert could offer no such solace, for he could see now how it all fitted into place.

'It had to be someone high up, didn't it? Someone with the necessary bird's-eye view of it all. It had to be someone who could access explosives and a gun. Someone who had the necessary leverage over Alec Jamieson and who could control the subsequent investigation. If you wanted to make sure this case wasn't going anywhere, who would you put in charge of it? An incompetent like Black, that's who. But why? What did he have to gain by it all? I expect we'll only find that out when we ask him.'

'We can't go and accuse a chief constable of murder. Black has explicitly told us to leave it alone.'

'No, sergeant, he explicitly told you to leave it alone. I am under an entirely different jurisdiction. And I'll be damned if I'm going to leave it. I've spent the last two weeks piecing together what was left of twenty-four men, women and children cut down by this obscene outrage. Giving them back their names is one thing, giving them justice is quite another, and until this moment I thought it was beyond me. I think I should speak to the chief constable alone. Let me collect some things, and then I suggest we go and pay him a visit.'

Hogg's desire for justice was equal to Cuthbert's; however, he understood the risks better than the pathologist and doubted whether any kind of meaningful justice could ever be won when people like Harper were involved. People for whom the rules simply did not apply.

*

When they arrived on the top floor of police headquarters, Cuthbert nodded at Hogg, silently indicating that he remain in the outer office, and then knocked on Harper's door. He did not wait for permission to enter.

The chief constable was seated behind his grand desk, the oil paintings of his Victorian predecessors glowering down at him through their whiskers. When Harper looked up to see who had invaded his sanctum, he looked disappointed.

'Do we have an appointment?'

'Do we need an appointment?'

'No niceties this time, Dr Cuthbert? But, then again, you do look like a man in a hurry. Are you here to bid us farewell? No need. I understand the forensic investigation is complete, and I expect you're eager to get back to London, so please don't let me keep you.'

Cuthbert strode across the thick carpet and took a seat in front of Harper's desk. The chief constable frowned and reached for his phone to arrange for Cuthbert's removal, when the pathologist asked, 'The thing that eludes me, chief constable, is why?'

Harper replaced the receiver he had barely picked up and shook his head in puzzlement.

'Why would a senior police officer engineer the assassination of a right-wing political candidate? I thought at first it might be some deeply held political conviction, but you really don't strike me as a communist, or even a sympathiser.'

Harper's brows knitted in a deep frown as he listened to Cuthbert.

'Then I wondered if it had been some kind of accident. Perhaps the wrong victim was killed, perhaps it had been meant to kill the protesters or even the Brigton Boys, but you're not the kind of man who makes that kind of mistake, are you?

'It had to be more complex, more subtle than that. What were the consequences of this assassination? I asked myself. There was concern at the heart of government, outrage from the right, the stoking of hysteria and a call for retribution. Screams of "down with the Jews".

'Henderson's death makes him a martyr – so much more important than he would ever have been had he stood for a seat he would likely never have won. In death, he becomes a much more effective recruiting sergeant for the fascists. Is that what this is about?'

Harper remained silent. He lit a cigarette and inhaled deeply.

'But what does all that do for you specifically? You've reached the pinnacle of your professional tree. There's nowhere else to go from this office, so what's a man like you to do? You're conscious of your image, you take greats efforts to cultivate the press, and you are acutely aware of who holds the power – or, perhaps in your case, who you think will hold the power in the years ahead.

'Perhaps you are a fascist, but I suspect not. I think you simply see that's the way the wind is blowing, and you've decided to throw your hat in the ring with Mosley and his brutes. You're a political animal, chief constable, and I believe you see your future in that particular arena.'

Harper was no longer frowning. He had relaxed, and he was almost smiling as Cuthbert described him.

'And I ask myself how much did Mosley know about this? Did he order the assassination in order to create exactly the furore that it has? He's certainly capitalised on it in his recent speeches. I mean, look at the newspaper headlines. He's enjoyed many more column inches in the last couple of weeks than he deserves. Doubtless he sees it as a godsend, but I also suspect he knew nothing about it.

'Am I right? I think this is all you, Chief Constable Harper. I think you thought that once Mosley and his gang knew where the credit lay you might reap the kind of political patronage you'd been looking for. A new career with the New Party. Maybe you even had it in mind to offer yourself as a replacement for Henderson. A local man, with all the right connections and a darling of the press to boot. How could they possibly refuse you?'

Harper was still saying nothing, but his expression now betrayed his irritation.

'And you planned everything to the last detail, didn't you? Why did you use Alec Jamieson, though? You must have been able to call on a lot of favours, but I would have thought any association with that violent little man would have been somewhat beneath you.'

Harper shrugged ever so slightly and thought for a moment that he might explain himself but pulled himself back.

'I don't doubt that he would have been useful. You needed someone who could plant the bomb and have no thought to the consequences, even for his own men. And I expect you supplied him with the gun. For unexpected difficulties? Not really his style, though. I expect you had to persuade him to take it.'

'Not at all, he was really quite enthusiastic. His eyes actually lit up when I gave him it. I think he felt he'd finally graduated from his razor days and was now joining the first division.'

Cuthbert knew that once Harper started to talk, it was his time to be silent. Everything he had said until now had been little more than speculation designed to provoke a denial. What had been interesting, though, is that throughout the one-sided conversation, Harper's eyes had never once revealed any kind of contradiction.

'Yes, I did plan everything very carefully, and I was proud of it. I anticipated everything – except you. If I'd only had to deal with the bumbling police surgeons who normally work in this city, and with Black in charge, little, if anything, would have been found.

'But then you arrived in Glasgow and Whitehall called me to inform me you were to lead the investigation. That was a surprise. I'm not sure why, but they were obviously keeping an eye on you, Dr Cuthbert. They knew you were here before I did.'

'But why on earth would they order you to give me the lead in the forensic investigation?'

'Come, come, doctor. They wanted someone they trusted on the ground, and they certainly didn't trust me. Let's just say my dealings with the Met have made me some enemies. I have, shall we say, a *difficult* reputation, and they weren't going to leave anything to chance, so you were their easiest option.

'You were here, you were trusted, and you were incorruptible. When I called you from London, you were really not that intimidated. In hindsight, that was an error of judgement on my part.'

Cuthbert was quietly relieved to hear that he had not in fact been pressurised to commit professional fraud by a member of His Majesty's Government, but he was annoyed with himself for having been so taken in.

'How did you find your way to me, if I might ask?'

Cuthbert took the Luger from his pocket and placed it on the desk between them. It still bore Morgenthal's handwritten evidence tag tied to the trigger guard.

'Of course. That was also clumsy of me. I should have known Black might be the weak link. Ambitious little men like him are so easily controlled by the lure of patronage, but he was always too stupid to be really useful. Unlike Alec. He was cleverer than the rest of them put together. It's a pity about the gun, but he obviously had need of it, so perhaps I did the right thing after all giving it to him.'

Cuthbert watched Harper as he spoke. He had clearly

enjoyed the complete control of the situation and the manipulation of so many lives. The deaths on the other hand seemed meaningless to him when stacked against the potential for political power that the bombing might have given him.

'Well, Dr Cuthbert, this is all very awkward, especially for D.S. Hogg, who I presume is waiting outside to take me down to one of my own cells. I would like to phone my wife before I go, if that would be acceptable to you. She has done nothing in all this, and I think she should hear it from me before she finds out from my fair-weather friends in the press. Would you do me that one courtesy?'

'Of course, she deserves that at least.'

Harper picked up the receiver and Cuthbert got up to leave, but as he was closing the office door, he swung back, realising he had left the pistol on the desk. Harper was still seated behind his desk as he stared at Cuthbert and pulled the trigger with the pistol barrel in his mouth.

Sergeant Hogg came rushing in and tried to push past Cuthbert, who was frozen in the doorway. The shot was still ringing in his ears, and although he could see that Hogg was speaking, perhaps shouting, he could hear nothing. Hogg was holding his arms, shaking him, and then he forcibly turned his head, taking his gaze away from the blood- and brain-splattered wall.

'Sir! Are you harmed?'

'No. No, I'm fine. But it was my fault. I gave him the gun. I left it on the desk. I didn't know it was loaded. I thought the magazine was emptied. Why did I leave a bullet in it?'

Hogg had seen the look in Cuthbert's eyes many times before in the eyes of other men. He knew the pathologist was in shock and would soon become pale and sweaty and even faint if he didn't get him out of there and seated.

Cuthbert was a mountain of a man for Hogg to move on his

own, but he used his own weight to manhandle him out of the office and push him into one of the chairs in the waiting room. He pulled a hip flask from his pocket and ordered Cuthbert to drink.

'It was my fault, all my fault.'

'Nonsense, sir. He would have done away with himself, one way or another. Men like him don't come quietly.'

'No, I'm to blame.'

'Stop thinking that, right now, Dr Cuthbert. That man was responsible for the deaths of more than twenty people, and he knew he would hang for it. He was the one who pulled the trigger in there, not you. It was the only decent thing he's done; this way he's spared us all a lot of work. Come on, son. It's over now.'

*

The following days were a blur for Cuthbert. He spent them in his room at the Central Hotel trying to escape from the torment of introspection by losing himself in his precious copy of Juvenal's *Satire*s.

Hogg visited each day to check on him and tried to protect him from the details of all that was happening as a result of Harper's suicide. What he could not do, however, was save him from the phone call from the procurator fiscal.

'Dr Cuthbert, Douglas Moffat, the fiscal on the Harper case. I'm sorry to disturb you, sir, but I have some questions for you.'

'As a preliminary to the inquest, I presume?'

'Oh no, sir, there will be no inquest. This is Scotland. The procurator fiscal will conduct a private investigation to determine the circumstances of the death. There will be no jury and no publicity.'

'But this was a suicide.'

'I'm sure I do not have to remind you, Dr Cuthbert, that unlike in England, suicide is not a crime in Scots law. We have long taken the much more reasonable approach, in my opinion, that man has the freedom to dispose of himself; he may well be answerable to his God, but not to his fellow man.'

However, the thought that Harper would be answerable to God, not just for taking his own life but for the twenty-four who died on the Green, was no consolation to Cuthbert. The questions Moffat asked were hardly searching and gave him no opportunity to elaborate beyond the most basic facts of the case.

Cuthbert dutifully gave his answers and heard no more until Hogg informed him that a death certificate had been issued and the matter closed.

'And what did they come up with as the cause of death, sergeant?'

'Accidental shooting, sir. It saves the family and the force from having to answer any more questions. And I think everyone wants to draw a line firmly under the whole affair.'

'Everyone? I didn't. I wanted some justice. But that's not going to happen now. At least it was a wet death.'

'Sir?'

'... *few usurpers to the shades descend, by a dry death, or with a quiet end* ... Just some lines of poetry that seem fitting and so very true. Look, I'm truly sorry for everything that has happened, sergeant. I think you deserved a better outcome from all this, given all your efforts. I can honestly say it has been a pleasure to work with you. I know I was far from your ideal when we first met, but I hope I have restored myself somewhat in your estimation. Perhaps we could share a dram or two before I leave for London tomorrow evening?'

*

At six o'clock sharp, Hogg met Cuthbert in the hotel lobby where he had first met the doctor almost three weeks before. He was pleased to see that, unlike the last few days, he was now standing just as tall as he had then.

'Sergeant, it really is good of you to come. Let's make ourselves comfortable in the bar. They have a fine selection of single malts here, and I can assure you we'll be sampling the most expensive ones they have.'

Over their drinks, Cuthbert turned the conversation back to the case. 'So tell me, sergeant, what about Alec Jamieson? He's as guilty as Harper of these murders and especially so of the McDiarmid boy's. Does nothing happen to him?'

'And where is our evidence, sir? Anything we have was left smouldering at the scene. And the only one who can put the gun in Jamieson's hand took his testimony to the grave when he blew his brains out. Sure, we have the thug's fingerprints on the bullets, but that doesn't prove he fired it. This is as far as we go, Dr Cuthbert, at least this time. But it's certainly not over. We'll get Jamieson sooner or later, and he'll swing. You have my word on that, sir.' Hogg raised his glass and drank to seal the promise.

'What about Black?'

'Oh, I expect he'll be in line for the chief constable job. That's the way it is with him — always has been. We have a saying here in Glasgow — if he fell into the Clyde, he'd come up with a salmon in his mouth.'

'And what about you, sergeant? Retirement?'

'Loose ends still to tie up, sir, and let's just say I've been given a second wind. And you might be interested to know that W.P.C. Anderson is transferring to vice. It'll be Detective Constable Anderson then.'

'Good for her. I expect you had something to do with that.'

'We all need a little push every now and then. And there

are interesting openings for women these days. You mark my words, she'll probably end up running the place.'

Cuthbert cradled his glass, warming the rich, golden liquid within. He sipped it, relishing the deep, peaty flavour. 'You're right, sergeant. We all need a little push at times otherwise we get stuck. Now, I really cannot keep you any longer. Thank you for guiding me through all this and for the support you gave me at the end. I will never forget it.'

'And I won't forget you, sir. But don't think I've quite forgiven you for being an Edinburgh man.'

This time Hogg smiled broadly and took his leave. Cuthbert watched him go and drained the last of his glass before rising himself to attend to the formalities at the hotel reception.

His bags had already been brought down from his room, and he had one final thing to do before making his way into the station for the London train. He used the house phone and placed a trunk call to his home.

'Madame, it is so good to hear your voice.'

'No better than to hear yours, monsieur. I hope everything is well. Your investigation, has it come to a completion?'

Cuthbert knew he could never lie to this woman who was incapable of any deceit. But he felt ashamed, and he hesitated.

'Monsieur, has something happened? Are you well?'

'I am fine, madame, and I'm coming home tonight. I will be back at Gordon Square in time for morning coffee.'

His housekeeper suppressed the surge of joy she felt at his words because she knew he had said them with just a tinge of sadness in his voice. Something had happened in Glasgow, but she knew she had no right to pry into his work. Nonetheless, she offered him an opportunity to talk. After a moment, he told her of Harper's suicide and how he blamed himself for what had happened.

'No one will answer for the crime now, madame. When he

took his own life, he left behind a vacuum where there should have been justice for all those men, women and children who died. I feel I have let them all down, madame, that I've failed.'

'We are all marked by failure, monsieur. But failure is just a bruise; it is not a tattoo. Come home and heal. There are many more victims who need you here.'

*

Standing on Platform 1, the porter carrying his luggage behind him, Cuthbert turned to look back at the great cathedral of a station. Acres of cast iron and glass roofed the vast space filled with noise and rush and soot even at this late hour. He had arrived three weeks before, intending to stay only three days, but of course that was before all that had happened.

The porter opened the carriage door for him and took the bags to Cuthbert's berth. It was quiet and comfortable, and he could hear the stewards preparing to serve drinks in the first-class lounge.

Cuthbert sat by the window, taking a final look at the bustle outside. Last-minute travellers overladen with luggage, children being hushed, porters doing their best – all of them trying to catch the night train. Shortly, the minute hand of the great square clock hanging from the station roof moved to twelve, a whistle pierced the smoky air, and flags were waved. The London train would leave on time as it always did, and Cuthbert closed his eyes. He knew he was going home.

As the train pulled out of Central Station, there was a knock on the door of his berth. Cuthbert realised it would be the steward to take his breakfast order. However, when he opened the door, he was met by a smiling Erich Jaeger dressed in a fine, grey tweed suit and a pale green silk tie the shade of his eyes. Cuthbert, in his surprise, breathed in sharply and caught the fresh citrus scent of the man's cologne.

'I hope you'll forgive the intrusion, Cuthbert, but I saw you getting on the train. I'm on my way back to London again, and I wondered if you might like to have another chat, maybe even a whisky or two to while away our sleepless night.'

Cuthbert had almost forgotten the perfect smile, the cleft of his chin and the swept-back blond hair. But now he was instantly back in that first moment when he had run from this beautiful man.

He stood looking at Jaeger, just as unsure as he had been the last time they met, but this time he managed a smile in return. He could feel his heart pounding in his chest as much from fear as anticipation.

'Well, can I offer you that drink, old chap?'

Cuthbert swallowed hard and thought in a flash of everything that had happened in the last few weeks. He had come to Glasgow looking for the possibility of a change, even a new beginning. He had failed to find that and instead had been taught that failure of a different kind was as much part of his job as success.

He was going home to recover the life he had left behind, to slip, unchanged, back into his everyday routine. Now, however, it seemed that fate had a different plan. At last, Cuthbert relaxed and felt his heart slow. He held out his hand to take Jaeger's in greeting, but this time he did not want to let it go.

Finally, he found enough breath to give Jaeger his answer. 'I think I would rather play cards.'

Author's Note

This is a work of fiction set in the 1920s and 1930s, but I have tried to make it as historically accurate as possible. While the characters and settings are fictitious, they are all modelled as far as possible on real people, places and circumstances. Where I have had to invent, I have always been mindful to keep it plausible.

A century has passed since the time that the events in this book are set, and there are few people left to ask about what it was like then. Fortunately, much has been written both by people who lived through those years and by those who have devoted their careers to studying that period of history. I am indebted to them and a few of my most valuable sources are listed below.

Sydney Smith's 1959 memoir, *Mostly Murder*.

John Glaister's 1915 3rd edition of *A Text-book of Medical Jurisprudence and Toxicology*.

Ralph Glasser's 1986 memoir of his childhood, *Growing Up in the Gorbals*.

Alexander McArthur and H. Kingsley Long's 1935 novel, *No Mean City*, which is based on eyewitness accounts of Glasgow's razor gangs.

Aarron Davis's invaluable 2006 guide to the Luger pistol: *Standard Catalog of Luger*.

Glasgow City Council's 2014 guidebook, *Glasgow Green Heritage Trail*.

Ben Braber's 1992 PhD thesis, 'Integration of Jewish Immigrants in Glasgow, 1880–1939'.

Linda Fleming's 2005 PhD thesis, 'Jewish Women in Glasgow *c*. 1880–1950: Gender, Ethnicity and the Immigrant Experience'.

Calvin H. Goddard's 1926 paper, 'Scientific Identification of Firearms and Bullets' in *American Institute of Criminal Law and Criminology 254 (1926–1927)*.

The Bridgeton Library Local History Group's 2014 publication based on oral histories, *Bridgeton: Recollections From a Time of Change*.

Christophe Champod and Paul Chamberlain's chapter 'Fingerprints' in the 2009 textbook, *Handbook of Forensic Science*.

Robert Shiels' 2019 paper, 'The Investigation of Suicide in Victorian and Edwardian Scotland', in *Dundee Student Law Review*.

There is, however, one other source that I must acknowledge. She grew up in the East End of Glasgow in the early 1920s but never committed her memories to writing. Fortunately, I was able to listen to the endlessly funny and thrilling tales of her childhood firsthand for she was my mother. Margaret even finds her way into the pages of this novel, and I think it is fitting that she makes such a crucial contribution to the investigation.

THE DR JACK CUTHBERT MYSTERY SERIES

BOOK I *The Silent House of Sleep*

Death is a lonely business

No one who meets Dr Jack Cuthbert forgets him. Tall, urbane, brilliant but damaged, the Scottish pathologist is the best that D.C.I. Mowbray of Scotland Yard has seen. But Cuthbert is a man who lives with secrets, and he is still haunted by demons from the trenches in Ypres. When not one but two corpses are discovered in a London park in 1929, Cuthbert must use every tool at his disposal to solve the mystery of their deaths. In the end, the horrifying truth is more shocking than even he could have imagined.

BOOK 2 *The Moon's More Feeble Fire*

She was someone's daughter

In 1930, the killing of a Soho prostitute is hardly a priority for Scotland Yard. But when a second, similar murder comes to light, and then a third, everything changes. Cuthbert and his team find themselves in a nightmarish world of people-trafficking, prostitution and drug use amongst the upper classes. Using all his forensic skills, Cuthbert sets out to solve one of the most baffling cases of his career. One final question remains unanswered until a faded photograph reveals its tragic secret.

BOOK 3 *To the Shades Descend*

The dead all have stories to tell

A visit to Glasgow for a job interview in 1931 unexpectedly places Cuthbert at the centre of a devastating crime. Unwittingly, he finds himself working at the intersection between rising British fascism, anti-Semitism and the infamous Glasgow razor gangs. To solve the case, Cuthbert needs to rely on all the expertise he can gather from those around him. But who can he trust?

BOOK 4 *The Shadows and the Dust*

Sins never stay buried

Like all pathologists, Cuthbert finds dealing with dead children the hardest part of his job. However, when the body of a young boy is found in the grounds of a church orphanage, Cuthbert not only has to steel himself for the task ahead, he is also forced to revisit his own childhood grief. The boy in his shallow grave has been interred with some ritual, but just how did he die? And why was he killed? Working closely with his assistant and the team at Scotland Yard, Cuthbert slowly and painstakingly reveals the terrible truth.

Acknowledgements

While the Dr Jack Cuthbert mystery novels are historical crime stories, for me they are also as much about the lives of the cast of characters who tell those stories. And, in particular, the protagonist Jack Cuthbert himself. The chance to be able to develop such a character and to reveal him gradually over a series of books is a great gift to an author. The enthusiasm of both my readers and my publisher, Polygon, for Jack, and their desire to find out more of his history and his exploits, have made that possible, resulting in this, the third book in the series.

As with the first two Dr Jack Cuthbert novels, I am indebted to all my early readers, especially, Ellen, Alec, Anne, S.J., Maureen and Alex. I must also thank Sharon Mail for important editorial input. All their comments were invaluable in helping shape the final manuscript. My expert editor at Polygon, Alison Rae, has once again helped me polish the manuscript. She and the rest of the remarkable Polygon team have worked hard to ensure the finished book you now have in your hands is exactly as I hoped it would be.

Lastly, but by no means least, my thanks go to Moira, without whose constant support and encouragement I would not be a writer.